Stolen Caresses

"Did you dream it would be so easy, MacAmlaid?
That I would willingly be branded your whore? One
night I was weak, I admit to that weakness, but I'll not
be so again. You shall have nothing of me without
force, and your keep will be haunted by the sound of
my curses."

The flamelight danced over his bared torso as he
moved to the door, closing and barring it. Dara
showed no fear at this evidence of his answer but
stood her ground even as he covered the short distance between them.

"If you would scream, lass, or curse me, begin
now."

His hands fumbled in the coils of her hair, the pins
dropping to the floor as he withdrew them. Like liquid
copper her hair fell loosely to her waist. She held rigid
beneath the hunger of his kisses until he broke away,
cursing her.

"You proved not so unwilling last night, my lady. Is
your virtue summoned on whim?"

HIGHLAND CAPTIVE

SUSAN TANNER

LEISURE BOOKS ▐▙ NEW YORK CITY

For Janice

A LEISURE BOOK ®

September 1990

Published by

Dorchester Publishing Co., Inc.
276 Fifth Avenue
New York, NY 10001

Printed in the United States of America.

Prologue

I n the year 1499, Henry VII and James IV, rulers of England and Scotland, negotiated a peace between their kingdoms which was to be sealed by a royal marriage. The countries, at war for centuries past, saw, for a brief time, a cessation of the turmoil along the borders that had witnessed overmuch of ancient hatreds and bitter bloodshed. Only one incident marred this peace and threatened to destroy a union wrought of kings . . .

Chapter I

The sharp mid-October moon found nothing on the leather-jacketed and breeked borderers to reflect its cold light. Daggers were tucked from sight, and bog muck muddied iron spurs. A long wind swept low over the moors, bringing with it the thin, faraway yipping of foxes. Sparse trees stood like twisted sentinels, guarding only heath and bog on this desolate stretch of border march. The silent, damning advance of the raiders through wind-clawed hills was unmarked but for the steady drum of iron-shod hooves.

The Scots approached the English stronghold in the stillness of midnight with none to bar the way save a few lax guards. In a trice, their hacked and bleeding bodies were but a prelude to carnage within. The walls gleamed of smooth, white stone as the invaders swung the heavy gates wide and streamed through. Relentless blades made short work of the defenders of Chilton Castle. Only half-awake, the English poured from guardhouse, stable, and hall, armed with whatever weapon lay closest at hand, too often poor if not utterly useless defenses. Pitchforks and scythes wielded by house servants and stablehands were no match for warrior-driven broadswords. Sleep-dulled men-at-arms fared little better.

Unslowed the raiders came, murdering and pillaging, destroying what could not be carried away. Only one man paid no attention to the English riches. Eyes aglitter, Ruod MacAmlaid roared a challenge to the lord of the hall. He stood waiting, tall and powerful and menacing, and none dared near but the Earl of Chilton.

Full of thunderous hatred, Kerwin Ryland stepped among the bodies of his people. "So, you dare where others do not! You will die for your courage!" There was bone-deep, gut-bitter fury in his voice.

Ruod smiled unpleasantly. "You are overconfident. 'Tis your death this hour will see! I but finish the bloodletting that you began, Chilton. Are you prepared to die as well as the Scots you have murdered? They are legion!"

For answer the Englishman swung his heavy battleaxe in a wide arc, but Ruod was no longer in its path. He stood aside, mocking his foe with laughter before engaging him in combat so deadly there was no space for mockery or taunts between hard-drawn breaths.

The earl was less heavily built and so had less

weight behind his swing, but his strength and endurance equaled the Scotsman's. Neither man considered the possibility of his own defeat —not when defeat meant death.

The faces of the conquering marauders, weapons gripped loosely at their sides, betrayed grim enjoyment as those mighty axe blades whirred, cutting through air with each dodged slash. No sound was heard but that of the struggle played before them. The cries from the courtyard and upper hall had all but ceased, a testimony of victory.

Paralyzed on the stairs above, Dara Ryland watched, seeing the combatants' feet slip on rushes wet with blood, seeing the sweat drip from her brother's forehead to blind him, from his wrist to loosen his hold on the stout wooden handle of his axe. Never had she felt such fear; it was an icy, screaming agony. A heavy cross of jewel-studded gold was in her hands as she prayed for the Scotsman's death. At her feet crouched a lean hound, his throaty growl a warning to any who dared near her.

A moan choked in her throat as the masked raider threw his axe with a mighty bellow and Kerwin stumbled beneath its impact. The sharp blade destroyed completely the chest that had been her childhood's haven and spilled his loved and loving life in great wells of blood. The cross that had lent no support to her pleas slipped unheeded from her fingers.

She rushed down the stairs to find the Scotsman bent over her brother, wrestling the axe from his dead grip. She stumbled over the bloodied torso and stooped to grasp the gleaming dirk that lay next to the outstretched hand. Blindly, she flung herself upon her brother's murderer, dirk raised to strike.

He struck the weapon from her grasp, and a blow to her temple sent her limply to the floor. In the fragment of time before she dropped, a flash of white, fur and fang, leaped in attack upon the man who had harmed her. Before thought or action seemed possible, the hound's supple body lay in Kerwin's blood and his own. The bitterness of Dara's grief at this loss was scarcely less than the others before it and lent strength to her resistance as she was dragged to her feet.

She had not strength enough, however, for the dim flicker of the hearthfire had revealed to Ruod her beauty.

Her twisting, fighting terror was nothing to the iron muscles of this man, even hampered as he was by the weight of her brother's axe, a trophy of his victory. He carried her to the courtyard and his horse. His ringing command called his men to him and away from their atrocities. With a fresh burst of fury, Dara saw that one of the men carried before him the youngest and fairest of the house servants. She was limp and unresisting in his arms, a blood-matted wound on her pale forehead.

Ruod silenced Dara's vented outrage with heavy-handed force, and nausea rose in her at the pain. Her sight was dulled by the blow, but nothing could blur from her memory that last backward glimpse of Chilton. The slain lay cradled in the arms of the living, their tears fading the darkness of flowing blood. But Dara had no tears. Her grief burned too deep and bitter for any such release.

A bruise ached where Ruod had deflected the blow of her attack and another throbbed at her temple. The wind was a constant chill, but it cleared her vision and her thoughts as they drew ever nearer the border. Once across, their pace slowed. There was, after all, little likelihood of pursuit. So unexpected had been the attack and so complete the advantage that few had been left capable of following. And those few would not waste time in so foolish and so futile an attempt, not when the wounded cried out for help.

The moors seemed barren hills this night, devoid of life or beauty, but Dara knew it was despair that made them seem so. She loved the moorlands, though there was no remembrance in her now of merrier times and younger days when she had crossed them with her brothers laughing at her side. There was only that last picture of Kerwin to carry with her.

She had given up the unequal struggle to free herself from the ungentle grip of a sinewy arm and merely clutched with numbed fingers the horse's dark mane. The arm around her ribs was bruisingly tight, and the saddle harsh against her bare thighs. Her mind was filled with a silent keening for those slain.

She started apprehensively as another rider spurred his mount even with Ruod's. His wolfish features were arranged in a grimace that only faintly resembled a smile.

Strang was the most favored of Ruod's men,

the one person he came closest to trusting. "Laochlain will little like this night's work."

"Damn Laochlain! I am master in his absence. I've dealt with the English dog as he would never dare to do."

Strang objected, mainly for the sake of torment. "It was not a lack of daring that stayed his hand, as well you know. 'Twas loyalty to James' interests. And they're not best served by stirring up trouble along the border when it's an English princess he's agreed to marry."

"Think you Henry will be put off by our deed? Bah! He's schemed too long to have James take Margaret to wife. If she had any looks about her, 'twould please our James, but 'tis rumored that neither her looks nor her disposition are pleasing. James would do better to marry one of his mistresses, be she humbly bred or no. At least they are all good Scottish lasses!"

At this point, he was forced to silence rather than admit the truth of Strang's warning. It was fact that James had cautioned his border lords against just such raids as they had made this night. James wanted no forced end to the peace he and Henry had agreed upon—at least not until he was suited to see it broken. But, for the present, it was not his king who would have to be outfaced but his brother. Aye—damn Laochlain!

He repeated it aloud, drawing Strang's animal grin, barely visible in the moonlight.

"Admit truth, Ruod. You would do more than curse him were you not so fearful of his might."

A savage jerk of the arm that held her startled Dara into renewed fear. Ruod's tensed body revealed to her an anger emphasized by his response to Strang's taunt.

"Guard your tongue, cur, lest I cleave it from your mouth! Your witless prattle ires me!"

"Ho, witless is it? I speak what is true, and well you know it. Laochlain holds all that you desire, and you have yet to take it from him. Wealth, lands, power, and his king's trust."

Strang rode at a distance now, wary of Ruod's long arm, and Ruod eyed him wrathfully. "'Tis well that you stay from my reach, fool. I fear no man! And Laochlain holds naught that I cannot and will not gain. James can have no trust in a dead man, and my might will hold these border lands with Laochlain in his grave!"

"You ill use your time in snarling at me. I do not bar your way nor seek to." Strang paused to smile craftily. "Even so, there is much you would have that you cannot—his birthright and the title that James bestowed on him within weeks of gaining his throne."

"Little enough use I'll have for aught but his wealth and his men. My power will surpass the boundaries of his, and even James won't deny my ability nor Duncan my attainment."

An owl hooted on the clear, carrying wind, and the horses pricked their ears at the long, echoing sound. Strang answered as the last faint echoes died.

"You care too much for Duncan's opinion. He's an old man and dependent on Laochlain's bounty."

Angrily, Ruod stripped the mask of a raiding border lord from his face, revealing features both handsome and cruel. He pulled Dara close against him. "Well, seldom does even Laochlain gain an English wench to pleasure him."

With a sickening dread, Dara felt his hand move slowly down her body to linger on the flatness of her belly, a burning warmth through the linen of her nightgown. Her struggles seemed only to amuse him, for his chuckle came harsh in her ear as she twisted furiously. His mouth moved from her ear to her neck, disgusting her with hard kisses. In rising panic, she thrust an elbow backward into his ribs, and in retaliation he sank his teeth into the curve of her neck, forcing from her a cry of pain.

Strang watched with covetous interest and rising desire as Ruod tugged the hem of her shift even higher than her position had forced it and caressed the pale skin of her thigh. Mayhap Ruod would share the prize after he was sated; the possibility increased his lust to painful proportions, and he leaned closer at a brief hint of dark hair against ivory flesh.

Ruod noted his interest, and an ugly smile curved his lips. "Well, mistress, if you suit me not, there are others less particular. Does Strang seem to you a more welcome bedfellow?" He laughed coarsely at her shudder. "It would be best for you to cease your fighting and prove more amenable."

Dara knew without a doubt what her fate was to be, for there was no dearth of blood-chilling tales along the border. Women unlucky enough to be taken in raids were tormented and debased in ways without number. When this man was done with her, there would be others to continue. If she survived their depravities, she might be ransomed, but more likely she would simply be murdered, for it was less troublesome, with less opportunity for reprisal. Who could know her fate but those who had every reason not to tell?

They entered ponderous iron gates as the first glimmer of dawn edged the sky. Dara gave little thought to the fortress beyond the fact that it appeared impregnable and inescapable. She had expected no less. Weary and sickened, she knew that her worst degradation was forthcoming. There was no doubt of her captor's complete bestiality, and she expected no mercy from him nor help from his people.

Staring unseeing at the massive rise of the castle walls, she waited, hating her own helplessness, until Ruod's snarl made her quiver in apprehension. Unbelievably, his arms slackened about her, and she found she was not resigned to her fate as she instinctively took the opportunity to slip free. He realized her intention too late to halt her descent, but his outstretched arm pinioned her close to his knee. Thwarted, she raised hate-filled eyes to him and found that, again, he had all but forgotten her. His lips were pressed in an angry grimace, and his eyes were narrowed in vicious regard. Her pulse erratic, she turned wonderingly to see what could effect such fury.

A great Scot, too fierce to be handsome, was before them, astride a mighty stallion. Not a single marking broke the shimmering perfection of the animal's deep copper coat, but more than the beast, it was his master who caught the eye. Tall and powerfully built, he sat his mount with forceful presence, glaring at them through hawk-keen eyes. Heavy brows were lowered over a high, thin nose. A sudden gust of wind ruffled his near-black hair and caused Dara to shiver.

"What whoreson's folly have you pursued this night?" His voice was deep and as harsh as his ruthless features.

Ruod's answer was loud with an assurance that was not bravado, his manner dangerously intense. "No folly, Laochlain. 'Tis a service I've rendered Scotland!" He reached to release Kerwin's axe from the trappings of his saddle. Boastfully, he hefted it before him and then flung it on the flagstones before the stallion's huge hooves. The clatter caused not a quiver in the animal. Ruod spoke again. "The Earl of Chilton lies dead in his own hall, surrounded by the blood of his kin."

"You lily-gutted son of a bitch!" The words were a slow, angry rumble. "I leave you unattended for less than a fortnight and return to such deviltry!" He paused, turning his wrath on the now-wary raiders. "And you—all of you—followed this puling bastard into madness, and as eager as he, I'll warrant!"

His sweeping gaze cowed the brawny borderers, who returned his look abashedly. Dara scorned them that they should let such abuse go unchallenged. Her contempt, clearly shown, drew the Scot's piercing look. A flush stained her cheeks as his eyes raked over the slenderness of

16

her figure, each curve and hollow molded by the same wind that stirred loose-hanging curls.

If she was fearful under his intense regard, dark-fringed eyes hid it well, and his gaze burned long and thoroughly over her before flicking back to Ruod. "And the girl—she is more of your valor?" His contempt made a mockery of the term.

Ruod snarled his answer defiantly. "She is booty. I claimed her by rights of the victor!"

Dark brows furrowed in a thunderous scowl. "You have no rights to claim! You, no less than any man here, owe your fealty to me."

All but his challenger waited tensely for Ruod's answer. There would be little he thought worth an open battle with Laochlain, but this girl might well be counted such a reason. Not a man among them would relinquish her without regret, but once Laochlain laid claim, none would by so much as a look give him reason to doubt that yielding.

Ruod was silent, and as if to speed him, Laochlain spoke again, very softly, the steel buried but audible in that calm. "You've pricked too long, a thorn sharp in my side. I welcome the day you give me leave to remove it. Will this then be it, Ruod?"

Dara stumbled when the pressure of Ruod's grasp was abruptly released from her shoulder, and she stared in disbelief as he wheeled his horse towards the stable. She knew he was no coward; he had faced the most savage of England's borderers unhesitatingly, yet he yielded to this man without contention.

The rest of the men remained mounted in place, awaiting commands, and Dara's eyes swept over them. She found the one she sought quite easily, marked as he was by the burden he carried. A burden that was ominously still. She knew despairingly that the girl was beyond aid. Anger made her brave as she turned back to Laochlain. Her voice was clear and unwavering.

"That man carries my servant. I fear she is dead. Will you release her to me?"

He swung down from his motionless horse, and his nearness was disconcerting. He towered over her, her head reaching only to his shoulders though she was of good height. Without comment, he glanced over her shoulder to the hapless borderer. The man needed no more than that steely look to bring him forward where he shifted restlessly, wishing himself slain at Chilton.

"So, Fibh, is the girl dead then?"

"Aye, my lord, I fear 'tis so. 'Twas not my intent. 'Tis that I hit her overhard. She was a pretty lass. I didna' mean to kill her." In his nervousness, he spoke too much, too fast. Realizing it, he fell abruptly silent.

"Then you will have her tended, readied for the grave."

Fibh took himself off with stammered assurances, but Laochlain had already turned his attention back to Dara. Furious that he had not acceded to her request, she returned his stare without flinching.

He was dressed as her brothers might for court in a doublet of dark green velvet with full, banded sleeves. A jewel-laden dress sword was at his thigh, a dirk tucked in his belt. A chamois cape swirled over one broad shoulder, and it was this he unfastened and swept around her own shoulders after his gaze had measured the lack of cover afforded by her nightshift. It was a welcome warmth and shield, but she could not be grateful to its owner, especially not while his cold, grey eyes judged and assessed her so calculatingly.

"What are you called?"

"Dara, my lord, of Chilton Castle." Her eyes sparked a hazel fire, daring him to trespass further.

"You are its lady?"

"Kerwin Ryland was my brother, murdered by yon brigands."

"He earned his death, mistress, and your capture as well."

His callousness filled her with blinding rage, and she flared defiantly. "My brother was a better man than any loutish Scot! This keep will rue the day of his dying, for Rylands take their revenge on all who do them ill. Kerwin is murdered, and I am held powerless, but there is another Ryland free, and Brann's vengeance will be swift and sure."

"Athdair fears no man, and you speak over-brave for one whose safety lies in another's power."

It was not his warning that drained the color from her face, but the realization that it was the MacAmlaid she faced, Earl of Athdair. Born to a savage Highland clan, but long a border power, his unhesitating retribution was feared and dreaded by his enemies. Understanding at last Ruod's submission, she stiffened. "I've asked no quarter."

"True." He studied her tilted chin without rancor. "Perhaps you'd rather I left you to Ruod? I don't doubt he can be very pleasing to a lass."

She shrugged, suddenly weary. "Will I fare any better in your hands?"

"That is yet to be known, but, lass, you could fare no worse. Even Ruod is not to be expected to treat an English maid with impunity however fair she might be."

His words chilled her, though she concealed it well. The events of the hours just past were too fresh. Her gently curved lips tightened in a sneer. She would put an end to this baiting.

"And you, my lord Scot, does your dislike of the English stop short of their women? I assure you my hatred for all of Scotland equals that of my brothers and is just as deadly."

A frown greeted her outburst, and the cruelty of his answer cut deep. "You forget, you have only one brother living to revile my country."

"Hatred does not die — only men!"

Tears glinted in her eyes, and she turned her face from him only to whirl back as he spoke again, ordering her into the keep. Her protest died at the sight of Ruod striding towards them. Willingly she obeyed. Only at the wide double doors did she glance back to see the MacAmlaid turn purposefully before Ruod, barring his way.

Chapter II

The great stone hall was warm with the blaze from a whole log whose length dominated the cavernous fireplace. The walls were hung with weapons and wool and bearskins; the floors covered with thick rushes. A long table sided by massive oak benches filled its width, and the only other furnishings were trestle seats drawn near the hearth and a serving table against one wall. It was nothing to the grace and beauty of Chilton, but it was comfortable and typical of border fortresses, both English and Scottish.

Her glance encompassed the room before turning to the two men seated near the fire-blackened hearth. One was aging but vital, his greying hair suggesting an age that had little relation to his bearing; the other young and

assured with the same hard, fine-lined features
as the MacAmlaid. After an uncomfortable moment, she realized that neither of them could
have taken part in the raid on Chilton. Their
dress was casually elegant, and mugs of sack
steamed in their hands. They stared at her with
penetrating interest, but before either could
speak, the door opened to admit Laochlain.

His tall frame daunted the empty space of the
hall as he moved closer, drawing their attention
to him.

The old man greeted him morosely. "Well,
Laochlain, a happy homecoming." His tone belied his words.

"Aye, Duncan, I ken Ruod had no time for
your counsel?"

"No the time or the desire." Duncan
MacAmlaid spoke with little ill will, for Ruod's
disrespect was no rarity. "He was resolved on
this raid and on Chilton's death."

Laochlain's gaze moved consideringly to
Dara. "I did not seek Chilton's death, but I do
not decry it. Had Jamie not bid for peace, I
would have wielded the blade myself. But Ruod
may yet feel the weight of royal displeasure."

Dara had not moved or spoken from the
moment Laochlain had entered, but she felt a
bitter anguish at his casual discussion of
Kerwin's death. She wrapped the MacAmlaid's
cape tighter around her shoulders as if she could
shield herself from further pain. Not one of the
three men appeared to notice her distress.

The youngest of them, silent until now, remarked quietly, "James would stay his hand if he

thought you gave the command for the attack. Does Ruod think to protect himself with your favor?"

Laochlain's eyes met his in a look of warm affection, even though the anger within him had not been entirely expended in his outburst against Ruod and his men. Niall was the youngest of Duncan's three sons, and between these two brothers was a bond of considerable strength and endurance, tested and proven by frequent separations and strained loyalties. Laochlain was somber as he answered.

"Who can say what thoughts Ruod holds in his head? He is a MacAmlaid, is he not?"

A brooding silence enveloped them, and none seemed inclined to break it until Duncan thumped his mug down firmly on the scarred oak surface of the table.

"And what of the lass? The Rylands are not to be disdained, for they are a mighty clan, and their power widespread. Vengeance would not be wreaked on Ruod alone, though the blame be his."

Watching Laochlain's face, Dara tensed apprehensively. Saved from one Scotsman, would she yet suffer at the hands of another? Could she expect any more clemency of this man than she had received of his brother? There seemed little to choose between them, though this one looked to be far more relentless and far more implacable. He did appear to lack at least the baser, cruder qualities of his brother, but could she place faith in appearances? Of only one thing was she sure, to escape from Laochlain

MacAmlaid would be no easy matter. His speculative gaze caught her stare, and she burned with embarrassment, for it seemed he must surely know her thoughts.

"She will bring a fair ransom. No Englishman would dare leave her long in our hands. They'll pay well to have her safely home."

Duncan nodded satisfaction and wondered if his son would make use of the girl. More fool he if he did not. Her kin would not anticipate forbearance of him, nor believe it if any claimed it was so. Best gain the greatest enjoyment, for the penalties would be the same as if he had.

Aloud, he merely warned, "I do not doubt they will pay all you demand, but Ruod will try to claim her yet. He is not so easily diverted from his purpose."

Laochlain shrugged his unconcern. "He has been warned, and I am sure Lady Ryland will take care to keep from his path."

Dara looked at him fully and steadily, and not without antipathy greatly increased by his utter disregard for it. "From both your paths, my lord. I have as little liking for your attention as for his."

His attention, and possible retribution, was drawn from her at the entrance of Athdair's warriors seeking their breakfast. As they ranged around the table, they did not trouble to conceal their curiosity about the fair English girl. They seemed normal men, bold in their stares, uncouth in their hunger, but Dara could not help looking on them with a kind of horror. So few hours past they had swept through Chilton like fiends from hell, their swords dripping with the blood of people who had loved and served her all her life.

They stared in turn, seemingly oblivious to her revulsion. Her soft curls flowed over the MacAmlaid's cape, and her eyes were luminous above pale cheeks, making her well worth the men's consideration. Even Laochlain's eyes were upon her as a place was made for her at the end of one bench next his tall chair which stood at one end of the long table. Niall was at her other side, and Duncan opposite. Both avoided her eyes.

There was little speech as the table was laid with pork and mutton and fish on platters, great bowls of porridge and thick, amber honey served with crusty oatbread. The servants were sturdy and efficient and, with the exception of one, not particularly attractive. That one was called Kinara. She was very young, little more than a child, with light green eyes and freckles to match her pale hair. The grace and fluidity of her movements lent a beauty she did not really possess to a body that was too thin and lacked the glow of good health. When necessary, the borderers addressed her kindly and courteously, but none jested with her as they did the others.

Ruod entered only after everyone was seated and eating, his eyes immediately seeking Dara. Under his stare, she reddened and pulled the cape closer about her. Quick was her chagrin at realizing her action had amused him. He did not speak or join the others in breaking fast but leaned against the wall, surveying the scene and quaffing the mug of heavy ale that Kinara had served him without request.

When at last he spoke, it was mockingly to Laochlain. "Are you no better resolved to my deed? Our poor sire declares himself finished with me. From me he demands filial obedience, but then I have no riches to offer in its stead, have I . . . Brother?"

Niall half rose from the bench, flushed and angry, but a gesture from Laochlain halted him. Reluctantly, he sat. Duncan's face revealed not anger so much as disgust. His hands were laid flat upon the table, his back rod straight as he stared at his son.

Laochlain spoke with insulting deliberateness. "Mine is the blame, Ruod, for leaving only Duncan to curb your insanities. For whatever your crimes, I know he'll use no force on you. It was careless of me to take both Niall and Gerwalt with me. I should have left at least one to deal with you."

Ruod's face burned an ugly, angry red. "They live only because you did not. I'd split the skull of either one who dared to stand in my way!"

A stranger to hatred between brothers, Dara looked on in apprehensive bewilderment. There was far more here than a moment's anger at a rash deed, or even their battle over her. It was palpable, bitter strife, and no less with one than the other, though Laochlain's emotions were mastered while Ruod's were scarcely held in check. She could perceive clearly now the resemblance that marked them brothers, emphasized by anger, in the lowered line of thick, dark brows and the unyielding set of hard jaws.

A tensely silent moment passed before Ruod turned away with a grating bark of laughter. He hesitated but a moment as Kinara passed near, and then his hand shot out to fasten on her arm. She flinched but made no protest, nor did any of those who watched. Dara realized she had erred in thinking the servant a child as shining corn-silk hair spilled over the arm Ruod had flung about her shoulders as they went from the hall.

Suddenly drained, Dara turned to find Laochlain studying her with intense interest as if he were judging her reactions to the scene. Resentful, she glared at him, and he met her flashing look with something akin a smile.

"It would seem Ruod is easily consoled of your loss, mistress."

Her hair caught the glint of firelight as the curls shimmered with her quick movement. "I would not have it other, my lord, though if the girl were aught but a Scottish wench, I would pity her!"

A discernible flicker of anger touched his features and was gone. "I doubt that Kinara would want your pity. And perhaps it is you who have hers. She, at least, is free and certain of her position here."

Dara frowned. "A Ryland is never to be pitied."

"Mayhap, lass, but do not be overconfident until you have tested my limits."

With determined dignity, she rose to her feet. "My lord, I have had no sleep this night. Will you permit that I rest now?"

Even his lazy look of contempt could not make her regret this somewhat cowardly means of escape, for she was exhausted and had little reserve left to uphold her.

The upper hall was wide and dim and drafty, the stone floor bare. Torches, extinguished at first light, lined the walls in cold stillness. At the end of that straight expanse of shadows, Dara lay in exhausted wakefulness. Her strength for battle was gone from her, and nothing, not the mean, bare room nor the heavily barred door, had the power to pierce her dreary resignation.

The rough covers of the bed were undisturbed beneath her though the grate was without a fire. She was warm, for the MacAmlaid's cape was still about her though she could not help believing that he had intended her to rest in chilled discomfort for her arrogance. But his cape was thick and well-lined and smelled of horses and leather and forests, a comfortingly familiar scent.

Her mind, unable to cope with thoughts of the night just past, had turned to earlier memories whose sorrows had dulled to a whisper of pain much easier to bear than those of the present. Her mother she had missed and longed for all of her life. She had been little more than a babe when Josceline Ryland had fled from the unendurable rigors of the northlands of England, leaving behind a husband who cursed her memory. His demise fifteen years later had begun the third tragedy when Kerwin, too young to govern with his father's wisdom, had commanded instead with ungovernable recklessness. Again and again in the months since Thayne Ryland's death, he had attacked every Scottish border village within reach, burning, plundering, murdering, until his very name was loathed and feared.

But for all his misguided savagery, Dara had loved him as she loved the quieter Brann. Those brothers, so fierce and impatient, had never disdained nor ignored the younger sister who worshiped them. Inseparable in youth, so they were in later years until their father's death had sent Brann to court in a useful, enviable position and had made Kerwin the new Earl of Chilton. Even then their love had abided, bound by cords of loyalty and enduring need. She clung gratefully to the knowledge that Brann would not long leave her bereft and imprisoned. Weary beyond comprehension, she at last drifted into sleep as restless as the thoughts turning her dreams to nightmares.

Chapter III

Athdair readied itself for attack, and Laochlain assured himself that all was well and secure in his domain. The sun's frugal warmth did not quite reach the shaded paths of the forest and a chill lay upon the shadowed riders. There was no tranquillity to the wind-buffeted afternoon nor on Niall's grimly set face. Laochlain had waited the morning through for an explanation of his brother's dour mood, but none had been forthcoming, and at last he questioned him.

"Have you beheld Satan that you scowl upon the world and me as well?"

"Ruod is not far from so! Have you no worries of what he has done?"

A bird's call sounded harshly through the forest, and Laochlain paused to hear it answered before replying. "Aye, why else would I bid my crofters keep close to their hearths with weapons at hand? This Ryland may follow his brother's example of burning homes and murdering whole families. We must be prepared, but Ruod is adept at causing intrigue and entanglements. I've become accustomed to dealing with the results as they arise. This, too, I will settle."

"You find yourself too often occupied with his misdeeds," Niall chafed. "You owe him no loyalty, and he surely grants you none. He was a bane to our mother from the day of his birth and an evil to us all. I would not do for him what you have done!"

"Ruod's bastardy is none of his own doing, blame Duncan for at least that much." His tone did not make it a rebuke. "Nor can he be blamed for the grief he caused our lady mother. I regret the day of his birth, but I do not hold him responsible for it."

"Nay then, so he is not, but what of his actions through all of his life? He has done nothing that was not intended to harm at least one person in his path. And it is you, Laochlain, that he hates and for you that he would seek the greatest evils."

He spoke vehemently and saw with relief the expression on his brother's face. There was strength and determination there that bespoke no future leniency for Ruod. Niall was young, but he was a MacAmlaid and astute. He knew Laochlain's sharp sense of responsibility for every MacAmlaid and often feared it would be his downfall, particularly when Ruod was foremost among those accepting his succor.

"I know far better than you what Ruod intends," Laochlain said flatly. "Do not fear, Niall, that he will take me unaware."

"Best rid yourself of him then before he does further harm!"

Their horses separated to make their own way through a tangle of brush, and when they again drew abreast, Laochlain said, "I learned long ago that it is far better to have a venomous serpent on the path before you, within reach of your weapons, than dangling from a branch above, out of vision."

They passed in silence from forest to the stubble of carefully harvested fields. Niall knew more than to persist in his warnings of Ruod, but he was far from satisfied. Years spent in observing his half-brother's tactics had nurtured in him a respectful distrust for that one's deadly accomplishments. And yet, each time, Laochlain had bested him in their continual battle of wits. It had yet to come to a test of arms, but the path was winding towards it with inexorable slowness.

The MacAmlaid was not the brother that many might desire; he was neither lenient nor openly affectionate, but it was he who provided every opportunity of worth, and his was the authority that had molded. However ruthless he had been in quelling weaknesses and youthful quaverings, he had never shown scorn or betrayed impatience. His greatest gift to Niall was his pride in him, reason enough for every effort, instilling self-assurance and resourcefulness—traits invaluable to the man Niall had become.

Invigorated by the crispness of the air, the horses stepped springily upon the browned turf. A flock of geese fled before the wind, and the blue smoke of burning leaves and rubble drifted upward from a croft protected by the hillside. A stalwart figure led his oxen on a climbing, winding course in the distance before them. There was nothing to mar the peace of the day.

It was darkening when they reached the fortress. A lad shoveled muck from the flagstones, pausing respectfully as they passed. Niall lingered to enjoy the warmth and welcome of the stables, but Laochlain turned his stride towards the hall. He paused at a shadowy corner to study the clarity of the evening, feeling again the tension of authority settle over him. It was a perceptible weight but not depressing. He had sought power and responsibility at an early age and found neither a burden.

His eyes were attracted by a shine of light as the hall doors parted silently for a slight figure to pass. A stealthy pause aroused his suspicions, and he pressed closer into the shadows that hid him. The figure started forward with gathering swiftness, and he tensed in anticipation. There was no hesitation in the movement that brought him directly into the fugitive's path.

Dara was stunned by the impact. She had awakened to shadows that spread and darkened until there was no light but that from a candle left at her bedside while she slept. It had illuminated a basin of now cold water, a clean gown, and a coarse, country tea of bread and butter and preserved fruit. Only after the use of all of the offerings had she discovered that her door had been left unbolted. She had scarcely dared believe in success as she crept through the hall, but gained confidence upon reaching the great outer doors.

She was dismayed to find herself pinioned firmly, a leather doublet rough beneath her cheek. She kept her face pressed tightly against it until a gauntleted hand raised her chin and she was forced to look up into stormy grey eyes slanted in an anger that creased further still the lines about them.

"Whose carelessness set you free?"

"It matters not; you will find it difficult to hold me!"

He tightened his hold slightly. "I think not; it would be a simple matter to have you chained." He watched her eyes widen in distress before adding remorselessly, "I would have your promise not to make further efforts to escape. Will you give it?"

She knew there was but one answer she could give. Irons would be no less binding than her word and far more unbearable. And she did not in the least doubt the veracity of his threat. Still, her mouth set mulishly, and darkened eyes glared at him in furious resentment.

"It will be as you wish, my lady, your word for your freedom."

Her fingers curled helplessly. "You have it."

He studied her for a moment as if assessing her honesty, and just when she would have had no more of it, he nodded and stepped away, retaining only his grip on her arm. The evening was suddenly dark and hostile, the rising moon cold as they walked back towards the hall. She sought desperately to repay him.

"My brother will come for me! He will repay all that your men have done, and you will suffer as much as they!"

"I do not doubt that he will try; I am ready."

She faltered. "You would kill him?"

His expression was guarded, noncommittal. "That lies with him. His is the next move."

Numbed by sudden fears, she moved forward. Brann would come for her without any caution or thought for his own safety, for he held her as dearly as she did him. Would his care for her bring him to the same fate as their brother? Kerwin's death was a grief, deep and bitter. Brann's would be an agony.

They entered a hall warm and bright with torchlight and noisy with ribald laughter. The MacAmlaid's men sought comfort and ease in this heart of the castle and found it. Laochlain was free with his meat and his drink with those who stood loyal to him. Only one of their number was known not to do so and yet was allowed to remain. But this night Ruod was not among them.

Laochlain's entrance with the English girl drew curious looks but no comment, for he did not welcome questioning. Though his attention was no longer on Dara, he did not release her. His hand was heavy on her waist, and she could not elude its pressure.

They were served mugs of sack still sizzling

from the red-hot poker, and Dara felt its warmth slowly repulse the chill that had seized her. The woman who tended them was the same that had shown Dara to the room where she had slept so restlessly. And, by her nervousness, Dara felt sure that it was she who had so carelessly released the MacAmlaid's prisoner.

Lethe's apprehension lay plain upon her full, smooth face and in her dark eyes. It was Kinara who had failed to bolt the door, but Lethe had full responsibility for the MacAmlaid's keep. She was not so young as might appear, having been married for eleven years and widowed for four. Her shoulders were quite capable of bearing such a load, and she was no hired servant, but a distant cousin of Laochlain's. As he seemed neither displeased nor blaming, she relaxed as she saw to the serving of his supper.

To Dara, the meal was overwhelming. The dripping juices of roast pork vied with the sizzling crispness of woodpigeon, and casks of wine stood near to quench hearty thirsts. She ate with good appetite but kept her eyes on the table before her, avoiding an exchange of glances with anyone. Only once did she lift her gaze, when Laochlain addressed a large, quiet man with thick, red hair.

"Eat well, Gerwalt, you've a ride ahead of you this night. I've a need to know Ryland's whereabouts. There is a message I would have him hear."

His eyes clashed with Dara's as Gerwalt answered, "So, I'll lose my sleep to a border ride."

Dara looked away first, cursing her helplessness, and Laochlain answered, "Aye, and ride swiftly and cautiously, my friend. There'll be no safety for you across the border, and I've no wish to lose a good man."

Dara toyed with a slice of thickly buttered bread, seeking not to hear the words forming plans that alarmed her. She could do nothing to hinder or to change them. Her food was pushed aside, for her appetite was lacking. Her attention was further engaged when Laochlain remarked on Ruod's absence.

It was Duncan who answered, roused from his dark silence. "He drowns the reality of his place in life drinking cheap ale with a skinny, white-haired wench."

Laochlain spoke calmly. "But for being a bastard—a fate you gained him—he chose his lot."

"As I chose mine?" There was a spark of animosity in the look that passed between father and son. "Jamie repaid well those who fought to place his father's crown upon his head . . . and punished sorely those who opposed his treason!"

All eyes were on the two men who faced each other challengingly, and relief sighed through the hall at Laochlain's controlled reply. "Royalty commits no treason. 'Tis well over ten years since we chose opposite loyalties, Duncan, and the past is reconciled. James the Fourth is our rightful king, and no man doubts it now his father is long dead."

"Aye, dead. Murdered, poor man, at Sauchie-burn. And do you think it forgotten that a son of

38

the Chief of Clan MacAmlaid did not stand loyal to him? And you but a lad less than twenty to turn his back on all. Not that there are many left to remember," he pointed out bitterly. "Far too many died upholding him that was our rightful sovereign."

"And to no good!" Laochlain's voice was thunder. "The man was no king. And Jamie never wished his father's death, only the power he could not control! It was no fault of mine that you should leave Gallhiel. Well I know you love it—as do I. But the past is dead, man; there must be an end to it!"

Duncan slumped. "Aye, so there must."

His eyes turned broodingly towards the fire. Nothing was gained by this battle of words, for Laochlain spoke true. The present James had ruled these many years, and none questioned that he did so with far greater success and popularity than his unhappy father had ever attained. And yet, the past could not be completely forgotten, for the bitterness lingered.

As Duncan brooded on his regrets, so Dara did also. She must bide her time now, for a Ryland's word, once given, must be kept whatever the cost. She felt no remorse for Lethe's blaming glance. It was nothing to her if the woman had been chastised for leaving the door unbarred. They were all enemy here, to be hated and defeated—for Kerwin's sake if naught else.

A basin of water and a clean linen towel were offered to her, and she washed her hands and dried them. Laochlain rose and offered his hand to her, but though she also stood, she disdained his hand and was rewarded by his angry flush. He seized her arm roughly and guided her towards the stairs, prodding her forward when she would have held back. The hall fell silent at their exit, and she knew that the faces of all present would hold avid interest if she could but see them.

Her heart raced sickeningly, for she feared his intent. She could see little of his profile in the uncertain light provided by torches bracketed onto high, cold walls, but what little she could discern was not encouraging. His mouth was still grim with the anger her insulting action had wrought. His hand burned into the sleeve of her gown, not painful but unrelenting. She would have little hope of resistance were he determined to have her.

He led her to a comfortable room of generous proportions, and she was relieved of two fears, though lesser ones. It was neither the tiny, barred room in which she had spent the day nor was it his own chamber. This room had most certainly been in disuse, for although a freshly laid fire burned in the grate and the furnishings were newly dusted, the smell of musty closeness clung to it still. Rose-damask hangings were pulled back from around the large feather bed, and her own nightshift lay across the turned-down covers. She turned back from her swift appraisal of the room and found Laochlain disconcertingly near.

His eyes were fixed on her, taking note of the borrowed gown. Soft and warm and blue, the laced bust was too snug, the plain hem inches short. She stood silent, waiting, the color gone from her face. Her hair had need of a comb for it fell in tangles of auburn curls, and worry and strain had left their traces in the smudges beneath overbright eyes.

She flinched, lifting a hand as if to shield herself, though he had not stirred. Unbelievably, he left her with no parting word, the door shutting quietly but definitely after him. The strength of her knees forsook her, and she sank into the deep leather chair drawn near the hearth. The fire crackled and settled its warmth about her while Laochlain stood outside her door, attempting with difficulty to put her face from his mind.

He returned to the hall where Duncan sat in solitude, keeping the unwed servants from the floor of the hall which when laid with pelts was their only bed. He poured two drinks and joined his father by the fire.

It was close on midnight when Ruod returned to Athdair, ugly with drink and his own sour broodings. Duncan nodded at his approach, but Laochlain gave no indication that he was aware of Ruod's presence until he spoke sneeringly.

"Ho, brother. It appears you found it no easy matter to bed the wench. Could it be that a struggle would not whet your appetite for the prize, or have you lost your stomach for rape?"

"That was never my way, Ruod. Are you so drunk you would place your crimes on me?"

Ruod swayed slightly, his expression belligerent. "There's naught a lass who wouldna' welcome me to her bed. This one's the same as any other for all she's English and fine-mannered."

Only then did Laochlain rise and face him squarely. "I'll warn you no more, Ruod, for well you know my measures when crossed. Stay clear of the girl or repent it sorely!"

Duncan spoke wearily as Ruod's fist rose in aggression. "Sit, man, and drink. 'Tis late for brawling, and I'd no enjoy the sight of it after so full and rich a supper."

Ruod, chin thrust forward, glared at his half-brother in drunken indecision before moving to take the earthern jug his father was offering. He drank deeply and stumbled to the table, where he slumped down in baleful contemplation of Laochlain.

Only when his snores filled the hall did the old chief relax. Ruod was far from wise, for Laochlain's forbearance had marked limits though he had treated them well and generously. Even, Duncan found, he was able to forget for much of the time that he was no longer lord of his own keep. He grimaced; at least Athdair was damnably more comfortable than the ancient highland stronghold of the Clan MacAmlaid.

He felt Laochlain's hand on his shoulder. They rose, leaving Ruod and the hall to the servants.

Chapter IV

Dara stood near iron-grilled gates and looked out over well-kept crofts set in lands as beautifully hilled as any of England and wondered about its people. Chilton's tenantry was ever staunch in support of the Rylands, willing to discard scythe and rake for dirk and axe at the first call. Their faith was constant, their loyalty unwavering to each succeeding lord. Unquestioning and unhesitating, they would slay any man among them whom their lord named traitor, so great was their pride in this loyalty. Could the MacAmlaid claim as much?

The muted flame of her hair against stones shaded grey drew Niall as he crossed the courtyard to the stables. His plaid hung gracefully from broad shoulders, and his spurs struck the flagstones as he came.

Dara turned at the sound and marked again his likeness to Laochlain though he lacked his brother's hardened expression.

His was no idle reason for approaching. "My lady," he said. "Do you ken that Laochlain was more than tolerant with your brother? He had far more reason for vengeance than Ruod, who had nothing to lose."

"Do you seek to defend him?"

"Nay!" She had angered him. "I would only know if it will be held in account by others of your clan—those who may seek retaliation and further bloodshed."

"Mayhap, but 'twas his household that rode on Chilton, whether by his order or not. Brann will have that knowledge within him when he seeks my freedom."

"So . . . he will continue in what has been set?"

Her hazel eyes were frank and clear. "That I cannot say. He misliked Kerwin's bloody deeds, but with his murder at Scottish hands . . ." Her voice trailed, then strengthened. "My capture will enrage him, but his actions will depend much on your brother. Brann is a just man though a fierce one."

Niall nodded. It was as he suspected. Laochlain would have to tread easy were he not to fan this flicker of Ruod's lunacy into the blaze of border war. James would little like such a disturbance with his marriage in the offing, and for all his faith in Laochlain, he would lay the blame on his shoulders.

In thoughtful silence, he moved away when he saw that she had turned her back to him. The lass was a bonnie one, but he, no more than Laochlain, was of Ruod's ilk. If she did not wish his company, she would not be forced to it.

It was midafternoon when Laochlain returned from a ride that had encompassed much of his holdings. He brought activity to the drowsing hall with his dominating force. Kinara leapt to serve him, and Duncan greeted him loudly. Food and drink were spread before him, and logs were added to the fire until it roared and sent a shower of sparks dangerously onto the nearest rushes.

From her place near the fire, Dara fancied that his eyes searched the hall before coming to rest on her. She turned her reddened cheeks away from him until instinct warned her, and she glanced round to see him almost upon her. She jerked her gaze from him, and his voice came deep and low at her side.

"Your brother tarries."

"He will come."

"'Twould be a mistake. He can do nothing to bring your brother to life nor to release you until I desire it. Nor will he find me unprepared."

She turned to him then, the pain revealed deep in her eyes, her voice bitterly low. "Then your luck holds truer than did Kerwin's."

"A man dare not rely on luck when he is at war."

She stared. "And do you war now?"

"That is on your brother. If he provokes it . . ." He did not finish, nor was there need.

Aye, he'll not quibble at the murder of yet

45

another Englishman, she thought. Nay, likely he will welcome such opportunity. Her feelings were so fierce she could scarcely keep from trembling as she accused, "Aye, and if he does provoke it, you would cut him down as Ruod did Kerwin. But Brann is not so unwary, nor easily bested. He will have before him an example of a Scot's honor. Mayhap it will be Scottish blood that flows!"

"Art a savage maid and eager for bloodletting, but it may be that it does not come to that. He will soon know my offer to ransom you."

"I will pray he does not heed it!"

A clamor rose in her veins as he took hold of her arms and pulled her to her feet. He had discarded his doublet, and she was near enough to see the tiny stitches of his cream-colored shirt. Too near. But his arms would not yield her any ground, and at last she raised reluctant eyes to his face.

Dark and fierce, his features were stamped with a reckless strength. His brows arched enquiringly above steady, grey eyes. "Have you so great a liking for Athdair?"

"You know I have not, but I have no desire to see English crowns yielded to a Scots brigand!"

His body was the hardness and strength of steel as finely tempered as the blade of a treasured weapon and so close she could feel his strong heartbeat under her palms pressed against his chest. His arms encircled her, and she leaned back against them, away from him. Her hair fell in rippling curls over his arms, the light of the fire caught and held in that silk. It

46

was a stance of lovers, but there was no tenderness in either.

"'Tis more than coins I would have yielded to me."

Her gaze traced his face from challenging eyes to thin but finely curved mouth before sweeping lashes veiled her eyes. In wild trepidation, she felt his lips close on hers, searing, searching. Never had she been kissed in such a manner, and she was without the experience and the knowledge of how to resist. Nor could she. Soon her hands no longer repulsed but rested lightly, steadyingly against him as a tumultuous weakness possessed her.

When he lifted his head, his lips were curved slightly in triumph, and his eyes held a bold promise. "Know you, lass, I do not forgo that which I desire."

She felt humiliated and defeated. "Then do not desire me, my lord."

His eyes did not leave her as she turned from him, and she mounted the sharp-rising stairs knowing he watched. A draft swept the iron-bracketed torches, throwing uncannily distorted shadows across her.

In the haven of her room, she lit a candle at the hearth and set it near as she combed her hair with long, heedless strokes. The sound of Highland pipes came from below, and she knew the others would be eating. She could give no thought to her hunger as she stretched upon the bed and stared at the shuttered window. She knew it was shut firm against the wind and the cold and could be opened if she wished, but it seemed to be shutting her in, away from freedom.

That long night passed as did two more, endless and anxious, until the day Gerwalt returned with news of Chilton Castle. Even then another period of waiting was thrust upon her, for Laochlain chose to hear his news in private while Dara chafed in silent anguish, fearing she would be kept in ignorance.

That was not Laochlain's intent. For the moment, he had all but forgotten her. His quick commands had sent servants scurrying for food and drink, and, curbing his impatience, he bade Gerwalt hold his news until he had eaten. They sat in a tiny room whose light, borrowed from the sun, was permitted entry through a high window with shutters thrown back. The only furnishings were a fancifully carved table, two stiff-backed chairs, and a deep, cushioned one which neither man had chosen.

Gerwalt ate with hearty bites that disdained manners and slaked his thirst with gulping draughts of malmsey. His plain, broad face was lined with weariness, and his clothes were stained with the soil of three days' wear. When at last he finished, pushing the platter of gnawed bone and crust from him, he spoke of the tidings Laochlain had waited so patiently to hear.

"There's no much to be seen at the castle but barred gates and a heavy guard. The crofters keep to their homes, and the villagers are no less wary."

"And Lord Chilton?"

"For certain, the new lord has not yet returned home. If you sit quiet in their wee tavern,

48

you hear no little and not a man knows the sound o' your voice. Aye, and I heard aplenty. The Ryland has been at court these months past, and we'll hear naught of him before this week is spent." He hesitated, then added, "I paid a lad well to carry your message to the castle to await him."

"So—no one has yet decided to take matters into their own hands?"

"Nay, Laochlain, there be no stirrings on any side of the border but for our own men. Chilton's men are not without wits. They wait for him, but they make ready and they'll ride with him, lusting for Scottish blood."

When he had gone, Laochlain sat in silence, not even feeling the chill of a fireless room. He had heard no more than he had been prepared to hear, though events and decisions could move forth in an astonishingly small space of time. He neither expected nor desired any interference in what would undoubtedly be Lord Chilton's course. He reached for a red-brocaded and tasseled bell pull above the table, and it brought Lethe to him so swiftly he knew she must have been awaiting his summons. He sent her to fetch Dara to him and waited without sound until she was before him, poised in the doorway.

"Come closer, and release the hangings."

Dara did so, and with the arras covering the door, the room became suddenly intimate.

"Sit." He was annoyed at her hesitance in entering the room further. "It is your attention I want, nothing more." Ignoring her deep blush, he said abruptly, "Chilton Castle is still without master, though I do not doubt your brother is fully informed of your fate and your brother's. When he arrives home, he will find my requests awaiting him."

"Requests, MacAmlaid? Surely demands would be more truthful?"

He checked his anger. "Very well, then—demands. Do you think he will heed them?"

"I cannot speak for my brother's intentions or even claim to know what they might be. And you already know my wishes."

She left her chair and stood before him, beautifully defiant. Her soft curls of firelit auburn fell loosely against her shoulders, adorning her borrowed gown. Generously offered and reluctantly accepted, it was one of two that Lethe had altered to fit the English girl's slighter build. Of palest yellow, it fit snugly from a square-cut bodice over her hips where it began a swirling fullness; tight sleeves were made in the same pattern, flowing out from below the elbow.

Laochlain rose also and crossed the room to hold aside the curtain covering the door and let her pass. The faint fragrance of scented soap touched him, and when she was from his sight, he scorned his folly in letting her go.

The next morning, Athdair wakened to a sharply cold, rainy, and dew-dropped world, a bold day reminiscent of youth and stirring in Laochlain the excitement and anticipation of the hunt. This particular cast of day, drear and cold before the snows fell, would ever fire his blood with a longing to heft a spear in his fist and see it quiver in its target of flesh, releasing hot blood to steam in the chill air. The keep held men aplenty ready for a hunt, and horses no less eager. A tenseness gripped the beasts as they were mounted and they recognized the boar spears and remembered their purpose.

The rain ceased, but the day grew steadily colder under clouds that threatened. Even in this season of dead bracken and browned heather, the land was beautiful, the cold creating a sharp artistry of its own. Twisting among the dull tree trunks, the hunters resembled the colorful figures on an exquisitely stitched tapestry. But no colored silks, however bright, could catch the vigorous sounds of shouting voices and snapping brush underfoot, nor the invigorating cold borne on winds that had gathered strength over the bare hillside.

They returned late and brought with them the scent of the woods clinging to their clothes as the bog clung to their boots. The vigor of their exuberance, whetted by the chase and the kill, swept each corner of the hall. Cheerful and boisterous were their voices, and no one could fail to share the full measure of their merriment.

Dara entered the room fresh from a hot, soapy tub and, chilled by the dampness that penetrated her clothing, moved near the hearth while half a dozen great rough men moved aside to make a place for her. She was a lady, true enough, and mannered, but, being men, it was her soft beauty that wooed them. She thanked them quietly as she chose a seat not too near the flames.

Finishing his drink, Laochlain set his mug on the table and came to stand before her. It was in his mind to speak, but he stared too long.

Dara felt irritation rise with embarrassed color. She let her eyes take in his lack of grooming, for his hair had yet to feel a comb and mud from flying hooves still splattered his clothing.

"Have you had no time to wash, my lord? The sweat of your horse and the dirt of the forest are still upon you."

His expression did not alter, and she wondered that she had failed to rouse him. When he spoke, however, she knew her mistake and regretted it.

"I go now to bathe," he said, his hand heavy on her arm as he pulled her to her feet, "and you will wait upon me."

In her indignation she had spoken too loudly, and his anger was sharpened by knowing she had been overheard by his men. He had been master of Athdair too long to let an English wench overturn his authority. There was no resisting the strength of his pull, and they were at the stairs before she succeeded in twisting free. Her escape, however, was brief, for he was the swifter and caught her close again before she could flee.

Tense and white, she stared into his set face and, not for the first time in her life, wished her tongue had learned wisdom. Lowering her head, she spoke, with no hope of clemency. "I beg your pardon, my lord. My schooling was not so lax as it would appear."

He was silent, and she lifted her eyes to his. They had softened as had his mouth, a relaxing that was as near to a smile as he had had for her thus far.

"And I, too, lass, was taught more courtesy, but I was very young and it was many years ago. My way of living has not fostered gentleness or civility, and I fear them entirely lacking in me."

He released her and stepped away, bounding so quickly up the stairs that he gave her no chance to speak. Passing a lad in the hall, he sent him to draw a bath, and in his room, he stripped, throwing his clothes in a heap on the floor. He felt a familiar burning and knew he desired Dara Ryland.

When his bath was ready and he was alone again, a young girl slipped in silently and caught her breath at the sight of him, naked and bronzed in the glow of the fire. Eiric was a young servant and new to the hall, but without hesitation she moved so close they nearly touched.

"I thought to ask if you had need of aught." Her voice was low and husky.

His eyes swept over her cloud of brown hair and the curve of her cheeks before dropping to her already-matured body. He stepped away and settled into the steamy water, tossing a sponge which she deftly caught.

"Aye, girl, you can bathe me."

She was young indeed but knew the pleasure of a man and how to give pleasure in return. They soon lay entwined upon the bed, her gown sodden and discarded upon the floor. He pulled her close as his hands sought those places which gave joy to them both, and his mouth burned over soft flesh. Her hands slid from the damp curls at the back of his head to his muscle-tensed back, then lower when he had aroused her unbearably. He pulled her tight against him, and she matched her body to his, eager and ardent, caring nothing for the morrow.

It was a bitter evening that Dara endured with the skirling of the pipes catching at nerves already strained by Duncan's glares and Ruod's leers. To give direction to her gaze, she fell to watching Kinara and could only marvel that such a light and graceful girl should lend herself to Ruod's baseness. He clearly considered her a possession, and she did nothing to disabuse him of the notion. His hands were constantly upon her, prodding and caressing, even as his eyes stripped Dara's gown from her body with sly cruelty.

Duncan's stares were no less unpleasant. It was hard to discern what thoughts lay behind his heavily bushed brows, but they were far from amicable by the scowl which drew his mouth to a thin-lipped line. Dara had early sensed the blame he lay on her for this new altercation between his sons, but the injustice of it failed to ire her. Beyond a doubt, the old man suffered from things of the past and would do so long after the memory of her was faded from his mind. But it was disconcerting to feel the blue flame of his eyes stabbing with the viciousness of his condemnation.

Laochlain seemed to take no heed of the discord surrounding him. The talk among the greater number of those at the table was of the day's hunting, and it was this that held his interest. Boasts and witticisms grew with the number of drinks imbibed as one young and outspoken man jibed another for his lack of skill. A good-natured argument arose, supported on each side by enthusiastic attestations from those who had been present. The MacAmlaid was finally called upon to settle the matter, but he laughingly disclaimed any such responsibility.

"'Twas seen that every man's spear was bloodied, and I'll not claim to know which was the death blow for any beast. Nay, Fibh, and you, Bretach, will have to judge the matter between you."

He lifted his mug in toast and ignored their amiable jibes of cowardice.

The pipes played endlessly, and an ache settled in Dara's head, intensified by every raucous laugh. She stood abruptly and fled the table with no word or look to Laochlain, who frowned and beckoned to Kinara.

Ruod scowled darkly as she slipped into the kitchen. He drained his newly filled mug, looking no less displeased when she reappeared some moments later with a tray laden with an earthen tea kettle and cup. He barred her way with a vicious snarl.

"What are you about?"

"Lord Athdair bade me take something hot to Lady Dara. He fears she takes ill, and I do not doubt it for she was fearful pale." Kinara spoke hastily, thinking to avert a blow from Ruod's open hand. It was clear that he was in ugly humor, and she had paid the price of his foul moods too often not to beware.

"That English bitch needs a taste of something

other than tea. Put it away! You'll tend me, girl, and no other!"

"I dare not!" she hissed, preferring his anger to the MacAmlaid's.

The words were barely spoken before his heavy hand caught her across the shoulder. The tea splashed and scalded as she stumbled, and sharp pain followed the numbness where the blow had landed. Bretach helped her to her feet, but she twisted from his assistance as soon as she was upright. She knew what the men thought of her and cared not—but she needed none of their pity or their help.

Bretach was more than a little drunk, and that fact, coupled with an inherent dislike of Ruod MacAmlaid, urged him on to a chivalry he did not normally possess. Turning from Kinara, he drew knife on Ruod, his drunken taunts fanning flames already fierce. There was nothing so frivolous as sparring in their circling nor so clear-headed as strategy. Their swaying inebriety at once safeguarded and endangered them as their blades encountered flesh in haphazard fashion a half dozen times before Laochlain lost patience. His command sent more than enough borderers to separate the antagonists.

He came to stand near them, disgusted and impartially furious. "You've neither of you enough wits about you to murder the other or save your own skin. The matter is done, and if either of you deem it otherwise, I'll have you flayed! I'll have no man lost for the sake of a wench. Now take yourselves away and tend your wounds."

Kinara gathered the shattered crockery and fled to the kitchen for a fresh brew, and when she again passed through the hall, she was sick with apprehension as the MacAmlaid followed her progress with a stony glare. She sent Ruod a look of sharp disgust. The trinkets he gave her would not be worth banishment should the MacAmlaid decide she was the cause of too much difficulty.

It was no help to see the English girl's eyes widen in curiosity at her damp, stained bodice as she explained her presence.

"I've brought ye a tea at Lord Athdair's command. He feared ye were unwell."

Dara frowned slightly. "Did you meet with an accident?"

Kinara shrugged. "'Twas Ruod's hand and no accident. He was angered that I served you."

"That man has much to answer for, and none of it good," Dara said darkly. "I am English and his enemy, but you are his countrywoman and scarce more than a child. 'Tis shameful that he should treat you so!"

"'Tis no child that has known such a man as Ruod for near two years," Kinara returned slyly, wondering which of them the English girl would think more a child if she were witness to Kinara's nights alone with Ruod. But, lest she speak too freely and find it repeated, she brushed aside Dara's hand as it lifted to stay her and left the room. She was not in the least surprised to find Ruod waiting for her in the hall, and she smiled as he took her roughly by the arm.

Dara paced the rug-softened floor and cursed

Ruod for every vileness he had spawned. And was his brother any less to blame? Was any man free of guilt who would let such malevolent practices go unhalted? Clearly he had power over the man; this was his hall, these men his, even Ruod. Nay, she could not see him blameless. Her restless movements were halted midstride by a knock at the door. Her eyes flew to the tell-tale candle. The light beneath her door was the culprit that had revealed her wakefulness at such a late hour. She stood mute in unreasoning panic as the door swung open at a touch.

Laochlain's shadow-veiled eyes took in the length of her nightshift before he stepped forward into the light. He saw at a glance the cold, undrained tea and the undisturbed bedcovers.

"You do no service to yourself in refusing sustenance and rest."

"You should have a care for those of your hall—if such decency is not beyond a Scotsman and particularly a MacAmlaid!"

"You talk without meaning." His lazy-lidded look was replaced by a knitting of dark brows.

"Do I, my lord? Kinara is your servant, and it is your brother's abuse that she endures. Have you ever sought to aid her or place any hindrance before him? I cannot think your power limited, so it must be your compassion that is lacking."

"That girl has yielded herself to Ruod and has yet to seek my aid or any other's in avoiding him. If you mislike our customs then it is you who must overlook them, not we who must change."

Delivered of this coldly furious speech, he turned on his heel, leaving the door standing wide. Dara stared after him, disbelieving that even a Scotsman could be so callous. Moments later the slamming of her door reverberated along the corridor.

Kinara, lying in Ruod's now-slackened arms, burrowed more closely against him.

Chapter V

Brann Ryland crossed into Scotland just after midnight, leading a group of men well and carefully chosen. Each one of them was strong, skilled, and loyal, and none had anything less than a murderous hatred for Scotland. They presented a formidable force, and an unwary foe would have added to that advantage, but Laochlain had riders guarding the border so that the English approach was noted and he was quickly apprised of the fact. His men needed no urging to ready themselves for battle; they were as eager for it as the English.

Dara's light sleep was shattered by a heavy pounding at her door. Before she could move, the door was flung wide with a virulent oath.

Laochlain lifted his torch high so that it illuminated her slight form, defenseless against the wide expanse of bed. His eyes raked over her without mercy, and his voice struck harshly into the silence.

"I go to meet your brother. Pray for his safety, if you wish it. I'll grant him no quarter."

She made no answer, and he turned and was gone, the sound of his boots ominous in the empty hall. It was long before she could force herself to move, and then she could not control the trembling of her fingers as she dressed. With her candle lit from the embers of the fire, she looped her hair at the nape of her neck and secured it with the precious few wooden pins Lethe had spared for her use. She had not yet found the words for prayer, and the lack disturbed her. Her faith in God was a part of her life, and she had never thought to have it waver. But, she could not help the thought, of what avail had been her prayers and her faith to Kerwin?

Her candle did little to banish the absolute darkness of the upper hall where doors opened into empty chambers, mute evidence of hasty departures. She descended the stairs slowly, hardly knowing whither she was bound. The torches of the great hall were extinguished, but an uncertain light emanated from the fireplace where Lethe crouched with a maidservant, their silent glares marking her path to the door. From their faces, she could name her fate if Laochlain did not return in safety. She would be torn apart long before Brann could force his way into the keep. She felt no fear, though there would be more than womenfolk to contend with, lads considered too young to fight, men too old, and perhaps a brawny few left to defend Athdair. Her only fear was for her brother. With head held high, she walked with steady strength through hall and courtyard, never pausing until she reached the gates where, hands clenched about cold iron, she stared into the murkiness that covered the fells.

Laochlain met Brann in the shadow of the hills, out of sight of Athdair. His sharp command held back his restless borderers, who would have attacked at their first glimpse of the English.

The Ryland halted his band and rode a few paces ahead to stand and wait. Although it couldn't be seen in the fitful light of a moon frequently obscured by clouds, he was dressed as richly as King Henry's court had ever seen him in a silk doublet stitched with scarlet vines and a black velvet cloak, sleeved in sable. But the weapons at his side were not for dress, they were strong, sturdy blades with but one purpose.

Laochlain stopped his borderers and came forward to meet the Englishman, Niall a few paces behind him. Duncan stationed himself before the men, ready to give the word for attack should there be treachery, a command that would scarcely be needed by the battle-eager men. The old lord's heart was proud as his eyes followed his sons, their broad backs sternly held, draped with the plaid of the MacAmlaids which swung heavily above woolen-hosed calves.

Ruod held his horse on the fringe of the group, communicating his restlessness to the animal as it danced and snorted at being re-strained. With hate-filled eyes on Laochlain, a sneer on his face, he was unknowing that Gerwalt's steady eye scarcely left him for a moment. The red-haired warrior was prepared for any measures should Ruod decide to ignore Laochlain's explicit command to wait.

Face to face they met; border lords both, weathered, wary-eyed, tense, swift-moving. Laochlain waited impassively, and Brann spoke at last, his voice carrying clearly to both bands of men straining to hear.

"I've come for my sister. If she is returned to me unharmed, we will leave as we came, for it is as my king bids. But," his voice turned bitingly ugly, "if she has suffered in any manner, you'll not live to see another day, Athdair—no worry whose edicts I defy!"

Laochlain's reply ceased the murmuring that had arisen on all sides. "Your threats have no authority here. My men are the match and more of yours, and your sister remains barred and well-guarded. Should I not return, I can make you no guarantee of her fate—but a likely guess." His next words forestalled Brann's angry eruption. "She is unharmed. Whether she remains so, you will determine by your actions."

"I came for her, think you I will leave without?" Brann's words were heavy with anger.

"You can do nothing more to ensure her safety than accede to my demands. Leave Athdair and Scotland. It will cost you a goodly sum to free her. Your actions declare her worth your life—is she worth your gold?"

"All I possess and more, but you bid me have faith in a Scotman's word. A man whose warriors wreaked a bloody defeat on my sleeping household, a man whose brother slew mine. Shall I leave my sister to such doubtful mercy? What guarantees her safety if I do so?"

"My word, and my arm will guard her."

Brann did not answer immediately, but sat his mount in tense silence, weighing his chances of success in freeing Dara. These equaled the Mac-Amlaid's as far as this battle was concerned, and he would ever place faith in his men, but victory here might well mean danger, even death to his sister. Even now a blade might be held to her throat, awaiting the outcome. Nay, the stakes were too dear for the gamble. Before he could speak his yielding, a single man rode forward to his side, a square-built contrast to Brann's slender height. His face was twisted with anger and hatred, his eyes gleamed with desire for battle.

"Would you listen further to Scottish treachery, man? What of Kerwin? I would not leave my friend unavenged! Would you your brother?"

"Nay, Tirell," Brann's answer was grim. "I would not, but Dara is of far greater importance than is vengeance. My brother is dead, my sister I would keep safe. She is all of my family, now, save an uncle who has only little more liking for me than for a Scots." He turned from disappointment and answered Laochlain. "Aye then, MacAmlaid, I'll go, but I give you not long to prove your honor. Should it be false, I'll leave no stone of your hall unscarred and no one of your people unslain."

He turned his horse without waiting for an

answer, his back held with easy dignity. Laochlain could admire such quiet courage and recognized that Dara possessed it to the same degree as her brother. He had marked it on more than one occasion, deeming it rare in a lass. Aye, the Rylands were worthy opponents on any battleground with any weapons. Watching the departing English, he did not see Ruod lift his weapon at the same moment he set his heels to his mount, but he did hear Gerwalt's roar and wheeled to see the powerful redhead bar Ruod's way with his own mighty horse. Their weapons clashed midair, and Gerwalt's greater force flung Ruod's axe from his grasp.

Laochlain's words cut through Ruod's fury of curses. "Were better you offered gratitude than abuse, Ruod. Gerwalt's timely intervention has saved you from my anger. You think yourself inviolable, but no man is who disobeys me!"

Heedless of Ruod's frustrated rage, he set a swift pace for home. Athdair waited in the rose-grey dawn, a great square of ancient stone. Stark against a background of shadowy woodland, its solid face bespoke centuries of strength and endurance. The gates were flung wide for their entrance, but Laochlain's swift eye caught a slender shadow poised against the stone. He halted the red stallion, but signaled his men on within the walls.

Dara stepped forward as pale as the fleeing mist. Her hair glowed with the color her flesh was denied as she lifted her head to confront him. "Has this cursed land at last claimed all that I hold dear?"

Her rigidly controlled voice betrayed none of her fear, but Laochlain was not deceived. She had withstood the death of one brother and was now faced with the loss of another. A struggle with an unfamiliar and unwelcome emotion harshened his voice as he answered.

"Your brother lives."

Even as he spoke, he spurred his horse forward with a suddeness that took her unaware. Trusting to the animal's training, he swooped sideways and lifted her into his arms.

Braced against him, she wondered that the forced embrace of one enemy should feel so different from that of another who was surely no less so. There was safety here and no cruelty in a grip that held her secure.

When he dismounted before the stables, he reached up for her as Ros took the reins. Taking her from the horse, he did not release her but carried her up the wide steps into the hall lit with warmth and welcome for his return. Placing her lightly on a high-backed trestle seat, he stepped away, his eyes still upon her face.

The trestle was placed so as to catch the heat of the fire, but it was not that which brought color to her cheeks. She longed to turn her eyes from his but felt tested by his gaze and knew a need to meet that test, unmindful of the consequences.

"You show no concern that your brother failed to free you."

It was no question, but she answered all the same, sure of her standing. "He'd not have left me here without an assurance and promise of my safety, and I doubt not that you threatened him with my danger, should he press."

"Aye. Do you share his trust in my word?"

She stared at him, feeling a tremor in her pulse. "You are known for a dangerous man, Laochlain MacAmlaid, but not a dishonest one. Aye, I would give you my trust."

His gaze touched her face in a bold caress. "Keep you from harm I will, but, lass, I gave no promise to release you. If your brother took it so, 'twas his error."

Foreboding swept her, and long after Athdair was abed, chambers dimly lit and plentifully warmed by hearthfires, the hall filled with servants sleeping soundly on their pallets, that foreboding kept her from sleep, tempering as it did the relief she had savored all of the long day through. Brann was safe. A merciful God would keep him so.

That hope was a consolation through the endless days of torment. She had resigned herself to dull hours spent in the confines of her room if she were to avoid Ruod's presence when Laochlain was from the keep. It was true Ruod offered her no physical threat, he was too cautious for such madness, but his eyes were ever upon her, crudely and unpleasantly so. Niall, Gerwalt, or any one of the others would have barred his way from less passive crudities, but only Laochlain could quell that lustful stare.

Duncan's torments were no easier to bear though far less obvious. His animosity had the substance of taunts and glares of loathing which not even Laochlain could bring to a halt. The old chief had no good to say of the English girl. Her English blood was a malediction, her beauty an evil as was her charm. She had brought no good to Athdair, he swore, and could not. His bright gaze rebuked her at every turn, his eyes as blue and punishing as his bastard son's.

On one evening when Duncan had pushed too far the limits of patience, Laochlain silenced him with a sudden, angry exclamation. "It is enough, Duncan! Your tongue is as evil as an old crone's and as sharp as the blade of my axe. I'll not have another evening soured by your ill humor."

A silence fell on the hall that could have been pierced with the point of a blade. The old man rose to his feet, saying no more than any man watching, but his glare was a curse on Dara's head.

Niall hacked a slice of oatbread into a mound of crumbs as he considered rising to his father's defense, but respect for Laochlain and a realization that Duncan had wrought his own humiliation stayed him.

And humiliation it was, for the hall was filled with men, none of whom betrayed a consciousness of the scene save Ruod, whose bark of laughter evoked an even more venomous look than the one his father had bestowed on Dara. When the old man finally quit the room, talk and laughter and the clatter of mugs resumed with almost painful determination.

Dara was stunned by the incident and stole quick glances at Laochlain. He did not appear in the least disturbed by the contretemps but jested with Gerwalt over an obstinate colt's resistance to being ridden. His face was alive with his love of horseflesh, and Dara realized he gave no more thought to the incident. She also realized that there was no respect or affection in him for his father beyond what lingered from childhood.

She could not know the naturalness of this, for to her it was not. Her own father had been of a different mold, a man to be reckoned with, but Duncan had yielded to misfortune in earlier days, and though he bemoaned it, he made no struggle against it.

Laochlain caught one of her quick looks and held her eyes quizzingly, almost smiling. She blushed with a confusion of emotions and turned her eyes from him. Whatever his reason in excoriating Duncan, it had served to ease a hurtful situation for her. The thought that that might have been his intention drove every other thought from her mind as she considered the implications of that possibility.

Hours later when candlelight had darkened the rose of her damask bedhangings to a shade barely above grey and the night wind hurled itself against her shutters, a knocking sounded at her door which could not be confused with the buffeting of the wind. She had been comparing the comforts of the room with her own at Chilton and had not found it lacking. Doubtless, she had fared better than any other of English blood imprisoned within these walls over centuries past. Such thoughts turned her pensive, and this mood was reflected in her face, giving Laochlain pause as she opened the door to him.

He carried a bundle awkwardly and thrust it at her, saying abruptly, "There will be visitors for All Saints, Niall's betrothed and her family. I would have you fittingly dressed."

He left as quickly as he had come, giving her no chance to refuse or accept. Once more alone, she stroked the softness of fine fabric and remembered the look of him as he had stood before her.

Before she could descend for breakfast the following morning, Lethe was at her door with a tray of food and a dainty chest of sewing implements. And once there, Lethe was firmly ensconced with a willing hand as finely skilled at needlework as Dara's. Whether resentful or pleased at this intrusion into her daily routine, neither Dara's practical conversation nor her calm countenance revealed.

Chapter VI

All Hallow's Eve. The night was sharply cold, and wisps of cloud hinted of rain as they veiled the waning moon. Stars glittered between cloud drifts, jealous of the leaping flames on the fells below. Lads and lasses danced about bonfires and loved in defiance of Samhain, lord of the dead. This was his night, the time in which he roamed the earth gathering the souls of those dead who inhabited the bodies of animals. 'Tis but a pagan belief, the revelers assured themselves even as they built their fires higher to guard against the witches aiding Samhain in his search.

Athdair feasted, welcoming with food and wine and laughter the guests that had arrived just on nightfall. The Kermichils' servants had revealed themselves leery of the gathering darkness as they pressed close into the light of the hall. An old servant scolded with easy familiarity when the daughter of the family proclaimed herself wishful to join those drawn about the open fires upon the hill.

"Ach, Miss Anne, you'd be taken up by a witch, ne'er to be seen again!"

The girl's trill of laughter drew answering smiles as Niall pressed forward to take her hand before bowing gracefully to her parents.

"I trust you traveled well, sir."

"Well as could be when there are womenfolk to portend disaster and complain of cold and discomfort at every league."

He looked a dignified gentleman to Dara who stood in the opened doorway of the hall. She would not have chosen so conspicuous a position, but Laochlain's hand gripped her arm and where he would stand so, perforce, must she.

Lord Kermichil escorted his lady to greet Laochlain, leaving his grown children, son and daughter, to follow with Niall.

Laochlain grasped his hand firmly, warmly. "We expected you ere now. Had you trouble?"

"A bit with a horse gone lame, but 'twill soon mend."

He turned questioningly to Dara, who blushed uncomfortably as Laochlain answered that silent query, presenting her to Lord and Lady Kermichil. "Lady Dara Ryland. She . . . abides with us at present."

Dara was almost amused at the ease with which he would have passed over explanations, but it was not to be, for Lord Kermichil had stiffened at the introduction and even his wife's shocked expression proved them familiar with the name.

Kermichil's voice held outrage as he exclaimed, "I had not thought Athdair asylum for Scotland's enemies!"

In the heavy silence that followed, Dara felt anger redden her cheeks and would have given answer had not the pressure of Laochlain's hand on her arms warned against it.

"If you fear the lass, you've leave to bring a man armed into the hall."

This time it was Lord Kermichil's face that burned with color at Laochlain's brusque answer. Laochlain gestured them into the hall, and the matter was wisely dropped.

Dara was familiar enough with MacAmlaid pride to know that Laochlain was angered by the questioning of his actions, even from a welcomed guest.

She left the hall as Lethe saw the Kermichils served with hot brandied milk. Her room was a warm, glowing refuge, and a hot bath awaited her as Lethe had promised earlier. She bathed slowly, enjoying the silk of water frothed with the soft, scented soap. Pins held her hair up from her shoulders as she leaned against the back of the tub, relaxed and comfortable. There she remained until the water cooled, and with a feeling of dread, she knew she must return to the hall or risk Laochlain coming in search of her as he would surely do.

Her dressing took no great deal of time. Her hair yielded readily to her nimble fingers, the clean, shining curls forming a crown of dark russet. The gown she and Lethe had cut and sewn from a length of apricot satin had the beauty of simplicity. There was nothing to delay her return belowstairs.

The guests had already assembled in the hall. She descended the stairs with obvious hesitation, for, although she had not expected to be at ease, she was unprepared for the timidity that swept her. She was glad when Gerwalt stepped forward to take her arm and she was no longer a solitary figure.

The hall was clothed in the heavy colors of furs and skins, and rushes lent no brightness to the room as carpets would have. But the Kermichils had changed from traveling dress to clothes of rich elegance, and Duncan and his sons wore doublets of costly cut and varied hues, stitched with threads of gold or silver. The effect was one of color and brilliance, making the hall an alien and no longer comfortable room for Dara.

There was no doubt that Athdair's guests had been apprised of her situation, for Lord Kermichil nodded civilly enough while his wife seemed almost sympathetic—to Dara's wrath. She had no wish for a Scotswoman's sympathy! The younger Kermichils' greetings were more acceptable. Anne was warm and cordial while her brother was quite definitely admiring.

Dara was somewhat surprised to find herself seated, as usual, at Laochlain's side. Lord Kermichil was disapproving; his acceptance of her presence did not extend to any desire to see her honored. His feelings were communicated to his wife, and they took pains not to allow their glances to rest on her. Dara was amused until a serving maid paused to meet her eyes in a look that was meant to be reassuring. Yet, even then, she was not without humor, and before her indignation could blossom, she felt laughter rise in her at the incongruity of the situation.

Watching her, Laochlain wondered at the smile that came to her lips.

Niall was noticing nothing beyond his future bride. She was seated at his side, their joy in each other obvious. Anne was not a beauty, but her neat features were full of lively good humor, and her short stature held grace and manners. And there was no denying her devotion to her betrothed, flirt though she might with others.

Creag Kermichil's nature was akin to his sister's, but they bore little resemblance physically. He was tall with bluntly squared features, and his hair was flaxen where hers was red, pale, and silky. His eyes of golden brown held none of the changeability of Anne's mixtured ones. And where his sister displayed pretty manners, sharing her attention with all in reach of her conversation, he had eyes for none but Dara. So much so that Laochlain had marked it grimly and unfavorably.

Inevitably through the evening, the talk turned to the coming union of James of Scotland and Henry Tudor's daughter.

"Aye, our James is a well-loved man, not like some Scotland's known. There's no gilly-gawky manner about him. Listens to his council but makes his own decisions when all's been said." Lord Kermichil paused to strip a leg from a crisply browned fowl. "Though it's been said he passes over the good counsel as well as the bad."

77

Niall grinned. "Aye, and some say he walks a fool's path at present."

"This peace with England is bitter for some to swallow."

It was Laochlain who answered Kermichil's scornful tone. "Then they are ones who've not thought how our borders are continually weak from raids and skirmishes. Our crofters have little chance to plant their fields when they must hold a weapon in the one hand and sow crops with the other. James looks to his own."

"Aye, but does not Henry, also?"

A murmur of assent greeted this observation, and Dara made a concerted effort to remain silent.

Femininely, Anne remarked on James' reputation, ignoring the more serious overtones of the conversation.

Her father gave a snort of laughter. "Well, he's a different proposition from Henry, I'll be bound."

Again Dara bit her tongue, and curiously enough, it was for Laochlain's sake that she did so. His guest, however, appeared determined to enrage her, for Henry's parsimony and fidelity to his queen was as well cited as James' extravagant generosity and sensual appetites. Henry was as good and noble a ruler as James but lacked the worship the Scottish king was accorded.

Dara's eyes met Laochlain's in a contemplative glance before she yielded her attention to the importunities of the Kermichil heir, who appeared oblivious to his sire's disapproval. Creag's blandishments, however, did not make her forgetful of the man close at her side, nor did his flattery engender the same elation as the unspoken approbation in a pair of reckless grey eyes.

The pipe seemed tireless, and one lay above all others caught in her mind. A song of the Highlands, wild and bittersweet. It held the stamp of the MacAmlaid and seemed to be of the stuff of which he was made. Brooding strength, unbending, but with rare moments of half-revealed tenderness. It was these rare moments she knew she must fear.

It was the swift, pulsating tunes the others preferred, those to stir the blood and set the feet askimming. Several wenches had come up from the crofts to aid in the serving, and their laughter rang above the sound of the pipes as they made playful moves to evade questing hands. Their faces were flushed with wine and excitement, their hair tumbled and their clothing disarranged, but morning was time enough for any shame they might feel at their abandon.

Kinara held herself aloof from them, her expression revealing her disdain for their commonness. She moved freely about the men, knowing that none dared fondle her even in play, for, drunk or sober, Ruod was quick with the knife he carried with him at every waking moment.

Watching Ruod openly place his hands on the serving girl at every opportunity increased Dara's hatred of Ruod and her provocation with Laochlain over the situation. Kinara was much too young for the use being made of her. Casting an angry glance his way, Dara found the MacAmlaid watching her with the certainty of one who knows another is thinking of him and that the thoughts are not favorable ones. His expression did not change as she jerked her glance away from him to a meal that had long since satisfied her hunger.

As with any feast, there seemed no end to the variety and quantity consumed. Men no longer hungry ate, and no longer thirsty drank. But while his guests and household gorged, Laochlain sat with mug in hand and sprawled against the back of his carven chair in complete relaxation. At last the platters of fowl and pork and beef gave way to sweets, pastries, and candied fruits, though the men would not yield their ale to the lighter wine as did the ladies.

Into sated quietness came excitement. A sturdy youth entered from the courtyard bearing a large, hooded falcon. The bird held herself proudly though she was carried blinded into a strange and frightening world. She was a bird to strike envy into sporting hearts, and there were murmurs of appreciation all along the table. The boy made unerringly for Laochlain, who gestured towards Anne.

She tensed in sudden, unwelcome realization, and his words confirmed her fear.

"My gift for the bride."

"My lord," she acknowledged, wondering how to continue. Her dislike of hawking was even more intense than that she felt for the hunt. She toyed with the heavy chain of gold and emeralds at her throat, Niall's gift to his betrothed. "I'm sure you honor me with your gift. Is the bird one of your own?"

"Aye," he replied, not bothering to name the bird's qualities. He had realized his lack of intuition immediately, but was more amused at his folly than disturbed by Anne's unconscious reaction. He saw the veiled relief in her eyes as he had the falcon returned to her caged room in the stables.

If Anne thought her gratitude sufficiently expressed, she erred, and several mornings later she sought bolstering from Dara. Her determination for friendship between them had been persistent, and much of Dara's stubborn pride had crumpled before the onslaught. There was no pity in Anne's manner. Beneath her calm nature, her dreams were as filled with adventurous longings as most young ladies', and Dara seemed to her to be envied rather than pitied. Only with the loss of her brother could she empathize, for she loved Creag deeply and would feel an anguish as deep as Dara's for Kerwin should he be slain.

As she slipped through the door Dara opened to her knock, her smile was quick and warm. Dara was dressed in Lethe's borrowed gown of gold, but her hair still hung loosely in a heavy, curling mass. She had not expected company at such an early hour and had been sitting idle before the hearth.

Anne's first words had nothing to do with her errand as she touched Dara's hair enviously. "Art a fool, girl. Nothing could lessen the color, but with it bound atop your head no one can see the lovely length of your hair. I wear mine loose from vanity, but it is not the match of yours."

Dara shook her head without speaking as she began to coil the object of Anne's admiration into heavy braids.

Anne grinned. "Well, I shall not insist against anything that disguises a rival's beauty."

Her soft voice was pleasing, and the accent not far different from Dara's own, for the north country of England and the lowlands of Scotland were not so diverse as was stridently proclaimed. The boundaries had ever been variable, according to the might of the defenders on one side or the other. So, although Laochlain, like all the MacAmlaids, spoke with the Gaelic accents of the Highlanders, Dara heard no strangeness in Anne's speech.

She shrugged. "I wore it loose at home, but here—here I have the need of dignity by any means."

Ever sensitive, Anne caught the hint of distress behind the admission and fell silent a moment, her eyes upon Dara's set face. When she spoke again, it was of another matter entirely.

"Niall has assured me I must do honor to his lordship's gift, and to show appreciation, it is needful to prove my pleasure. I have never cared for hawking, it seems a cruel and needless sport. And," she added with her quick smile, "I shall never convince his lordship of my pleasure in it. The man is no fool. Yet Niall is right—the effort will please him. And my father is also very concerned that he be pleased."

It was evident that her desire to please Laochlain had no connection with her father's as she said mischievously, "Poor Father has dreams of power, his wealth has ceased to content him. Ah well, it does me no ill to concede to his wishes when they are also Niall's."

Dara listened without speaking until Anne stated her request. "I want you to come with me. The MacAmlaid, for all Niall's reassurances, is quite likely to be critical, and I dread to be a girl alone amongst men."

"I think what you ask is not wise. Nor would it be granted."

"It is most certainly not wise that you are immured within this keep! You are no criminal! And as for anyone's forbidding it, well, I think you need not worry about that!"

Dara wondered if Niall had ever seen his beloved with quite that look of intractability upon her face. Still, whatever her reasons, Anne's suggestion was tempting.

"I am grown tired of these walls. If permission is given, I will go and gladly."

Delighted with Dara's acquiescence, Anne broached another aspect with a tact that denied shallowness. "I've a riding skirt that will fit you in all but length, and by the time we've breakfasted, Cearda will have attended to that quite nicely."

As they descended the stairs, Dara could not prevent a flare of hope. If her presence among the hawking party was not forbidden at the outset, she would enjoy the outing whatever the consequences.

There had been more formality to meals since guests had come to Athdair, and though most of the men still ate at dawn and took themselves away, Laochlain and Duncan, at least, joined Niall and the Kermichils at a well-laden table. Morning meals rarely varied even for guests. Dara had soon learned that the vast meal she had had before her that first morning was uncommon. The normal prospect was fish and porridge. Dara had little taste for either and generally contented herself with the bread that was served fresh and hot at every meal.

Life had remained more or less even for her in the days since All Saints', for Ruod apparently found much to keep him occupied and away from the keep. Lord and Lady Kermichil she avoided, him because of the cold stare he fixed upon her whenever they chanced to meet, and her because of the probing curiosity she exhibited, a thing intolerable to Dara's privacy. Creag and Anne, however, were delightful companions, accepting and sharing her confines, the walls of Athdair.

Anne's calm pronouncement that Dara was to accompany them was uncontested, though Dara stirred uneasily under Laochlain's quick look. Niall appeared agreeable, Creag even more so. Dara relaxed, ready to take what pleasure she could in the hours ahead.

It was a rare, fine day with the shine and crispness of October lingering into a month that was normally damp and grey. Dara felt at home in Anne's snug jerkin of soft chamois and a swinging skirt of dark green. Cearda was indeed adept with a needle, for none could have told that it had been altered in length; it might well have been a garment tailored for Dara herself. A small, flared hat of the same dark shade as the skirt emphasized the brightness of her coppery hair.

Firmly held horses stamped their eagerness on stones that intensified the sharp sounds. Niall grasped Anne's hand to pull her more swiftly forward, and Dara followed, troubled by sudden misgivings. Creag was astride, and near him, Dara recognized Laochlain's red stallion, snorting his disdain for the enforced wait. A movement from the stable opening caught her eye, and Laochlain led forward a sorrel gelding. His gaze went immediately to Dara, and his beckoning left no space for hesitation. She looked swiftly about for a groom to aid her, but it was the MacAmlaid's own hands that lifted her effortlessly into the saddle. She was left breathless at the power and restraint of his grip. This then, was the source of her misgivings. Until this moment, she had not considered the possible intimacy of the outing.

They rode in a close group, flanked by servants bearing the hooded falcons. Moorfowl and partridges, startled by their approach, fled in great rustlings of feather and dried bracken, but though the falcons stirred at the sound, they remained passive beneath their hoods. The fells were nearly barren now, occupied only by bare trees and the hardiest of brush, and the approach of winter was evident in every sign. With the wind unhindered, Dara had cause to be grateful for the warmth of her clothing.

On an unprotected slope, they drew rein and dismounted, Laochlain taking his falcon into his gloved hand. The peregrine was large, the length of the arm from crooked elbow to outstretched fingertips. The feathers on back and wings were a rich blue-black and lighter beneath her body, a greyish white. Controlled power lay in every plumed feather, deadly power in curved talons. She wore a scarlet hood, and scarlet streamers were wound through Laochlain's strong fingers, binding her to him. Very gently, he loosened the hood and slipped it from her head.

Dara felt as much as saw Anne tense as huge, lightless eyes scanned the hillside, missing no form or movement in that sweep. Anne's dread seemed untenable to Dara, who had hawked as well as hunted since childhood, taught and encouraged by rough young brothers. With no mother to instill gentler principles and a father who cared too little to provide any female capable of doing so, she had grown up with experiences few gently-bred girls were allowed to attain. She thrilled to the sweeping spread of wings, moving effortlessly above them, casting a shadow of imminent death on the creatures below. Distantly, she heard Niall speaking in murmurs to Anne.

"She kills only to eat, and no human need fear her. There's more beauty in the flight of the falcon than in a coffer of gems."

Anne's reply Dara heard only remotely, and Laochlain and Creag heard not at all as the falcon made a swift climb with powerful, lifting strokes. She had spotted her prey and would attack from above with the unmatched dive of the hunting hawk. Her prey was a lone partridge, the kill swift and sure. The talons struck, snapping bone and loosing feathers.

She brought her offering to her master, but did not release it to him. They waited until she had eaten and was safely on Laochlain's hand, streamers once again binding her to him, hood shielding the world from her sight, before Niall released Anne's bird. She was hooded in yellow, her feathers well sheened with health. A smaller bird than was the MacAmlaid's but no less skilled.

If Laochlain knew the effort it cost Anne to watch as this falcon, her property, killed and gorged upon a softly feathered, living creature, he gave no sign of it. Niall was justifiably and visibly proud of her as she stood unshrinking, her eyes not once wavering from the scene, no portion of her disgust revealed upon her face. She realized the necessity of accustoming herself to a harsher world than the one her parents had provided for her. In no one bearing the name MacAmlaid would less than courage and strength be tolerated.

As they rode homeward, Niall's gaiety, and Anne's, almost covered Creag's morose silence. His expectations had been blocked by a silent, almost grim figure of authority. He had no opportunity to flirt with Dara nor to capture her attention in any serious manner. The MacAmlaid guarded her unobtrusively, but effectively. Even the mount he had provided for her served to that effect, for it was not a docile animal to permit others to crowd too near. Creag had developed no real affection for Dara though his interest had been captured by the novelty of her situation, but he was intrigued by her and wished her well. His chagrin was complete and angering when, almost upon Athdair, Laochlain conferred briefly with Niall and then pulled abreast of Dara, commanding her attention effortlessly.

"Ride with me."

It was not a command nor wholly a request, and without speaking, she turned aside to join him, readily and unquestioningly.

Creag had no choice but to ride forward, returning with the others to the fortress.

Laochlain held to a steady pace until Dara, feeling the inherent recklessness of all Rylands invade her blood, spurred her horse into a speed that abandoned caution. The red barely needed his master's swift signal to leap forward, and they raced side by side over autumn's turf of dying heather. The rough wind pulled Dara's hair free of its coils and flung it back in a welter of tangled curls. When at last they halted, her cheeks and nose were brushed with the deep color of cold and excitement.

Dismounting, Laochlain held up his arms for her, and she slid slowly into them. He took the reins and led the way down into a shallow ravine sheltered by a ridge of trees across the winter side. The dryness of fallen leaves and weedy stalks was a crackling beneath their feet.

Dara moved ahead to sink onto that coarse, brown carpet next a tiny burn, hidden by bushes but betrayed by its whisper of rushing sound. The water was icy to her fingertips.

Laochlain came to a stand behind her after tethering the horses. His voice was as quiet as the little valley. "In the spring, that burn will flood this hollow, fed by rains and snow melting in the Highlands."

Something in his voice caused her to look up swiftly. The yearning of that last word was repeated in eyes darkened to slate.

"You miss your Highlands."

"My heart is there," he replied starkly, "and the heritage of the clan. There is no place so cruel or so beautiful as the mountains of the north of Scotland. They master you no matter how great a man you might be. No mortal is the match of them."

"Yet you remain here, in the border lands."

In the silence that followed, she dropped a leaf into the swirling water and watched as it was swept against a tiny boulder which had created its own eddy. The leaf was sucked under.

"My loyalty is with James and Scotland, wherever their need is greatest. For many years, that need has been here. The border must be secured, but I will not remain here forever."

"Secured against England."

He nodded, ignoring the flare of angry feeling she made no effort to suppress. She rose restlessly, and his hands came down upon her shoulders, gently but securely, turning her, drawing her near.

Without protest, she let herself be molded to him and accepted, even welcomed, his strength. Her spirit was weary of the struggle against his influence. Her head lifted for his kiss, and the onslaught of his lips was sweet, unlike the encounter that seemed so long ago, yet was measured in time less than a fortnight. The pleasure of it grew frightening in its unfamiliarity.

He felt her shrinking and lifted his lips, protesting hoarsely, "Nay, lass, do not go from me."

It was a blast of icy reality, that plea spoken in passion, and the shock of it broke through the lethargy that had taken possession of her.

Her eyes were anguished. "'Tis wrong! I betray my name and my brother. My people you would conquer, my country is your enemy. Release me now," she pleaded, "let me return to Chilton!"

The fire was gone from him and in its place was cold implacability. "No, not until I will it. Not until my terms are met."

"Met by whom, my lord? By my brother—or by me?"

She was left without an answer as he turned and walked away. She followed reluctantly, and felt only pain where there should have been fury. The ride back was accomplished in heavy silence, and when Laochlain lifted her from the saddle in the darkening courtyard, she pulled swiftly away and fled into the hall.

He stared after her, angered and perplexed, and it was late that evening before he left off drinking in the great hall. And though it was Dara who tormented his thoughts, he did not send Eiric away when she crept into his room in the hour after midnight.

Chapter VII

It was a weary band of riders that reached Chilton Castle in the cold hours of early evening. There was very little light left from the vanished sun, barely more than a pale tint upon the low-hung clouds and over the fells beneath them. The countryside was silent and still as they passed through, and the flickerings of light from the crofts seemed a promise of comfort ahead.

Chilton's walls loomed protectively about the keep, and the gates, alertly and heavily guarded, remained secure until Brann Ryland was identified among the riders. He wore none of his accustomed richness, nor were his servants dressed in the colors of Chilton. Their dress was dull and rough, able to withstand the most grueling wear, and their faces were begrimed and unshaven, making of them a seemingly crude lot though they came from His Majesty's winter court.

Only within the safety of the walls did they relax to speech, and the sound of their voices, mingled with the stamping of hooves, heralded their arrival to those within the hall. A warmth seemed to emanate from the opened doors, and two men detached themselves from the milling group and hastened towards that warmth.

An old woman stepped back at their approach, and Brann took her age-withered hand in his and drew her into the room. He entered the great hall without really seeing any of its elegance—that was left to his guest to marvel over. Such gracious beauty in the supposedly barbaric northlands! Vivid tapestries covering ugly, bare stone. Tall candles in sconces augmenting the light from the hearth. There were backed and padded benches against the walls, their coverings stitched by generations of Ryland countesses. The long table was covered with fine linen, and bowls of dried flowers graced it in places, sending a soft perfume over the room to mingle with the pleasant odors of hot wax and burning apple logs.

The room received more of Lord Blaecdene's notice than it might have as he sought, in courtesy, to keep his face and thoughts averted from the scene behind him. The words, however, he could not help but overhear.

"Nay, Mildraed, it came to naught. We'll have no aid of Henry, and he's bound my hands in the paths left to me. If Dara is to be freed, it will be at Lord Athdair's convenience, and upon his terms. Else I will incur our sovereign's wrath and penalties."

"Rylands have defied their king ere now. We of the north give our allegiance where we desire! Where it is worthy!"

Lord Blaecdene could not help turning to seek a closer look at the woman, though he had given her no more than a cursory glance upon entering. Hers was the fierce, independent spirit he had looked for and found in Brann Ryland. The defenders of the northlands had long been a law unto themselves, holding themselves apart from the greater part of England and, at times, the authority of their king.

Brann allowed the weariness and frustration he had endured since his audience with Henry to show in his face as he agreed. "And so I could now. Defy Henry and lead our men against Athdair, but I fear that if we attack Athdair in force, we shall but rescue a corpse."

Mildraed's moan brought him swiftly to repentance. "Forgive me, Mildraed, I should not speak to you so. Take heart. I will find a way from this labyrinth. I must."

His words were brave, but his tone was despairing and moved her to say, "Have you thought to seek aid elsewhere? Owein?"

"Nay!" Her suggestion ignited the explosion she feared. "My father's soul would damn me. I'll look to him for naught!"

"Your pride is witless, Brann!" She spoke sharply as she had been wont to do in days of boyhood recalcitrance. "'Tis your sister's life we bargain for, not anything so trivial as the matters your father and uncle quarreled over, bringing a senseless breach between their families! My Dara is lost, and 'tis left to you to bring her home. Do not disdain any man's aid. Not even Owein Ryland's!"

Brann stared irritably at her stiff, arthritic back as she left him. Even in old age, it was as rigidly upright as in the days of the schoolroom. And her familiarity was that remembered from the nursery. Those thoughts soothed his anger, reminding him that she spoke from the love of long years. Proven love, and the only such they had had from a woman since their mother's desertion, the only mother's love his sister could ever remember. Aye, Mildraed loved her always, but curbed her never.

Without realizing it, he smiled, and his companion remarked on it, returning him to the present. He turned to face Lord Blaecdene.

"Ah, Merlion, that poor woman has had little enough thanks for having given up her life to three determinedly independent children. Kerwin and I gave her miseries enough, but we were boys and no better was expected of us. It was Dara who grieved her most dearly. Too wild she is, and willful, but it was Kerwin and I who encouraged her in rebellion. Mildraed's pious teachings were canceled by our more realistic and sometimes devilish ones." He stirred restlessly. "I do not admit defeat, Merlion. There is a way, and I'll find it. Royal policy will not force me into abeyance."

"That way is fraught with ensnarements, my

friend. Have a care that you do not find yourself entangled."

Lord Blaecdene was no idle companion. Their friendship had grown quickly in the first months of Brann's court appointment before his hurried and troubled return to the north, and when Brann had sought an audience with Henry and been denied his intervention in the matter of his sister's abduction, Lord Blaecdene had returned with him to Chilton, offering what services he could extend.

"You caution me at every turn, Merlion, while an old woman goads me on. 'Tis an unflattering comparison."

It was not unkindly said, and his friend took no offense. "Perhaps. But I would see you succeed in your quest, and caution often prevails. And, after all, I, too, have a stake in the outcome —if your sister will yield to your wishes as readily as you believe. She is young and lovely by her portrait and willful by your own words. It may be that she would choose another."

Surprised, Brann replied, "No, Dara knows my love for her will always seek her happiness. And I hold all authority over her, now. She would never disobey me."

"We have yet to free her. The success or failure of our future plans must wait upon that," Merlion remarked composedly, and then looked thoughtful at the black scowl that settled once again on Brann's face.

Chapter VIII

Clouds threatened rain, and the inevitable wind found its way into the courtyard, but the air was clear of whiskey fumes, and the cold washed over Dara cleansingly. It was the last evening of the Kermichils' visit, and as the night progressed, it had become bawdier and the men more boisterous. Though Laochlain played the courteous host, his face had remained grim and his eyes unrevealing except for the times when they chanced upon Dara. It was those brooding, half-savage glances that had finally driven her from the raucous, close-packed hall. She had begun to feel like a rabbit caught tight in a snare. A gentle trap, with no sharp edges, but no less powerful for its lack of cold, biting metal. There was more reason here for fear than in Ruod's lust, for Laochlain was of a different force, one she was ill-equipped to withstand.

It would be false to protest herself indifferent to him, though he had avoided her in the days since they had ridden alone with such disaster. Dara privately professed herself glad this was so. She was shamed by the desires that had blazoned in her at his kiss—shamed and disturbed. By slow degrees, she had stirred and rekindled her initial animosity towards him, but anger and hatred yielded far too readily to less protective emotions. And, though he kept himself from her at present, she knew he desired her—and she feared her own reactions to that desire.

Shivering, she stared at the changing pattern of clouds against the barely discerned light of a hidden moon and stars. Three brothers, so alike in physical attributes yet so varying in temperament. Niall was the most easily placed, a young man proud of his heritage and sure of his position, a young lover in sight of fulfillment. Ruod held a baseness the other two lacked, whether bred into him by a wanton mother or taught him by the cruelty of life to a nobleman's bastard, it was there in his bitter jealousy and outlashings at all who dared near. And Laochlain, the enigma. The blending of power, reckless and harsh, made him a leader. No man would ever control him, and no woman would ever subdue. His was the power. His eyes could burn with hypnotic force, demanding and receiving subjugation. Too often this night they had held her in the bondage she had come to dread and finally sought to escape, here, under the heavens.

At last a creeping, numbing cold forced her to retrace her steps towards the hall, though reluctantly—and unwarily.

Ruod stepped from the shadows without warning and spoke with exaggerated courtesy.

"My lady, I feared for your safety when I realized you had left the hall. I found your room empty and sought you here."

Her eyes were cold. "My actions are no concern of yours, Ruod."

She was more fearful than she betrayed, for though he reeked of drink, he was steady on his feet and clear in speech. Her distrust was warranted. He was upon her before she could utter a sound, and in a very few moments, she had not the breath to do so. His arms encircled her in a grip of steel while his hands entangled in her hair and pinned her head still beneath his kiss. As she recovered from her first startled fear, blinding rage engulfed her. Her hands ceased pushing uselessly against the brute force of his embrace and flew upwards to rake at his face.

Howling, he flung her roughly to the flagstones while his fingers explored the furrows she had gouged in his cheeks. His eyes narrowed in fury, and he bent to her, jerking her to her feet with violent intent. "You damned little she-cat!"

He gripped her hair tightly with one hand as the other cracked flat-palmed against the side of her face. She was blinded by tears of pain and helpless against his strength.

Broad warrior hands pulled Dara free, and feeling his quarry wrested from him, Ruod cursed foully the only one he knew would dare even before a glimpse of Laochlain's furious face confirmed his knowledge. They faced each other grimly, no longer concerned with the bruised and shaken object of their contention.

Dara backed slowly away until she felt the solidity of stone at her back.

Ruod's leaping attack was savage but expected, and Laochlain was prepared for the force of his weight. With quick strength, he flung Ruod away, and his leather-skinned fists drew up as the other regained his feet.

"Whoreson," spat Ruod, "you will regret your interference. Too long have I played the knave at your commands. Yours and that whipped cur of a lad you call brother! He will find your gore spilled upon this stone."

"I think to see another end to this, Ruod."

Ruod ceased his slow circling and struck out with mindless ferocity. Laochlain blocked his first swift jab but received the next squarely, grunting with its force against his middle. He returned the blow but with better control than Ruod employed. Ruod's cheek split slightly under his knuckles, and Laochlain felt a surge of satisfaction.

Duncan had sons to boast of in their physical prowess, for their strength and skill were great and nearly equal. No fault could be found in lean, hard torsos or in arms that strained at the sleeves of their shirts. Their blows fell with stunning force, and each planted fist left damage. Only slowly did Laochlain gain any edge over his brother, and it was slight, but it led to further advantage though both men were tiring.

The sound of their breathing was a hoarseness in the night air. At last, staggering under a blow that swelled and bruised his eye, Ruod dropped to his knees. He braced himself with his palms flat against the stone but found he could not rise. He was spent.

Laochlain breathed raggedly, and sweat gleamed upon his brow, but he was strong yet, and his face was unmarred. Slowly, he drew his dirk from his belt, the metal gleaming with its own wicked beauty.

Ruod stared in frustrated exhaustion, his defeat made the more bitter by his consuming hatred. His face twisted to ugliness as he heard Laochlain's pronouncement.

"Only my father's blood in you stays my blade, Ruod, but you no longer have a place at Athdair. Leave now and do not return, for there will be no welcome but death for you here."

Ruod struggled to his feet and swayed there. "Do not think to rid yourself of me so easily— brother," his tone made the term a vile designation. "You will pay and dearly. I have lived my life under your shadow. No more! My moment will come, and I will return."

Malediction lay in his burning blue eyes as he backed away. Laochlain stood without movement as he lurched towards the stable, and Dara was held in place by that very stillness. Within moments, Ruod emerged, mounted and howling like the most primitive of his ancestors as he fled through gates flung open at his approach.

Only then did Laochlain turn his attention to Dara, waiting tensely in the dark and trembling with shocked reaction. Poised before her, he appeared some ancient warrior, his features held the prowess and cunning of his forebears. He stepped boldly forward, and words of gratitude tumbled from her lips only to be halted by the knifing slash of his anger.

"Are you so witless as to believe yourself capable of controlling a man such as Ruod? Wandering about alone, dressed as you are!" His eyes raked over her bared shoulders to the exposed swell of her breasts, and she flushed deeply. "Ruod or any one of my men, half-crazed with drink and lust, might have taken you here in the open like any common trollop. Or is that perhaps what you wish?" He gave her no time for answer as he drew her to him, his fingers bruising the flesh of her arms. "Is it I who have been blind, and Ruod the wiser?"

"Nay, MacAmlaid, never!" she lashed out. "And do not think I would look on you with any more favor than I do your bastard brother. You disgust me—both of you!"

Despite her words, it was fear that choked her to silence as she realized his battle for self-control. Yet, even in the midst of his fury, she thought she had never seen eyes so bleak.

Abruptly, he released one arm, but the other he held firm. "We'll return to the hall . . . together." His cold tone evidenced mastery over his rage.

As they neared the hall, his hand lay lightly upon her waist, but it was more than that light pressure that held her at his side, fighting for composure. Ruthless he was, and he would not hesitate in keeping her forcibly next him.

Lord Kermichil and his lady had retired while Duncan, one among many, slumped at the feast table in stupored sleep. Others were single-mindedly engaged in lively amorous strivings.

Niall turned with curious eyes at his brother's precipitant entrance with his hostage at his side. Creag, seeing Dara's distress, sent a quick, pleading glance to his sister for aid. Anne had already noted Dara's numbed look and Laochlain's steely countenance, and she reached them at the end of the table, eluding Niall's swiftly outstretched hand. If she did not intervene, she did not doubt that Creag would, and with disastrous consequences.

"Dara, we leave early on the morrow, and I would like to speak privately with you before then. Could we go to your room, now?"

Anne dared not look at Laochlain though she breathed a sigh of thankfulness that her voice had not quavered as she made her request. If the MacAmlaid suspected her motive, he would be less than understanding.

Dara did not speak but glanced uncertainly at Laochlain, who unhanded her as if burned by the contact. Anne ignored his sharp oath as if she had not heard it and took Dara's hand. She was dismayed to find it icy. Without waiting for misfortune, she led Dara swiftly up the stairs and to her room.

She stirred the fire to a solid blaze but could not induce Dara to get into bed nor even to sit in the leather chair placed near the fire to catch its warmth. Instead, she watched as Dara paced with the restlessness of nerves and futile anger and heard the words tumble in bitingly harsh denunciation. Anne, too much of a woman to lack perception, discarded the wrath and heard with increasing sympathy the underlying dread and uncertainty.

"He means to have me," Dara finished flatly, "and there'll be no one to stop him."

"I can offer you no more of hope than that the MacAmlaid is an honest man. I know, for Niall is like him in many ways," Anne answered softly. "If you perhaps convince him of your loathing . . . if that is what you truly feel for him."

Dara stared in speechless dismay. So quickly had this seemingly light-minded girl thrust to the reason for her fears. Rape she could endure, however brutal or debasing, for it would be an evil not of her own doing, but if she yielded willingly to him, a Scotsman, she would be damned by her own weakness. She felt Anne's hand on her arm.

"Perhaps you will be ransomed before the choice is thrust upon you. I will pray so, for I fear yours may be no choice at all. There is one thing in this for which I am indeed thankful— Ruod is gone. I have always feared and mistrusted him, and it would have been difficult to make my home in a keep he shared. Yet if Lord Athdair were not so concerned for you, Ruod might have remained for many a year."

Dara smiled wryly. "I am glad that good has come of this for someone, and better you than another. If I were Scottish, Anne Kermichil, or you English, I would be proud to seek your friendship."

"You'd have no need to seek, I would give it freely."

Anne left the room gracefully, and Dara closed the door after her. She found herself regretting the loss of something she had never known. And doubtless never would.

She feared it would be a long and wakeful night, but in the wee hours of the morning, only one candle burned in the whole of Athdair. It cast an unsteady glow on the missives Laochlain had ceased trying to answer some time earlier. He could not keep his thoughts from that moment in the courtyard when he had been hard put not to rape the girl he had wrested from his brother's arms. A girl who had denounced him with loathing in the next instant.

A sound from without, beyond the shuttered window, alerted him. Quietly he rose and moved to unbar the shutters, extinguishing the candle between his fingertips as he went. It was Strang who broke the night's silence, a bundle strapped to his saddle portraying flight. He approached the gate, and the guards, already given their instructions, allowed him to pass unchallenged. He disappeared quickly into the dark.

There had been no difficulty in anticipating his flight, for, after all, even mad dogs ofttimes remained loyal to their masters. Smiling at the comparison, Laochlain stretched upon the bed and slept, still fully clothed and booted.

Chapter IX

November rained, steadily and continually, straining nerves and tempers.

Kinara's dismay at Ruod's banishment was soon supplanted by a greater despondency, for already her belly was swelling with his unwanted seed; in early spring she would bear his child. Lethe, disgusted and scolding, nevertheless took into consideration Kinara's burden and permitted her only the lighter duties. She was no longer sent to fetch coals and kettles of water, nor made to scrub the great stone stairway and change the soiled rushes in the hall. Her body filled out with a woman's roundness, and her face lost its sharpest edges, but even though Ruod was no longer there to lay claim to her, no man sought her. Not because she disdained them, though she did, nor entirely because of the bairn. It was the look in her eyes that held them to a distance, a half-revealed hint of buried madness. That which had drawn her unerringly to Ruod was becoming ever more obvious.

Only Dara came near to realizing the full extent of her damning hatred, though not through any confidences. Kinara trusted her no more than any other, but she felt less need for hiding her bitterness and resentment around a girl who was really no more than a prisoner. These destroying emotions were aimed at all who remained while Ruod was gone and aimed most especially at the MacAmlaid and at the unborn child distorting her body.

Dara's pity for Kinara gave way beneath the realization that Kinara had indeed chosen her lot, but she feared for the babe's safety. If Lethe did not see it cared for, no one would, for Dara did not doubt she herself would be gone from Athdair long before its birth.

When taxed with it, Lethe shrugged. "If the bairn lives, I will tend it—if Laochlain does not send it away."

The winter's grey suited Dara's moodiness. She walked restlessly in the drizzling rain or its misty aftermath, her face tilted to its renewing freshness and her raw emotions somewhat eased. When her gown grew damp beneath her cloak and her hair hung in darkly wet curls, she would reenter the hall, passing those who hugged the hearth like grey grannies to an inglenook, and retreat to her chamber. Dry and comfortable, she would remain for hours, waiting and thinking, the crackling of the fire a faint accompaniment to her thoughts.

Lethe followed her up the stairs late one afternoon and spoke sharply as she eyed her dripping hair. "You will catch an ague and mayhap your death staying out in this nasty weather."

"Then you will not have to be bothered further with me," Dara answered almost absently as she discarded her wet gown, but Lethe's ready retort drew her full attention.

"Aye, but Laochlain won't be thanking me for allowing it."

"You might find him grateful but for the loss of my brother's gold."

Dark, knowing eyes swept over Dara from thick curls to lithe body, but Lethe only shrugged as she poured scalding water from kettle to basin. She stirred the fire and was gone, reminding as she went that supper was soon served.

As she washed, Dara was troubled by Lethe's discerning looks. Had all of his household marked Laochlain's desire for her? Did his men bandy jokes about it or place wagers on the outcome during their long evenings of drink and laughter? The possibility made her burn with shame. Laochlain had ceased to avoid her since that evening of violence in the courtyard, and she felt he played with her, baiting, snaring, and then releasing her to begin anew. She realized he but repaid her for the stark malice she had spat at him, placing him with Ruod in her estimation.

With these speculations taunting her, she noticed for the first time that evening that the barbs Duncan aimed at her were less obvious and less frequent than before. Had he, too, noted his son's determination to have her and bowed before it? Shaken, she studied each man in turn. Fibh, Bretach, all of them, were as ever, admiring but distantly so and never daring familiarities with her. Gerwalt, even Niall, treated her as Athdair's guest rather than its prisoner.

She spoke little until the meal was done and the men lingering over their ale. In quiet tones, she requested private speech with Laochlain, and though he did not mask his surprise, he agreed.

To her nervous dismay, she found herself closeted with him in the anteroom of his bedchamber, seated across from him at a small, littered table. It was not a large room, but it was a comfortable one. A fire burned in the chamber beyond, sharing its warmth and glowing upon the bindings of a few books lining a shelf, precious things and rarely come upon in a secluded border castle. Any one of them would have done much to ease the dullness of her days.

Not knowing the direction her thoughts had taken, Laochlain wondered if she perhaps regretted her request. "You wished something of me? Ask it, though I do not promise it will be granted."

She met his eyes, defensive at his tone. "I want no favors of you, MacAmlaid, naught but information I have a right to know. 'Tis no secret you have sent men to watch my brother and Chilton Castle. Have you had word from him—or of him?"

"I dispute what you claim for your rights, but

there is no reason I should not tell you this much. I've had no direct word from your brother, but I did not expect haste. He has sought the aid of your king and been denied. Henry eyes a greater gain than a border lord's favor."

"That is injustice," she flared. "Brann has served Henry well and does not deserve such careless treatment!"

"Are you indignant upon his account or your own, lass? Mayhap your anger is due to the fact that a king does not think you sufficient reason to risk the plans he has so carefully constructed."

"Damn you." Her voice was low and she subsided into furious silence, glowering at him through darkened eyes whose hazel depths defied him.

"No doubt you again scorn my manners, but yours are not always perfection, are they, my lady? But truth does not bow to convention."

"You abuse the word truth, my lord. I care nothing for what Henry thinks of my plight. Unlike you, I have never held royal favor. But Brann is a loyal subject and worthy of Henry's consideration."

"You are quick in your brother's defense, yet he seems slow in yours. He knows my demands."

"If he delays, there is reason. It may be that he has not the gold at hand that you have demanded of him. Or," she added darkly, "he may seek another method of freeing me. He has power in his own right!"

No longer baiting her and playing with her

reactions, Laochlain answered grimly. "He should consider that his delay risks your honor —and your virtue."

Shakily, she got to her feet. She was ashen. "You threaten, MacAmlaid?"

"I warn you, my lady."

He sat unmoving as she crossed the room and threw open the door. She paused there in the open doorway and remarked in even tones, "Your life would be the price of my virtue, my lord."

As she closed the door behind her, he leaned back in his chair and thoughtfully regarded the lusterless surface of the table. She had challenged him openly with no defense save her wits and her courage. Not many lasses would have had the courage.

For Dara the die was cast. Through the days that followed, she did not doubt that only time separated her from the MacAmlaid, he could have been no clearer in his meaning. It was a mercy when the date of Niall's wedding drew near, and she was no longer the focus of attention and conjecture. She had no wish to be exposed to the curiosity of strangers, however, and expressed her feelings fervently to Laochlain.

For once Duncan was in agreement with her, though his reasoning was far different. "A wench bearing the name Ryland would not be welcome at a marriage of MacAmlaid and Kermichil, good Scots both. 'Tis an insult to the Kermichils that you suggest it!"

Laochlain was adamant. "The girl will go with

us, Duncan, and I'll hear no more of it. You'll say no more! My decision is made, abide by it."

For him the matter was ended, but Dara was less fortunate. Not only must she live with her own increasing dread, but also with Duncan's secretively malicious mutterings. His sharp tongue hinted of dire consequences, improbable, she knew, but scarcely soothing to raw nerves. She began to avoid him more desperately and was thankful that he was willing for it to be so.

And, for her at least, the time of the wedding arrived too soon.

From the moment they arrived at Kermichil Keep, late in the evening two days before the wedding, Dara drew marked attention. Laochlain was inscrutable but took his revenge with calculating forethought as he made apparent his claim from the earliest moment. Without playing either the devoted swain or the tyrannical gaoler, he managed to convey the impression of possessing her, body and soul.

From the exchanged glances she intercepted and the titters that were stifled at her approach, she knew in what light his manner was regarded. And that he was no less aware than she of these things, she knew by the devilish light of enjoyment in his eyes and the look of satisfaction he so often wore. Her defiance was set at no small price.

In the whole of her life, Dara had never felt so alone as she did in that castle crowded with some of Scotland's noblest bloodlines. Not that any shunned her, she was too much of a curiosity for that. Indeed, she would have welcomed greater privacy. Her distress stemmed from the very fact of her popularity, for she was never deceived into believing that any of them looked on her as anything more than a barbaric Ryland. Kerwin had written their name in blood across the borderlands, and none doubted the ties of family. Those few who might have made her feel more at ease had no time to do so. Anne's hours were filled even without the continuous feasting and entertainments. Niall's were the same, while Creag shared the role of host with his father. And all the while, Laochlain played his devilish game.

Early upon the morning of the ceremony, Dara rose from the rumpled bed she shared with Lethe in a large room crowded with two more beds, also doubly occupied. The fire had died to embers, and she dressed in the cold without rekindling it. To do so might have awakened the others, and she longed too dearly for privacy to risk that. Without conscious intent, she made her way to the chapel, readied for the moment of importance with an abundance of fine wax candles and a gold-stitched altar cloth.

As she knelt before the holy altar, her face must have shown the strain of seeking prayers that remained from her grasp, for when she rose, she found the priest, Father Clarius, had entered. He remarked on her struggle.

"Are your prayers a burden to you, child? I have watched you through two mornings' Mass and seen no peace come to you."

"There is no peace for me. I find I have no

prayers—nor the faith that any I uttered would be answered."

"Then the fault is yours." He moved nearer and sat on the first hard bench, motioning her to do the same. Ignoring her reluctance, he continued. "I have heard your story, Dara Ryland, and I have a sympathy for you. These raids are an ungodly business, but I fear they will continue far beyond any efforts to halt them. Violence is bred into our border marches and the people here. Yet," he grew stern, "whatever your sufferings, your faith should hold firm, your prayers come readily to your heart. That they do not is your own shortcoming. If you wish it, I will hear your confession."

Dara got to her feet, feeling chilled by her negative reaction to his suggestion. "My confession would be false, Father, for I do not repent of my hatred or my anger. Forgive me, please, and pray for me. Your prayers, perhaps, will be answered."

With that, she whirled from him and fled the room. Never before had she so much as thought to defy a priest's authority, but the past weeks had dealt far more harshly with her than she had realized. They had left her bitter and defiant. Never again would she submit without struggle to any authority. Be it church or man.

That incident haunted her mind as she knelt in the little chapel for the second time that day. There was intense silence within the dark-paneled walls and without as the kneeling couple bowed their heads and waited for the priest's blessing. And then it was done, and the chapel, serene with the faith of centuries, erupted into joyful approbation.

It was a wedding feast that would be long remembered, marked by plentiful food and the entertainment of minstrels, jugglers, and morris dancers. The young couple greeted the villagers in the courtyard, accepting with shining happiness the carefully made toast drunk to their future. Once toasted, they led the way into the hall and took their places at the canopied table which had been draped with delicately embroidered linen and strewn with dried flower petals.

The guests feasted on peacocks baked whole in a covering of crisp dough, geese, plover, herons, and swan. Hunters had provided roe and boars with appled mouths, and wooden platters were piled high with roasted mutton and boiled and spitted beef. From the sea came flounder and herring, carefully grilled. There were sweet dishes of jellies, custards, spicy tarts, and candied fruits. Earthen jugs of malmsey, claret, and elderberry wine stood in frequent spaces, and mugs of ale were set at each place.

Trenchers were filled and refilled while musicians played unceasingly behind a silken screen. Hooded falcons were perched overhead on ceiling beams, and staghounds gnawed at bones flung carelessly from the tables. Both bird and hound were the cause of as many wagers as the barely-wed bride and groom. Braziers of burning musk and ambergris masked the less pleasant odors of the animals and the many close-packed, perspiring bodies.

Amidst the clamor of celebration, Dara sat as

silent as she was allowed to be and fervently wished she were elsewhere, though, determinedly and defiantly, she had made the most of her beauty for this occasion. Her gown of chocolate brocade was the result of hours of effort and had felt no needle but her own. Its daring cut emphasized the slight curves of her breasts and hips. She had no jewels, but the lack merely drew attention to the loveliness of her skin, as did her molasses-shaded hair, falling in long coils to her bared shoulders.

She had been relieved to find herself seated far from Laochlain's honored place near the head of the long table spread with the wedding feast. She soon found herself parrying bold compliments and bolder suggestions from men very little different from others she had known. Not witty, but possessed of humor, not sparkling in speech, but honest and earnest until drink made them brash. They were country nobility for the most part and not court gallants.

Midway through the evening, the bride stood, and a roar swelled to the ceiling as she was seen. She was lovely perfection in a gown of ice-blue velvet edged with ermine as white as the snow thinly covering the ground. Her hair was unbound as tradition demanded, its soft fox color reflected in her cheeks. Leather mugs went up in a final toast, and before it was completely downed, she and her ladies were fleeing the hall with the men soon in close pursuit.

The girls were gasping with breathless laughter as they slammed the door upon their pursuers, though their jostlings against it made Anne tremble as her hair was combed and her jewels lifted from her by loving hands. She strove to hide her confusion, answering with laughter the others' jests as they removed her gown and enveloped her in sheer sea-green gauze. Anne was determinedly cheerful until they left her, but once alone, she could not ward off her apprehension of what was to come.

She had not moved from before the hearth when the door burst open and Niall was thrust forward by numerous helping hands. Quips and witticisms followed him into the room, whereupon he shut and barred the door with laughing rejoinders. He had been roughly divested of his shirt and doublet, and he stood bare-chested before her, sweating from his exertions.

The fire was behind her, the flames silhouetting every curve of her body beneath material that was no hindrance to the eye. Her smile wavered uncertainly at the familiar look upon his face as he came to her. He kissed her gently, fighting the urge to crush her to him and release his pent-up desires. The lass was his wife and no six-pence whore, what he began here would last for all their life together. It was a time for patience. His fingers moved in whispering touches over her eyes and cheeks and lips. His lips touched softly on her ear, her neck, the hollow where her pulse beat at its base.

And, slowly, she lost her apprehension as he intended she should, and closed her mind to everything but this man, her husband, and the love that was between them.

Chapter X

The day was bright and winter-clad, the sun threatening to melt at least the top sheet of ice on the flagstones. Those who yet remained sought its warmth. Amidst the confusion of restless mounts and harried servants, Anne bade her parents farewell while Laochlain clasped his brother's hand in a firm grip and wished them Godspeed in returning to Athdair, for they were to go first to James' court so that Niall might present his bride to their king. He lifted her onto her palfrey, and though there was not much to be seen of her, muffled as she was in furs, a filmy scarf at her throat, she had the intensely happy look of a woman loved. Niall leapt to his saddle, and the small cavalcade went forward.

As they passed through the gates, Laochlain's

eyes turned from them and encountered Dara. She was plainly gowned and caped, but her cheeks were stung into color by the cold, and her hair gleamed copper where it escaped from her hood. He spoke to her abruptly.

"We leave now. Summon Lethe and the servants."

Dara stared after him, consideringly, as he moved away. His tone had been brusque and irritating. Might he not be as satisfied with circumstances as she had thought? Shrugging, she turned to do as he bade but determined he would yet learn she would not accept a servant's treatment.

Lethe was easily found, and she had already herded the servants together with their belongings packed into neat bundles. Traveling was a smooth process under her watchful eyes and careful regulations.

The land they traveled lay under a light, dry snow, and the branches of the trees were frosted with ice. The horses picked their way carefully through the light crust. November would soon be done, and the fury of December would bring fresh discomforts. Dara wondered if she would still be held on Scottish soil when the celebration of Christmas sounded through the land.

The ride home was, for the most part, a silent one, each of them intent upon their own thoughts. An occasional command to an intractable mount was the most of speech until a light snow began to fall. Then Laochlain reined his horse closer to Dara. She looked at him inquiringly.

"You are carelessly dressed for the cold."

His tone was still harshly arrogant, and she felt antagonism stir within her. He persisted in this unstated incrimination of her, hardly just in the face of his own faults. She was the one wronged, and yet he played that part. She glared at him.

"My lord, I have warmer things at Chilton, were I but permitted their use."

His eyes narrowed at her intended accusation. "Tis to be hoped, mistress, that discomfort eventually dulls your tongue lest your taming prove less gentle!"

He spurred ahead of her, and she was left to stare in frustration at the uncompromising set of his shoulders. She felt no guilt that her courtesy had not withstood the test of her captivity as well as her courage had done. Niceties were for those who could afford to employ them.

The unvarying countryside lulled her to introspection, but, disturbingly, her thoughts remained on the MacAmlaid. She soon found to her dismay that she had drawn nearly abreast of him and that they were some distance ahead of Lethe and the servants. Duncan and Gerwalt lagged far behind, deep in conversation, and the outriders were outflung about them all. She rejected the impulse to slow and wait for Lethe. That would admit the effect he had on her, and that she would not admit even to herself. So, when they reached Athdair in the gloom of dusk, he was near enough to notice her shiver of emotion as the reminding shadows of the arches fell over her.

She kept to her room that evening, preferring the quiet of solitude to the conviviality of the hall where Athdair's own celebration of the marriage continued. After days of having companionship forced upon her, she had no wish to seek it more. She spent most of that evening wondering unhappily why Brann delayed. The next night she was given the reason.

The day had been a quiet one with the men keeping to their quarters in the guardhouse and seeking the hall only at mealtimes. After an early supper made uncomfortable by Laochlain's grim proximity, Dara rose with the intention of returning to her room.

Laochlain's booming voice halted her. "My lady, I have news of Chilton."

She turned back to him, her face impassive, knowing how many watched, but her eyes reflected the light of a hundred dancing flames and her cheeks were brushed with sudden rose. Laochlain came forward and took her arms, not speaking further until they reached her door. They stood in the dimly lit hall, ignoring the chill draughtiness.

Dara's face was upturned to his, and Laochlain fought a desire to touch her. His voice reflected that struggle with harshness. "Bretach rode out immediately upon our arrival last evening. He returned but an hour ago. One who remains there, watching, sent back this word. Two weeks ago a messenger arrived at Chilton from Taran, it was answered, and there have been several exchanges since that time."

"No . . ." The word was barely breathed aloud.

He studied her blanched face. "So. You do

realize the implications—and the danger. If Owein Ryland seeks to aid in this matter, 'tis that his madness seeks glory. Would your brother be such a fool as to allow it?''

Her anger braced her. ''Would you call a man a fool who joins forces with his uncle against a common enemy?''

''Your uncle is the fool,'' he answered sharply. ''His hatred of Scots blinds him to all else. If he leads your brother into border war, Henry will turn his forces upon them, and will not the whole of the northland rise up in their defense? A civil war, mistress, with your brother and your uncle at the heart of it.''

''You cannot know that Henry would fail us! And if Owein and Brann were to win me free at the first, there would be no need of his intervention.''

''Do you think I will allow it, Dara? No man takes by force what I would hold; his life would be forfeit. It must be the fire that stirs in both your veins that turns your brother to this course. I do not believe it is greed. What man would hold gold above you?''

The low timbre of his voice transfixed her, and, looking up into grey eyes that flashed with a reckless light, she swayed. His hands steadied her. The touch seared through the cloth of her gown, and still she could not turn her eyes from him.

In her soft voice she struck to the heart of the matter. ''If you held the gold, the price of my freedom, you would still not release me, would you, my lord? Mayhap Brann fears your deceit?

He would not leave my safety to chance."

"What do you fear, lass?" he questioned huskily.

"I fear you, MacAmlaid, as I fear myself," she whispered.

Her words ended beneath his lips. She felt his palm flat against the curve of her back, felt his other hand cupping her face. His lips were warm and hard against hers. She knew it was madness to yield to his questing tongue, yet she did. He pressed harder against her, bending her body to his. Her fingers curled into the fabric of his shirt as she sought support for her trembling legs.

He became bolder. She felt a coolness on her face when his hand left it, then his touch on the flesh above her gown. His fingers traced a gentle caress over the swell of her breast. Waves of shame left a color on her cheeks that he could not see as strange feelings swept her. A sobbing cry rasped her throat as she tried to pull away, but he held her fast. He paid no heed to her breathless pleas or to her struggles, and desperation seized her.

"Oh, damn you, MacAmlaid," she cursed him. "I've nothing for you! Nothing!"

Her ragged voice halted him more surely than her hammering fists. The look of terror on her face struck at him, and he released her abruptly. She leaned back against the door, trembling, her face averted from him.

There was a long silence, and then his footsteps echoed away from her. When she raised her head, he was gone.

He stalked angrily through the hall, doors

slamming shut after him as he went out into the courtyard. He had seen the startled looks, had heard his name called questioningly, but he had no wish for commiseration or jocularity. There was irritation enough in knowing they speculated now on the wench's effect on him. It was sheer idiocy. Any other man would have bedded her the first night—and so should he have!

The disturbed stable was a restless background to his oaths as he fumbled through the saddlery. Hay rustled beneath shifting hooves, and low whickers sounded inquisitively, but the red knew his master and stood calmly as his saddle was snugly girthed. His coat was heavy for winter's cold, and his breath frosted the air.

Laochlain turned as an arc of light fell over him, his scowl unabating as Ros lowered his torch.

"Well," Laochlain barked, "what the devil are you doing up and about?"

The groom was disturbed by neither the dark scowl nor the apparent ire of his master. "A deaf man might could sleep amidst this collieshangie, I could not." He fastened his rushlight into a holder and came closer. "'Tis a wicked hour for a ride. Be there trouble?"

"Only of a fool's making," Laochlain answered savagely.

Ros watched in silence as his master led the stallion out of his stall and past Ros to the courtyard. The groom's face registered nothing. He had been many a year at Athdair and knew that the MacAmlaid answered to no one save, perhaps, Jamie. And Ros respected the rights of others to privacy and independence as jealously as he guarded his own. Whatever Lord Athdair was about was his own concern, but Ros looked thoughtful as the clatter of hooves sounded on stones and horse and rider fled recklessly into the dark.

It was a clear night and sharply cold. A hard, swift, dangerous run cleared Laochlain's head and left the stallion tired but strong still. They slowed to a walk, both listening to the utter silence of a peaceful night. The domestic animals were safely sheltered, their predators not yet forced down from the hills by the torture of starvation. It would come soon, the baying of wolves and the yowling of cats, for the snow would deepen and the small wild game would sleep undisturbed in their warm nests until spring.

Unbidden, the thought intruded. Dara expected to be gone by spring, traded for gold. It would be better so. He cursed. The uselessness of lying to himself, and to her, was grating. He did not mean to let her go, and there could be no continuing the unstated truce between them. Had he been wise, he would have disregarded pride and anger and freed her at the start and thought no more of her. It was too far beyond that now, he would not forget her. Her beauty had tempted too long and her willfulness had dared too often. She must choose her own way, without her brother's protection.

She has chosen already, though she knows it not, he thought. The teachings of family and priest would have her deny it, yet, if she would be honest, it was there in her giving this night until her own fears forced her to flight. If she will fight this—and me—so be it!

The stallion halted before a dark and still croft, forcing Laochlain's attention from his thoughts. He stared at the hovel. It was well secured with doors and windows tight against the snow and against intruders. The stock were carefully enclosed within a shedlike barn of more careful construction than the hut. On the open fells, a man must be ever watchful if he would keep what was his own. Yet no simple crofter could guard against marauders who attacked without warning, taking the only things of value that poor men possessed, their stock and their women. Among these knaves and villains who lived off the toils of the honest, the newest had proven to be a MacAmlaid. Word of Ruod had reached Athdair from more than one source. He had turned to brigandage through the middle marches of Scotland. Should he be slain, attacking or fleeing, none here would mourn his death.

Laochlain frowned, picturing Kinara's pinched and sullen face and swelling middle. He wanted none of her brat about his household, but there was no help for it. He could not turn the girl out whatever her sins—though, if Dara had the truth of it, Kinara had none and had been sinned against, forced to her submission. Curse Ruod, even gone he caused damnable difficulties!

He let his horse choose the pace home. The stars hung low in crystal air that cast tiny splinters of life with each deep breath. The peace and beauty of his lands could not be ignored nor the effect on him denied.

Ros was still wakeful and came from his small room as horse and man entered. Taking the reins, he sent Laochlain back to the keep. "Away wi' you. I'll tend yon laddie. You're near frozen."

The weapons above the hearth gleamed in the dark as Laochlain crossed the hall. Weapons of the present and the past, of son, father, and grandfather. He mounted the stairs swiftly and paused before a door that suddenly appeared impassable.

Dara stood at the opened window, an icy draught blowing on her and past her into the room. The fire danced in its wake. She had not removed her gown, but her hair was loose about her shoulders. It gleamed from endless brushing, the action a balm to her turmoil. Her thoughts had not been soothing ones as she waited, but they had been honest. She no longer blamed any other for the torments of her heart. She had the choice of denying her longings or yielding to them. In the first there was pain with honor, in the second there could only be shame.

She heard the door open quietly behind her and turned, realizing at last that the choice had never been hers. The realization brought no comfort.

"I saw you return."

"Then you had fair warning."

He came closer. His hand touched her face, then slid behind her neck, pulling her near. His lips were still cold from the winter night and

128

hard with desire. He raised his head, his eyes searching her face. She was mute, but there was pleading in her eyes. He gathered her swiftly against him and carried her from the room.

The ceiling beams of the corridor were lost in the black shadows above, and she felt lost, without direction as that darkness dropped and enveloped them.

Laochlain's bedchamber was sudden warmth and soft light after cellarlike gloom and chill. It embodied his character of stern and spartan strength. The walls and floors were covered with pelts, and the bedhangings were of forest-dark wool while the windows were covered only by heavy shutters. Empty shadows were held back by a vast bed of heavy, rich-grained wood, an iron-bound chest at its foot. The room lacked any ornamentation, but the sconces were of heavy gold and held the finest tapers, and the blades and handles of his weapons had been polished to a loving glow.

He stood her on her feet before a hearth almost as spacious as the one in the great hall below. Her legs were not steady, but she forced them to hold her erect as he barred the door. The action held a compelling finality. When he turned back to her, she could not keep her eyes from his face. It was hard with the need and determination to have her. Boldly, he swept aside the silken spread of her hair and unfastened the row of hooks down her back. Her arms hung limply at her sides. He was before her, his arms imprisoning her. She cried out softly, but his mouth subdued the sound to a moan as he eased the gown from her shoulders. It slid to the floor in a crushed heap, and she was once again clasped in his arms.

He felt her heart race as he lay her against the cold sheets of his bed, and he murmured reassurances to her before moving away. Her eyes swept up to meet his, but as he slowly began removing his jacket and shirt, she swiftly lowered her lashes against the sight.

His throaty chuckle sent the blood pounding through her veins. She felt his weight on the bed and then his lips on her face. His mouth touched low between the swell of her breasts, his fingers brushing gently against them. She panicked, erupting into the strength and fury of a wild animal as she sought to escape him.

He caught both her hands in his and held them effortlessly. "Nay, Dara. 'Tis too late for struggle. I will have you."

She twisted, and he flung his leg over hers to still her. The encounter of flesh drew a gasp from her, for she was acutely aware of the touch of him, the warmth of his flesh and his hard thigh forcing submission. The seduction of her body brought worse shocks. He was gentle, but when he gained entry, she knew only unendurable, burning pain. He stifled her cries with his lips and his thrusting tongue while his hands pinned her struggling body beneath his. Her sobs did not cease when he rolled away. It was his cruel words that shocked her to awareness and anger.

"I thought you had more fire and more courage—at least enough to admit that you desire me. Else I would have left you to your virgin's bed."

"I would that you had, but my shame is my own and no blame of yours."

"There is no shame in honesty."

He turned to her again, ignoring her moan of protest, and wooed her with kisses so expertly rendered and caresses so thorough that her body responded in spite of her tension. His hands stroked her softly, while his lips learned sweet hollows no man had ever seen. Unexpectedly, she felt a warmth kindle within her, evoking sensations too strong to displace. She discovered that she was not possessed of a cold nature, but that the passions of ancestors less civilized and long dead coursed through her veins.

A shudder wrenched her as his fingers stroked the silk of her thighs, and involuntarily her hands lifted to his face, guiding his lips to hers.

She stiffened as he arched above her, but he whispered against her lips, "This time there will be no pain, lass. I swear it."

His body moved to her, tight and strange, but as he promised, no longer truly painful. As he thrust, she felt a heat radiating, undeniably pleasurable though frightening as well for she could not control it. It built unbearably, and she cried out against his power over her. They had battled too long, and the battle was not yet done, not even when she clung, weak and spent, to him.

He settled to sleep, holding her to the warmth of his body. Dimly, she longed to rise and seek the sanctuary of her own chamber, but she found she was too weary to rise. It was unwise to be so without guard, yet her limbs were impossibly heavy, and even her eyelids seemed weighted with the need for sleep.

The day was still without light when a sharp rapping wakened them both. Laochlain halted her startled rising and slid from the bed, donning his breeks as he crossed to the door.

Lethe moved past him unaware, carrying a kettle of water and a fresh candle as well as her own burning taper. "The door was bolted, but you bade me wake you early. I . . ." She fell silent as she caught sight of Dara frozen in the bed, her chagrin well displayed.

"Aye, Lethe?" Laochlain could not completely disguise his irritation, and the brief hint of impatience in his tone stirred the woman to complete her errand. In silence, she emptied the kettle and lit the extra candle, leaving it on the washstand.

With the door closed solidly after her, Laochlain turned to Dara, his irritation gone.

She caught his look of contentment and bristled. "You enjoy my shame, my lord? Perhaps that was your intent when you bedded me. Will you jest to your men of how you wooed your way between English thighs?"

He frowned at her crudity. "Silence, Dara, or you'll find better reason for complaint."

"So, now you threaten, but I fear you less than ever. I despise you greatly, but fear you not at all."

Of a sudden, she found herself flat against the sheets, hard grey eyes boring into hers. "Despise me, lass? I think not."

His lips covered hers without warning and with a hard insistence that drew her unwilling response. It disturbed her to find she could not retain her anger, that it faded to a frustrated helplessness. When she responded with a shy gesture of surrender, he pulled her close against him where she could feel the beat of his heart and his warm breath against her hair.

It was with great reluctance that he finally rose and finished dressing. He paused at the door before leaving and regarded her thoughtfully.

"I shall send up servants with bath water, but the harshest soap cannot wash away what is done, Dara. Do not think it possible."

She returned his look in silence and willed all Scots to damnation before the door shut, leaving her alone with her angry thoughts.

The bath water was very hot and silken with the fragrance of soft soap, but Laochlain had been prophetic. Her efforts to wash away all traces of the night were in vain as Laochlain had warned her they would be. Not because of the soreness between her thighs to remind her, but because of her own confusion. The soft sponge could not scrub that away nor the water rinse her free of it.

The girl who had seen to her bath had been wide-eyed with the curiosity she was too well trained to speak. Dara had sent her away with a curt word for her ineptness, but though the wench drew her wrath, she was not the cause of it. Laochlain she tried to hate, but for herself she felt only contempt. She could not even be true to herself. She had desired him when he came to her room, and later he had said true, her struggles were too late.

Lethe had recovered her habitual calm by the time she returned to Laochlain's chambers bearing fresh clothing for Dara. She strove for normalcy in her tone. "Laochlain bade me enquire if you had need of me."

The color drained from Dara's face, then returned with dark force. "I am not his lady, and you are not my servant! I am hostage still. Do not make my shame more than it is!"

Lethe found herself relaxing in the face of this agitation. She had not expected it—haughtiness, perhaps, and a new disdain, but not this unhappy self-condemnation. And that surely was the girl's reaction to Laochlain's attention. The housekeeper felt more inclined to sympathy.

"Well, now, it grows late and you have not eaten. The table has been cleared, but the cook will find you something. She favors knowing you eat, mayhap 'tis because you are so thin."

There was despondency in the set of Dara's shoulders as she fastened the hooks of her bodice. She shrugged in answer to Lethe's suggestion. "I've no hunger now, perhaps later."

Lethe watched for a moment as she listlessly applied a comb to her wealth of tangled hair. "If you've need of me, I shall be in my sitting room. I've mending to attend. Laochlain will be from the keep until late."

Dara flushed. "Lord Athdair's whereabouts are of no concern to me."

She followed Lethe from the room, turning towards the stairs with a feeling of desolation. It was short-lived. Lethe had, of course, held her tongue, but not the young girl who had attended her bath. It was Duncan's malice that banished the lassitude that gripped her.

She found the hall empty but for the old chief seated at the table, sharpening a heavy, flat blade. His slow smile at her entrance was the first hint that the night's events were no secret.

He spoke most casually. "Ruod was wont to use my weapon for its strength and sharpness. Likely this very blade slew your murdering brother. And it may yet see another of them fall." He snorted at her cold stare. "Hah! Perhaps you would no longer care, now that my whelp has had his way with you!"

Her eyes flashed. "You speak in ignorance, old man, but your vileness must find other prey. I shall listen to no more of it!"

Her skirts swirled gracefully as she swung away from him. His cackle followed her from the hall. The courtyard was icy, even in the sunlight, but the stables exuded the heat of its warm-blooded, heavy-coated inhabitants. She sought the rangy sorrel that Laochlain had chosen for her to ride on the two occasions she had been permitted to leave Athdair. The gelding blew gently in her face, recognizing her, then pushed his head into her shoulders.

She felt an ache in her throat and tears burning her eyes. How simple the loyalties of a horse, and how difficult her own. Brann would give his soul to free her from a man she could never escape now, no matter how great the distance between them. They were entwined with bonds she could never deny. Fervently, she wished she had been imprisoned in the feared cells below the keep, wished she had not made the promise to Laochlain that had allowed her such freedom. They could never meet nor speak nor even pass, now, without memory of what had been searing her mind.

The gelding started at her impatient movement as she brushed away tears that fell despite her will. In the dark of the stable, with none to see, she stiffened her shoulders in defiance. She would not pity herself—nay, nor allow any to think it.

She left the stables with head high and back proudly braced, but there was no denying the dread of her next encounter with Laochlain. There was reprieve in his absence throughout the daylight hours, and when he returned, it was to go straight to his chambers. His supper was brought to him there, and later his bath.

When Duncan at supper in the hall questioned Lethe curtly, she shrugged.

"He is at his desk and has been the evening through. He should employ a man to deal with ledgers and accounts, but you know he will not. 'Tis years since war has made a need for such care and secrecy, yet still he trusts few."

"His distrust has naught to do with war and politics. He was ever secretive, even as a lad. Did I want knowledge of what he was about, it needs must be beaten out of him."

Dara stared at Duncan in disgust, doubting not that he had always been capable of the greatest cruelties. Likely his young sons had known their father's strength far more intimately than his affection. Ironically, he lived on the generosity of a son who must have reason to hate him. Did he think on the quirks of fate when he stared for hours into flames and downed his mugs of liquor?

With Laochlain absent, supper was not the ordeal for which Dara had braced herself. Duncan's barbs she could ignore, even return, and Kinara's twisted joy in another's disgrace was more pathetic than hurtful. The men treated her no less respectfully, though none were ignorant of the fact that Laochlain had claimed her at last. They had ever been reticent, few daring to make speech with her. It was still so.

Dara lingered in the hall, thankful she need not be alone with emotions that would not cease their torment. She longed to feel again the caresses that had destroyed her innocence, and that longing soon became an ache, bewildering and humiliating her. The bawdy songs and jests of the borderers were scarcely welcome diversions, but still she dreaded returning to her room. But the evening finally played to an end, and almost as one the men left for their own quarters. When Dara left the hall, only Duncan remained with the wenches cleaning around him.

She needed no candle to light her way, for Lethe had not yet darkened the torches. She entered her chamber and stopped short. The room was cold and dark, no fire glow to welcome her and no candle waiting to be lit from its flames. Her bedclothes, usually turned back for her, were undisturbed. Her eyes scanned the room. The coffer that held the few garments she could claim, the comb from her washstand, her nightshift, all were gone. There was no need for questions, no need for answers.

Rage consumed her, and with so little hope. What was there for her? Protest to the MacAmlaid's servants? to his kin? Approach him with anger? No. She had no help but what she could give herself, and no strength to withstand his force. Yet she could not meekly accept this arrogance.

The force of her anger carried her along the hall. His door opened readily at her touch, releasing heat and light. She entered quickly, without knocking or asking entry, but she did not catch him unaware. He had busied himself with the work always at hand, but he had waited and listened for her approach. She came to him and braced her palms against the table in front of him. He stood at her approach.

"Did you dream it would be so easy, MacAmlaid? That I would willingly be branded your whore? One night I was weak, I admit to that weakness, but I'll not be so again. You shall have nothing of me without force, and your keep will be haunted by the sound of my curses."

The flamelight danced over his bared torso as he moved to the door, closing and barring it. Dara showed no fear at this evidence of his answer but stood her ground even as he covered the short distance between them.

"If you would scream, lass, or curse me, begin now."

His hands fumbled in the coils of her hair, the pins dropping to the floor as he withdrew them. Like liquid copper her hair fell loosely to her waist. She held herself rigid beneath the hunger of his kisses until he broke away, cursing her.

"You proved not so unwilling last night, my lady. Is your virtue summoned on whim?"

The sharp denunciation cut through her icy control, and she jerked from his grasp. Turning wildly, her eyes lit upon his work, the papers and ledgers and inkpots lying as he'd left them, open to destruction. Her arm swept viciously across the surface of the table, sending everything crashing to the floor, all but an inkpot her fingers encountered and automatically gripped. The action satisfied her primitive fury as Laochlain cursed again, this time at the damage she had inflicted.

He turned from the debris, menace in his face, but she was too furious to be fearful. She sent the inkpot in her hand hurtling against the carved oaken mantel and was looking for another missile when his hands grasped her shoulders. Her anger proved no protection as he shook her with punishing fury until her teeth chattered in terrified pleas.

Searching her frightened face, his eyes darkened to a different emotion as he gathered her close to his chest. His hands eased up to the coolness of her hair and guided her face to his kiss.

She rested against him, spent of fury and defiance, wearying for peace.

"You drive me to madness, lass. I never forced

139

a lass to me before you, and I had no wish to hurt you so."

Her answer was buried against him as she took the strength he offered. Her hands crept up to cling to him, and he groaned with the desire she roused in him and swung her up into his arms.

Chapter XI

Messengers sped between Taran and Chilton as Owein scorned his nephew's peaceable intentions. Every missive urged retaliation and decried Brann's reasoning. Trust for a Ryland's safety could not be placed in the word of one of Scotland's most powerful earls. Particularly not when that Ryland was a young and lovely maid. Was not Kerwin's murder, with not a man punished for the deed, proof enough of the MacAmlaid's treachery? The old warrior's fiery persuasion fanned Brann's burning desire for reprisal. Rylands had ever used force of arms to gain their desires, Brann could do no less.

Apprised of his northland lord's intentions, England's Henry, hastily and belatedly, decided to take a hand in this ill-judged affair. In a masterpiece of diplomacy to the sovereign ruler of Scotland, he urged a swift and peaceful settlement of the feud. The result was a terse message dispatched speedily to Athdair.

At the border castle, the piper played an ancient rant, holding his listeners with the imagery of wild moors and mountains and bracken-strangled lands, of warriors, strong and dauntless, and of valor and sweet victory. The notes were strange spiralings enflamed with the beauty and the cruelty that was Scotland. Scarcely music at all, it suited far better the transplanted bit of the highlands that was Athdair than did the most mellifluent of lutes and lyres.

"She has bewitched him! Aye, with her cat's eyes and fox's hair. Devil's endowments!"

Fibh started at Duncan's muttered pronouncement. "What say you, my lord?"

"'Tis she, the devil's handmaiden come to cast a spell over my son. Aye! Satan is jealous of a man that earthly dangers hath never touched."

Glancing round to ensure that Laochlain's attention was elsewhere, Fibh implored, "Do not speak so."

Duncan raised his voice. "Ruod brought her here. He made a pact with hell, and even yet he awaits his brother's doom to become Athdair's master. Satan's reward." His blue eyes turned crafty as the younger man crossed himself. "Aye, Ruod brought her here, mayhap he could be made to take her away. And the devil be damned!"

A furious pounding, a rattling of bars brought

him leaping to his feet with a cry as if he feared that Satan's vengeance had been drawn by his curse. But it was Lord Athdair's name on the lips of the near-frozen man who was permitted entry. The guard's hand never lifted from the hilt of his sword, yet the comer brushed past him with no more than a glance. His fairly youthful face was intensely earnest above a short, full beard as he unerringly sought the man who was his destination. Stopping before Laochlain, he bowed low.

"I am come from Edinburgh, your lordship, from James. 'Tis a matter of urgency, and he bids your answer be not delayed."

"Rise then and deliver your message."

Thrusting a gloved hand into the breast of his thickly lined jacket, the messenger drew forth a scroll which Laochlain grasped with steady hand. As the royal seal was broken with a flick of a knife, the herald fixed curious eyes upon the girl at the MacAmlaid's side. So, this was she who had thrown the courts of England and Scotland into a furor. He was less incredulous of the fact now he had seen her, for she rivaled the court favorites in beauty and bearing. Should James behold her, the newest of his mistresses would encounter a reversal in her influence.

Laochlain re-rolled the paper and glanced at the herald, no noticeable change in his expression.

"What are you called?"

"Baltair, my lord."

"Then, Baltair, eat and rest. Prepare to leave at dawn, you shall have my answer then."

There were curious stares aplenty, but only Duncan spoke. "Hath James need of you again?"

"James' business with me is in confidence. What must be done, I will do."

"The borders be quiet," Duncan mused, undaunted, "but for the Ryland's foray and retreat." He cast a sly glance at Dara.

Anger glinted through the strands of Laochlain's control. "You would be unwise to think retreat Lord Ryland's final action. He rallies forces with Owein of Taran, and 'tis unlikely they will admit defeat while a man of them yet stands."

"None of which need be were it not for the girl! She is a curse upon our hall."

"Silence!" Laochlain's roar was like thunder through the high-ceilinged room, halting movement, speech, and pipes. "Lady Dara was brought here by force and held here by force. Lay the blame where it rests more honestly, if you cannot still your blathering tongue. Do you deny the truth of it?"

"I do not. Nor will your ass-eared ragings silence my truth! Send this vixen back to her lair, and we shall have no more trouble of her kin!"

Gerwalt's angry growl rose ominously in the silence that followed the old man's outburst, but Laochlain answered with more conviction than rage.

"Dara Ryland is mine now, whatever befalls. Should any think to wrest her from me, it will be their undoing."

Obeying his outstretched hand, Dara stood at his side. Her own hand felt cold in his, and fragile. His height and breadth made little of her own proud bearing, for he evidenced the power to crush her or protect her.

To onlookers, they presented an appearance of unity, but, in truth, the battles still raged between them. They were storms of passion and of disposition, for they were both strong-willed people. The contests of blood and loyalty, of Scottish and English, were thrust aside unreconciled, neither yielding nor hoping for victory.

Their bedchamber proved no haven this night, for James' command could not be ignored. Giving in to her entreaties, Laochlain had given it to Dara to read. She felt a growing numbness as her eyes moved rapidly over the decisively worded mandate.

"He greets you most warmly yet bids you return me to Chilton. There is no place here for dispute."

He stood beside the hearth, his shoulder resting against the mantel while she sat on the settle-seat below him. Her head was bent over the scroll spread upon her lap, and he could see no more than the warm bronze tones of her hair.

"James directs me to no more than your brother and your uncle seek. No more than you fought and pleaded for a short while gone. Has your heart changed? Is Chilton no longer all that you desire?"

She looked up at him. "Would you have it so, my lord?"

"I wish no false assurances."

"And you shall have none. You proved your strength over me and petitioned not for my

145

loyalty." Her eyes dropped from his to the scroll she twisted in agitation. "I long for my brother no less, but my love for him is such that I dread to see the destruction of his for me. My dishonor will destroy it."

She fell silent, restless, knowing they were no more attuned than ever they had been, yet unable to name what she wished of him. He remained uncommitted though stubborn in his decision to keep her, whatever the consequences, while she grew daily more vulnerable, undeniably drawn to him.

"You bear no shame."

She glanced at him quickly, then shrugged. "Worthless commendation."

His face tightened. "It matters not. You are lost to England and your brother."

"You will defy your king?"

He smiled mockingly at her disbelief. "I hold what is mine over any authority. Fear not, James will see my justification."

"Art sure? Your defiance promises border war? He could not wish it. And I wish for none of Owein's butchery, his methods are unspeakable. Far better I should flee ere they come."

"You cannot. I hold you to your pledge. You would avert no bloodshed even did you go. I would seek you there, and the end would be no different."

She paled at the ominous warning. "Why? You have no love of me. Do you pursue battle for pride's sake?"

"Is it not every man's reason?"

"Nay!" She leapt to her feet. "Some fight for honor and truth and justice."

He seized her arms. "All are no more than pride."

His kiss was hard, and their strife, unresolved, found release in passion. Forgetful of the bonds that tied them to separate loyalties, they strained to each other, denying all but the insistent demands of his body and hers. Desire flamed to life at his touch and filled her as wine flows into a waiting vessel.

Stripped of her clothing, bare skin against cool linen, her body arched to meet his mouth, warm and sweet against her. Her soft moans were of helpless encouragement, while her hands lightly caressed his face. In desperation, she writhed against him, brought to fulfillment's painful edge. He met her need with his own, and they fused into completion.

Even thus, they could not banish reality. They were set apart though their bodies touched—nay, clung. Her head on his shoulder, her breast pressed to his ribs, his thigh hard against hers. His was the leather of lean muscles, hers the silk of lithe curves. His shadowed face betrayed none of his secrets, hinting perhaps at the ruthless dominion he had created but not the deeds that had made it a necessity. She longed to break the silence, but words of worth eluded her.

It was he who spoke at last. "I must ride to Edinburgh at dawn. I dare send no envoy—not in this matter. I leave Gerwalt to guard you against harm. My trust in him is as secure as that in myself."

Her eyes roved to the weapons on and above the mantel, gleaming attestations of battle. "As your faith in yon blades?"

He followed her gaze and nodded. "'Tis well placed. They have been my constant companions in years past."

"When came the others to Athdair, your father and brothers?" She broached her question cautiously, but she was indeed curious of his past.

"They fought for the third James until his death. Afterwards, Jamie crushed his opposition by stripping the chiefs of wealth and title. Some were exiled, some impoverished. Duncan has never forgiven the aid I was able to provide, though he speaks of it not. Gallhiel haunts his dreams."

"Gallhiel." Dara tested the word softly.

Laochlain felt a peculiar surge of emotion at hearing the castle name spoken from her lips. It was not Duncan's memories alone that were wreathed with painful longings.

"Gallhiel," he repeated. "'Tis said a Norseman came from the seas and chose the stoutest keep within a day's distance of the shore. Slaying the laird, he took his daughter to wife, and she bore him two sons. When he returned to the sea, the elder sailed at his side. The younger remained to found our clan. 'Tis his name we bear."

"What of the Norseman?"

"He never returned, but it is said his woman remained true until her death."

"Such steadfastness is rare," she said slowly, lost in the tale.

His hand caressed her face gently before cupping her chin, lifting her face to his gaze. "And you, lass, would you be so true?"

She was apprehensive of his intensity but answered without compromise. "Aye, for my faith is not lightly pledged, but it can never be forced—it must be earned."

He leaned forward so that their lips nearly touched. "And where it is earned?"

"So it shall remain," she whispered as their lips met.

In the slate-colored dawning of the icy morn, Dara watched from an open window as Laochlain mounted the red stallion. A dark woolen cloak hung to his heels, covering breeks and a shortcoat lined with soft skin, and the flared brim of his hat shaded a face tanned even in winter. His mount was caparisoned in black and silver, and his fist on the reins was gauntleted in black.

Gerwalt, afoot, was at his side, and though their words were lost to Dara, she guessed accurately at their speech.

"Gerwalt, I charge you with yet another burden."

"Fear not, Laochlain, I'll stand you in good stead, my life the forfeit."

Laochlain smiled. "'Tis not one I'd claim."

"I'd not leave it to you to do so," Gerwalt answered calmly. "God go with you and sanction a speedy return."

"I trust rather in myself, friend."

He turned without ceremony, and James' messenger followed suit. With lifted hand, Laochlain beckoned his outriders follow. Their garb reflected the somber colors of their master, and they rapidly blurred to shadows against the colorless horizon to the north.

Far south of their destination, Taran quartered double its usual number of men-at-arms. Their weapons bore the armorial stag of the Earl of Chilton. Their expressions reflected their moods, ready and watchful but not anticipating the planned assault with any degree of grimness or even reluctance. They were borderers, accustomed to dealing in death and stoically accepting the fact that it might befall them as readily as their enemies. Defeat and disgrace were more to be dreaded than that familiar specter.

Within the hall itself, anger was rampant. At last had Owein dropped his pretense of concern for Dara. He barely remembered her as an unmannered, undisciplined girl of tousled hair and flying skirts and an unruly, impudent tongue. He wished only to see the Scots defeated, and as many slain as could be found. His niece's safety, the avenging of his nephew's death, both were overshadowed by blind, burning hatred.

Lord Blaecdene listened in silence as Brann angrily warned his uncle. "We will, from the outset, ascertain Dara's whereabouts and deliver her to safety. There will be time enough for reprisal when that is ensured."

"I'll not see the pillaging bastards flee to safety whilst you scour the hall for a wench!"

Brann leapt to his feet, the backless stool skidding from beneath him. His hands crashed open-palmed against the long table. His eyes blazed with fury.

150

"That wench is my sister! 'Tis for her sake that we ride on Athdair at all. I will not have her endangered by your damned blundering!"

Owein snorted in disgust. "You would place all after her, even the slaying of your own flesh. Will you let Kerwin's murderer escape unscathed to rescue the girl? Would she not give her life to avenge his death?"

"Whether she would or not, I will not. Nor will you! Goad me no more, Uncle, lest I ride alone!"

Owein toyed with his signet ring of bloodstone and gold. When he finally answered, he glared at his nephew from slitted eyes. "My men have orders. You'll not leave here without me. Not alive!"

Glancing at Brann's murderous face, Merlion intervened. "This quarreling is useless. We all seek this Scotsman's death, and with it will come Lady Dara's release. Your dissent does him no harm but yourselves much."

Brann subsided. "Aye, then, but if he brings her to harm, I'll not remember that he is my father's brother."

Merlion accepted this without comment, for he had made the same determination. He opened a new topic with the diplomacy learned at court. "We'd best strike swiftly, for Henry will not long delay with merely a warning. He will send forces to bar our way if he discerns we will not heed his commands."

As Brann nodded agreement, his uncle stared at the two young men. His eyes had faded in color but not in keenness. "I've yet to understand, Blaecdene, your part in this. To speak of friendship and loyalty is noble, but you risk your life and all you possess in a quarrel that cannot concern you. What is to be your reward? Gold?"

"Nay, Ryland, something of far more worth—your niece."

"So-o-o." The single, long-drawn syllable hid any reaction, and, reaching forward, the old man pulled a roughly sketched map closer before them. "A poor time for warfare this, we are like to freeze." A square finger traced a faint ink line. "This burn runs under the wall and waters the keep. If we block it, our siege will have early success."

"If Henry and James give us time enough."

"Do not worry, Blaecdene, we will have the time. James will stay his hand as long as possible to avoid war, and Henry also, for the same reason. He'd not dare send forces across the Scottish line, 'twould be an open declaration."

"Be not too sure," Brann interjected. "The MacAmlaid holds James' favor, and his peril would bring quick aid. But as for Henry, aye, you are right, he'll not send men into Scotland."

"Bah!" Owein was scornful. "These damned Scots are too proud to admit themselves vulnerable. Athdair would never send for help, and if we cross the border quietly and at night, none will know their danger. Athdair stands more than a day's ride from any neighbor save Kermichil, and I have a notion that can be used to our good."

His gaze slid from Brann's dubious frown to Merlion's passive patience, and a hint of a smile crossed his leathered face. He'd show these young bloods the fighting ability of a true warrior. They'd soon see that no Scot could withstand the onslaught of hell when guided by Ryland of Taran.

Chapter XII

A massive portcullis set in walls twelve feet
of stone guarded the Castle of Edinburgh,
with an esplanade the only avenue to the
city below. The great gates of High Street
shielded the city from the plains beyond. Up
Castle Hill, in the finer sections of the city, were
tall houses of stone, elegant city dwellings of
great nobles with armorial bearings carved
above the doorways. Below lay the marketplaces
with signs swung over doorways, naming taverns, iron-forgers' shops, butchers' shops, and
linen shops. Mean streets with narrow, twisting
closes ran off the cobbled thoroughfare, and in
the black of winter's predawn, cats, lean and
vicious, foraged through the middens in search
of rodents feeding on the refuse.

A tall, cloaked man, flanked by armed retainers, passed silently through the deserted streets and made his way up the grey ramp to the castle above. Terse speech gained his immediate entry.

The castle slept, but not so Laochlain. In the chamber appointed him, he bathed and shaved with meticulous care before donning breeks and doublet of dark amber. Far from the somber garb in which he had traveled, these proclaimed his wealth and nobility. A short cape fell from one shoulder, revealing topaz-and-gold-hilted weapons abelt. His boots were of soft cordovan leather, and a heavy, intricately twined gold chain lay against the expanse of velvet covering his chest.

Shortly before noon, James of Scotland received him in private. The room was a spacious corner chamber overlooking the city. James awaited him without any sign of tension, relaxed in a high, carved chair, his feet sprawled before him. He was a true Stuart, handsome and strong and dark, with brown eyes and hair a strikingly dark auburn. Laochlain entered and knelt before his king.

"Rise, my lord," he was commanded, "I'd have no ceremony of you. I am greatly curious of your journey here. It has been long enough since I've enjoyed your company."

"I regret that 'tis not pleasure that brings me here, Your Grace." Laochlain settled in a chair near the window, watching James for any reaction. There was none.

"I warrant not, by the look of you. Speak your mind."

"The girl," he began abruptly, "Dara Ryland, I would not release her."

"So . . ." James looked unsurprised. He had guessed right and with little difficulty. "You have not yet obeyed my command."

"I would have you know my reasons."

James was amused. "Think you I do not already?"

Reluctantly, Laochlain smiled. "Perhaps not entirely. I've demanded a ransom, but I've no wish for the gold. It was a delay. Once Lord Chilton regains his sister, there will be no bar to his vengeance. Little use to assure him that Ruod is gone from the border marches, and that Ruod alone is to blame. There will be many innocent to suffer. The crofts and villages along his path could ill withstand a firm attack."

"Valid reasons, Laochlain, but offset by England's concern in the matter. Chilton is one of the few northern powers that have proven more loyal to Henry than to themselves. Henry might well reward that loyalty. He neither warns nor threatens—he'd not dare—but he does remind me of certain agreements. I'd mislike giving him reason to declare himself freed of his obligations. At least for the present."

Laochlain remained silent, and James sighed. "I'd be a knave to forget your loyalty and courage in my behalf. And could I do less for such steadfastness than Henry? You place me in a quandary, my lord. Is Chilton's sister of such importance to you?"

"Aye, Your Grace."

"Then do as you will, but it cannot be with my sanction. I've commanded you to release her—that is the decision that will come to Henry's ears. For the present, you must leave Athdair

157

with the girl and tell few of your directions. Is she worth exile, my lord?"

Laochlain was relaxed now and answered with assurance. "I warrant so, she is a comely lass."

"Ever the root of a man's difficulties!" James remarked wryly, and Laochlain grinned in sympathy. James' mistresses were legion. "Would you wed the girl?"

The question caught Laochlain completely off guard, and his surprise left him with no reply.

James chuckled. "'Tis of little matter. I command your presence at my table this evening and another audience on the morrow, then you may return to your lass. Have you a destination when you leave Athdair?"

"Aye, Your Grace. Gallhiel. As you well know, 'twill be no exile for me there."

James looked thoughtful. "You might do well there for my interests as well as your own. The borders are nigh unto peace if this present affair passes, but the Highlands froth with rebellion. Aye, you might do very well there."

That evening, amidst the gaiety of James' extravagant and immoral court, Laochlain sought his brother. That was no small feat, for James was ever surrounded by throngs of people.

He seldom tarried long in one place but traveled continually from one castle and one burgh to another. In this manner, he remained accessible to his people, speaking with them and listening to them. Despite this accessibility, he was never less a king, nor less a Stuart. He enjoyed every manner of sport, loved his horses and dogs, spent freely and dressed with elegance. His own personal extravagances extended most generously to the needs of others, and no few had cause to bless his name. Noble to beggar had tasted of his munificence.

Dancing, dicing, and cards were but a few of the pleasures he embraced, yet in a surrounding of drunkenness and gluttony, he was moderate in all things. It was remarked that his regularity in worship and fasting was due to guilt for his father's death. None knew. Nor was there proof of the chafing metal belt that many swore he wore beneath his clothing. Beloved by his subjects, Jamie Stuart's energy and zest for life, his self-confidence and physical perfection, all held an infinite appeal. His eye for a lovely woman was forgiven (and perhaps secretly applauded) and his numerous illegitimate children were viewed with pride.

But above all, James the Fourth of Scotland was loved, and his court bubbled with enthusiasm.

Under a babbled mixture of foreign tongues, Niall pleaded with his brother. Having already been told decisively that argument was futile and seeing the stubborn set of Laochlain's face, he had little hope for success. They were seated at James' table, the other tables adjoining it to form a wide, open square around the pit of fire burning hotly in the center of the room. Everywhere was the glitter of jewels and the gleam of gold, with servants as numerous as the guests.

"What you suggest is worse than folly. Athdair is your life!"

Laochlain shook his head. "Athdair has served

159

me well, and I value it truly, but not above all."

Niall looked desperate. "Is it pride that forces your hand?"

Laochlain frowned. That had been Dara's suggestion, and he liked it no more now than then. "Pride is but a man's honor. Is that without importance?"

"I have no wish to quarrel with you, Laochlain, but I know the cost of your exile from another home. What need to endure that torment a second time?"

"The choice is mine as it was twelve years ago."

"But to give all for a girl . . . !"

Into Laochlain's mind flashed a picture of Dara, vivid and alluring. His response held a calm that did not deceive his brother. "I warrant you know me as well as any man could, Niall, and I tell you now that the matter is decided. You would be better served to turn your attention to your bride who awaits you with such sweet patience."

Startled at the sarcasm he heard in his brother's voice, Niall glanced at his wife chattering ebulliently with her handsome neighbor. He shrugged. "She is well disposed."

Laochlain considered Anne's partner in conversation, a middle-aged Spaniard whose accomplished speech was laced with smooth compliments. "Are you so certain of your lady that jealousy is lacking, or is it that you are lenient in her handling?"

"Never that. I brook no rivals, but I fear no deception at her hands."

Looking around at the full, pouting smiles and bared bosoms of the court ladies, Laochlain shrugged. "You're luckier than many. You'd think not a woman here was wed."

Niall laughed aloud. "Are you grown rustic or is it cynicism?"

Laochlain lifted his goblet in toast. "Neither. 'Tis honesty."

The servants began to clear the table, but few moved to rise. There would be jugglers to perform, wrestling to wager upon, and dicing and cards for those who wished. And always the music that was necessity to James as surely as were meat and drink. It might well be two hours or longer before he would retire.

At last Anne disentangled herself from her conversation and gave her attention fully to her husband. "Forgive my neglect, my lord." Twinkling eyes and a barely suppressed smile belied her dutiful words.

Laochlain looked past Niall to his sister-in-law, who had adapted well to court ways for a country lass. "You'd best beat her, Niall, else she'll lead you a merry dance," he remarked conversationally.

Anne blushed. She had not yet the confidence for bandying words with her husband's lordly brother.

"I regret, mistress, that you must leave your circle of swains. Niall is required at Athdair."

With widened eyes, she glanced at her husband. He had told her nothing of the matter, having hoped to change his brother's mind. He deemed it useless now and nodded to Laochlain.

"We will be ready on the morrow."

Not long after, when James had laughingly drawn Laochlain into a wager, Anne heard the whole of the tale from Niall. Her mouth pursed as she remembered Dara's troubled foreboding. "So, he had his way with her, after all."

Niall frowned, his eyes going to Laochlain's momentarily relaxed, even carefree, expression. "Aye, so he did. And he's apt to pay dearly for the pleasure."

Chapter XIII

Reparation had begun. In a night of frigid calm and bitter damp, a stranger awakened Athdair with a terrible tale and a plea for aid. The Earl of Chilton had attacked Kermichil Keep at dusk, and if no help were forthcoming, all would perish. As men scattered to seize weapons and saddle stamping horses, Dara stared at the stranger in horror.

"Art sure? Is there no doubt that 'tis Lord Chilton?"

"No mistake, my lady." His veiled stare did not miss her pallor and agitation. "He has begun what is needful."

The peculiarity of the low murmur passed unchallenged, for Dara was numbed by the realization of Brann's daring intention, and his danger, and no other had heard it.

Duncan had retrieved his claymore from above the hearth and was fastening a protective vest of strong leather about his massive chest. For once he ignored an opportunity to torment Dara, his attention was focused on Gerwalt.

"Come, man, we've no time to spare."

"My duty lies here."

"D'ye jest?" Duncan asked incredulously. "Our neighbors—nay, our kin now—are fallen upon by English whoresons, and you would linger as they are butchered?"

Gerwalt answered heavily. "My charge is of Laochlain and binds me until I am released of it."

"'Tis bastardy. That girl is naught. Her brother craves the lives of innocents, and you would shield her?" His flushed face twisted in fury. "Protect her then, you witless knave, but watch from whence her danger comes and know it for my revenge!"

"Take the men," Gerwalt growled. "I will safeguard the girl—whatever the source of her danger."

Cursing volubly, Duncan stalked from the keep. The stranger delayed, his eyes searching the hall with a thoroughness that missed nothing until, feeling Gerwalt's stare boring into him, he turned abruptly and left the room.

Gerwalt clenched his rough, scarred hands into fists, fighting the driving urge to abandon all and follow. Hatred of the English burned in his brain, but Laochlain's certain trust in him overrode anything else. He listened in frustration as a thundering of hooves signaled the men's departure. Though damning his helplessness, he never feared their defeat or the outcome. Athdair's men were a canny lot, brave and skilled in battle.

But danger is not always visible. So filled with fury was Duncan, so intent his warriors, that not a single one of them noticed when the stranger lagged further and further behind and finally melted into the shadows of the frozen hills. Nor, when nearing Kermichil Keep, did they have any premonition of the snare into which they rode. Surrounded suddenly and completely in a passage of hills, they fought bravely but against a foe half again their number and one completely prepared.

And, as they battled Owein's forces, Brann led his men upon Athdair, but another arrived before them.

None of the few left at Athdair had returned to their beds, although Dara returned miserably to the chamber she shared with Laochlain. It seemed to her there was renewed distrust in Gerwalt's blue eyes and in Lethe's dark ones. Distrust and loathing, and she would not plead with them to judge her less harshly. With the coming of dawn, she dressed and left the keep.

The first rays of sunlight sparkled on crystals of snow, giving the grey morning a brighter aspect than it warranted. The fells beyond the gates appeared deserted save for barren stands of trees. A voice from behind her was unexpected and startling.

"You make safeguarding you a difficult task."

She answered wearily. "Should you make the effort? If my brother succeeds, he will come next to Athdair."

"That has naught to do with Laochlain's bidding."

"His trust is well placed."

"No more than mine. We are milk brothers, and 'tis a tie closer than blood."

"I warrant so since he gains less loyalty from Ruod."

Gerwalt stared into the distance. "Their blood is but half shared, the ties are weak. When Duncan's lady was full with Gallhiel's heir, he begat another son on a serving wench, a bastard and with a wanton dam."

"What manner of woman was his lady, Laochlain's mother?"

His eyes returned to her. "Iseabal Camdene MacAmlaid was a rare woman, as strong and beautiful as the mountains. And willful—much like you."

She was thinking that with a sire such as Duncan, a mother such as Iseabal would be doubly missed by her sons, and she repeated idly, "Willful?"

"Aye, you should stay within."

"You are overcautious, Gerwalt."

"I await no chance," he averred.

Abandoning the argument, she returned her attention to the horizon. It was no longer deserted. Two riders approached steadily from the northeast, Kermichil Keep lay to the west. She suppressed a fluttering weakness in her belly as she pointed them out to Gerwalt.

His reaction was daunting. "Get within the hall and call Lethe to you."

"Could it not be the MacAmlaid?" Though she

strove for detachment, wistfulness edged the question.

"'Tis not the red. Obey me!"

Reluctantly, she did so, leaving her burly protector staring out from beneath his shaded hand. He pondered again his unease since Laochlain's departure. Duncan's peculiar, satisfied silences of late and his parting threat seemed more ominous than before. Mayhap he had been lax, rather than overdiligent as the lass implied.

The minutes passed slowly as the riders loomed closer to the heights of the stone wall. They entered. Dismounting, one of them turned slowly to scan the deserted courtyard and smiled behind a heavy growth of beard.

"Duncan promised he would contrive."

"He was aided, Ruod. The Ryland attacked Kermichil Keep—our men are there."

"All of them?" Ruod licked his lips.

"Enough." Gerwalt answered him succinctly, his eyes on Strang as he dismounted and sidled next to Ruod.

"I've come for the girl."

Slowly, Gerwalt drew his dirk. "I remain only to guard her, as Laochlain wished."

Ruod grew grim as he palmed his own blade, one that had proven worth his trust in the past weeks of thieving and plundering. He sized his opponent with a practiced eye and signaled to Strang surreptitiously. Gerwalt was too fit for Ruod not to take every advantage, fair or no.

They engaged with methodical savagery, each intending the other's death, and each coming chillingly close to success. But Strang knew his part well, and before Ruod began to tire, before Gerwalt could land a fatal blow, his own blade found hold between muscled ribs.

Strang grinned. He had thrown true.

Gerwalt swayed, not touching the knife hilted in his side. It would be useless. He would not have suspected even Ruod of such treachery. A struggle face to face, death to the defeated, aye. But not this craven breach of unwritten law. Ruod had been from the Highlands too long. Gerwalt was still groping for acceptance as his knees buckled with weakness from the loss of his blood pumping steadily upon the flagstones.

Ruod did not even trouble himself to watch his kinsman die. He swaggered confidently into the keep and found Dara and Lethe alone in the hall. He would have been better pleased had they huddled in fear, but they did not. His eyes roved leeringly over Dara, and her flesh crawled as though it were a physical touch. With set chin, Lethe moved silently so that her body shielded the younger girl.

Ruod frowned. "Do ye think to set a price for the wench?"

"I am no whoremonger, but doubtless you've plied that trade yourself, Ruod MacAmlaid."

"You'll gain Gerwalt's fate with your blathering, bitch!"

Lethe did not so much as flinch at his lifted hand, and he turned from her in disgust. It was an inopportune moment that Kinara chose to leave the kitchens. The stout doors which closed off the passage swung heavily closed behind her. Ruod's eyes went to the fullness of her belly, and his laughter was chilling.

168

"A welcome for me? The bastard to sire another and on a whoring servant as his father before him. I would ha' thought you'd rid yourself of it."

Kinara's sullen eyes flamed to life at his taunt. Her lust for him had long since turned to fury that he had not returned for her. "I tried," she spat. "I'll strangle it between my legs at birth as your mother should have done for you. Though likely she could not close them long enough for even such a worthy deed!"

The back of his hand split her lip against her teeth, and the taste of blood filled her mouth. Cursing, she spat blood in his face. His broad fist drew back, and she knew she had dared too much. She turned to flee and stumbled upon the rushes, falling heavily.

Ruod grasped Dara's arm as she bent to aid the girl. "Nay, you will drink with me."

Lethe stood, torn by her choice, before bending to Kinara. Her loyalty must be first to Athdair's own.

Ruod dragged Dara to the table. She shrank from his touch as he forced her to a bench. Taking Laochlain's chair with a sneer of enjoyment, he hefted the cask of ale that Gerwalt had opened earlier. He drank greedily and noisily, disgusting her as the excess dripped from his beard and beaded on his greasy, stained jacket. He shoved the cask near her hand and scowled when she made no move to touch it.

"Drink! You will drink with me as I have watched you drink with Laochlain. You will talk and smile with me as you do with him!"

Dara was mutinously silent.

"You damned little whore! Laochlain is no longer here to protect you—or to bed you!"

"Even your force has its limits, Ruod," she spat at him. "If you wish a companion for your foulness, it must be someone who fears you. I do not!"

Furious, he lifted the cask to her mouth and gripped her hair painfully as he poured its contents against her closed lips. The ale spilled over her, onto her gown and hair and into her nose. She choked and gasped for breath, pushing violently at the cask.

This was the scene that met her brother's eyes as he entered the hall followed by two men dragging the unfortunate Strang between them. Another man, a stranger to Dara, was at his side. Brann's fists were clenched in rage, and his eyes blazed with uncontrollable fury as he advanced on Ruod who fell back at his approach.

Freed from his grasp, Dara sank limply to the floor, only to find herself caught up in the stranger's arms.

Her eyes followed Brann as he wrested Ruod's dirk from him and flung him against the wall. The scuffle lasted little more than a minute, but left Ruod with a bruised and bleeding face. Brann was not inclined to mercy.

"You are the MacAmlaid?"

Ruod's lips twisted in a grimacing smile. "Such is my name whether lawfully or no, but I am not the Earl of Athdair."

Dara spoke slowly, fighting a thick mist. "This man slew Kerwin and brought me from Chilton —not the other."

"Aye, slut, but 'twas Laochlain who bedded you, was it not?"

Brann lunged at him again in rage, but the stranger who held Dara called forward two of the men who gathered into the hall. Brann shoved Ruod towards them, and he was roughly seized.

"I'll not sully my hands further! This one and his lackey are to be dealt with as we deal with any who lay hand to our womenfolk and do murder among us. And make haste, we've no time to spare."

Strang had begun a shrill, cowardly protest midway through this speech, and his pleas left a foulness after him as he was dragged outside with a silent and still defiant Ruod. The howls of the English were like those of starving wolves upon a coveted prey, and Strang's screams were drowned beneath them.

The sound echoed in Dara's ears until she pressed her hands against them in a frenzied effort to block out the noise. When Brann reached for her, she shrank from him in horror, scarcely aware that the stranger held her still.

"How many murders for my sake, Brann, how many?"

He halted before her, bewildered and a little angered. "I did what must be."

"I would not have had any of it. I would prefer my own death to one more slain for my sake."

Brann was two and twenty, only five years her elder, but he looked, suddenly, twice that. "Are you grown like mother, too weak to face reality?"

His words were a bitter pain, and she lashed out in return. "Nay, 'tis you who are too like Owein, brutal and cruel and . . ."

She stopped, aghast at her own cruelty to this brother she loved so well. Tears blinded her, and she lifted an imploring hand, but he turned away from her.

Her return to Chilton was far too much like her leaving. A second time she grieved for a brother, though death had no hand in it this time, and again she carried with her agonizing pictures of death. Gerwalt's body lay crumpled in the courtyard, and two unspeakable, unrecognizable bodies had been flung near his. And once again she was held in a stranger's arms, though it was no blue-eyed Scot of cruel temper this time.

Lord Blaecdene was dark and lean with a London-bred assurance. When he spoke, it was with a soft, clipped London accent, and his arms formed an impersonal shelter she welcomed with relief.

The uneven towers of Chilton were but blurs against the darkening sky as they passed beneath the castle's great arches. It was Christmas Eve, and she was home.

Laochlain's foreboding began some distance from Athdair, a curious dread that drove him to a faster pace though horses and riders were all weary, particularly Anne. She was unused to the grueling pace of travel they had endured since leaving Edinburgh, and the last miles had been arduous ones as the horses battled driving winds and stinging snow.

The presentiment became a chilling conviction as the brothers were greeted somberly by men who exchanged uncomfortable glances but volunteered no explanations. Laochlain insisted upon none; instead, he turned from their uneasy silence with growing dread and followed Niall and his exhausted young bride into the hall. There a brooding emptiness enveloped them.

Laochlain strode to the center of the hall and shouted so that his voice echoed Gerwalt's and Dara's names by turn through the silence.

"You'll have answer of neither. Nor of Duncan, Fibh, and a half a dozen others." Lethe spoke from the landing above, as neatly dressed and as composed as ever but indelibly aged. She came slowly down the stairs, her words making a reality of the fears. "You left the best of Athdair's men to defend your keep, and many are slain."

"Dara?" The word was an anguished question.

"Her brother came while our men were engaged. Ruod gained death in his lust for her."

"Ruod?"

"Aye, Duncan sent for him before . . ." She halted, glancing at Anne. "Niall, take your lass from here, she will have enough to bear without hearing the worst of it in this manner."

"Nay," Anne said firmly, arresting Niall's rising movement. "I am a MacAmlaid now. I'll not flee trouble."

Lethe looked at her compassionately, almost surprised that pity and sorrow were not dead in her. "Aye, you are truly a MacAmlaid now. Your father and your brother are dead. They led their men to Duncan's defense and were slain, though their added numbers dispersed the English."

Anne's face drained completely of color before she fainted quietly in Niall's arms. He held her gently as he heard the last of Lethe's tale.

"They lured our men with a ruse. Word came here of an attack on Kermichil, and Gerwalt sent all to battle. They were surrounded within sight of Kermichil Keep. And Gerwalt was alone when Ruod and Strang came, alone to guard the English girl."

"A fair fight with Ruod would not have seen him slain," Laochlain raged, swept by a shattering grief.

"Nay," Lethe agreed. "A fair fight would not."

"Where are our slain?" Niall questioned grimly.

"They are laid within Kermichil Keep." She looked to Laochlain. "All but Gerwalt. I had him taken abovestairs. He is there, in your chamber."

He started towards the stairs, then halted and turned. "And Dara, did she go willingly with that murdering whoreson?"

"She greeted him with words of anger—but she made no struggle when they took her from here."

When Laochlain returned to the hall hours later, Niall awaited him. Anne had been put to bed, weak with weeping. Lethe was above, tending to Kinara who lay cursing because her babe had not been stillborn. She had a daughter. As the brothers were served a hastily prepared meal, Laochlain saw only the bierlike appearance of his chamber where candles were lit in

174

vigil about one who was like his own flesh and lived no more.

As they ate, they argued. A decision was imperative, and, as yet, the two brothers disagreed. Niall was impatient, ready to mount arms and do battle, but Laochlain halted his raging.

"We've no' the men."

"Your name alone could raise all we need and more."

"To ride to their deaths," was the grim reply. "Chilton will be waiting for just such a move. And doubtless, too, Henry has forces scattered along the border. A man alone could pass, if careful, mayhap a handful, but no more than that."

Niall was watching his brother warily when Anne's soft voice startled them both. Neither had seen or heard her soft-slippered entrance. She was gowned for bed in a white softness that emphasized her frailty. Her eyes were red with weeping, and her lips were broken where she had bitten them to stifle her sobs.

"My lord, he is my husband, and my people also were slain. Who else is to avenge them?"

Laochlain answered her gently. "I grieve with you and for you. For your kin as well as mine. For men who rode and fought so many years at my side. But I'll no lead more men to their deaths, most especially not my brother, whose bairn even now you might be carrying. No," he glanced from one to the other, "what must be done, I will do alone."

Anne nodded slowly, realizing how easily she

might lose Niall to an English blade. She could not bear that, not now.

It was Niall who voiced the question she dared not ask. "What of Chilton's sister?"

Laochlain recalled his vows to hold her and smiled grimly. Without a struggle, Lethe had said. "She can watch her brother die."

"And after you've taken revenge?"

"I am for Gallhiel."

Chapter XIV

Kermichil Keep loomed without warning
from a shroud of mist, its inner recesses
pierced by screams and pleas for mercy.
The hills gathered close about the fastness ran
with blood, and a keening echoed between the
craggy slopes. Neither moon nor stars lightened
the ceiling of clouds, and the sense of solitude
was stifling.

Dara struggled from her nightmare in panic
and then lay tensely silent, fighting its aftermath
of unreasoning fear. Her breath came in dragging sobs, and her heartbeat was swift and
painful. She could not banish the lingering chill,
but at last her pulse calmed and panic receded.
She sat up and drew back the hangings of the
canopied bed.

The room was her own, the furnishings as

familiar as her own childhood. Oaken paneled walls gleamed softly from the flames in the generous hearth while floor-length curtains withheld the light of day from every window. Slipping her feet onto thick fur rugs, she crossed the room and threw wide the shutters of one tall aperture. Seven feet high and tiny-paned, it led onto a small stone balcony. It was late, for the sun had reached the forest top in the valley in its descent. A rueful smile acknowledged that her sleep had doubtless been aided surreptitiously by one of Mildraed's mixtures in her brandied milk. She sighed. It had been a difficult night after an almost unendurable day.

She and Brann had made their peace, but all wounds were not healed by gentle words of repentance. It was to her credit that she had not loosed the bitter condemnation she felt when Owein had arrived on their heels. She had held her tongue, but it had been necessary to seek her apartments in doing so. She could not bear to remain in the same room as her uncle. She had seen no one but Mildraed after that, and it was Mildraed who came to her now, almost as if she had sensed her rising.

Mildraed was welcomed gladly, for she would make no demands Dara was unable to meet. She had never been a gentle comforter but rather a stern bulwark, and never more needed than now.

She entered scolding briskly about the cold wind that blew upon her young mistress. "Will ye close the window or perish and give this family another grief? I've kept water hot for bathing since morning."

"I would have used it earlier had you not sent me so soundly to sleep."

"No impudence, miss, you're no longer among heathens."

Sheltered from drafts by an ornamented screen, Dara washed her hair and bathed, relishing the warmth and fragrance of the soap-scented water. When she was done, she stepped into the warm fleece mantle that Mildraed held ready. It was with a sense of displacement, almost of unfamiliarity, that she dressed in her own clothing. The gown she chose was not what Mildraed would have wished, though its deep green shade became her. The old woman complained of its plainness, for even the kirtle gathering it tight about the hips was of the same dark material.

Combing her hair dry, Mildraed left it loose in a cascade of auburn, threading one heavy tress through with a silk ribbon of green. Dara was amused as well as amazed at her own lingering over her coffer of jewels. She had not realized she was so fond of her few treasures. After long consideration, she chose a lovely strand of pearls that had long ago graced her grandmother's wedding gown. Her father's mother. Josceline had left no keepsakes behind for her abandoned daughter.

At her own request, Dara had occupied these tower rooms since her twelfth year. At the foot of the tower was Mildraed's domain, where she kept close night watch over the unwed maidservants. The next flight was Dara's morning room, and above this, reached by tiny, thickly carpeted stairs, was her bedchamber. Throughout, the eight-foot-thick walls of stone were paneled and the floors carpeted and rugged.

As she descended with Mildraed to the hall below, Dara could no longer close from her mind the cruel words she had flung at Brann at their reunion. Though forgiven by him, she was lashed by guilt. He had risked his life for her, and she more than shared his blame. It had been pride that held her to the pledge she had given Laochlain. Had she abandoned pride and fled, she could have prevented the bloodshed that must now lie so heavily upon her peaceable brother.

Dara paused on the landing of her morning room and, on impulse, stepped forward into the gloom. Mildraed followed, lighting their way with a single, flickering candle which she touched to the tapers in the candelabrum. The golden glow touched on dark wood and soft-hued coverings. Mildraed moved about bemoaning the dust that had insinuated itself into little-noticed corners and threatening terrible consequences to the lax servants. But when Dara ran her fingers across the stiff brocade and crevices of carved walnut, it was only to satisfy herself of their sameness. She wished no further changes in her life, not even of the smallest degree.

Brann, coming in search of her, was drawn from the stairs by the candlelight and Mildraed's sharp tones. From the doorway, he called her name, and she turned to him smiling.

"Nothing has changed here, Brann."

"Who would dare?" he replied, taking both her hands in his and placing a kiss on her cheek.

Neither he nor Dara noticed Mildraed's unob-trusive departure.

"No one, of course, but much has changed . . ."

They both fell silent at this until he rallied and mentioned their guest and supper waiting be-low.

"Owein," she questioned tensely; "he is not still here?"

"Nay," was the grim assurance, "he is not nor like to be again. The cost of his alliance was too great. 'Tis only Lord Blaecdene who awaits us."

Dara was not eager for the demands of con-versing with a stranger, she was still too unset-tled. She could not even recall his image to mind beyond an impression of sharp, handsome fea-tures and even sharper eyes. Yet she sensed the importance of their acquaintanceship to Brann and felt constrained to please him. Or would have had he courted patience.

"Merlion has been more than a friend to me, and he holds a position of worth at court. His counsel is valued as is his wit."

Dara smiled. "None of which are as important or of such worth as his loyalty to you. That has earned my gratitude."

"He seeks more than gratitude of you—and I have promised more."

Her eyes widened in disbelief. "Oh, no, Brann, make no such plans for me."

"My word is pledged, Dara."

She stared at him aghast. "Mine is not!" His silence rebuked her. "Do you truly not know the cost of these past few months? Let me recover in peace."

He could not bear her anguish. "It need not be soon. The time is yours."

"I need none for an answer, Brann. When I wed, 'twill be for love."

"As did Josceline, only to find love of less strength than adversity?"

Her hands clenched into stubborn fists. "Twice you have compared me to our mother, and perhaps not wrongly. We have been used to name her weak, but was she? Is there strength in enduring an intolerable existence? Is it weakness to take the future into your own hands, no matter how difficult the path ahead? Aye, selfish, I grant, but weak? I think not, Brann."

She whirled from him, leaving him to follow as he would. He wondered suddenly that he had ever thought his sister biddable.

Merlion did not make that mistake as he greeted them with no sign of impatience. He saw, rather, a strikingly lovely girl with an expression at once composed and determined. His bow was low and courtly as he took her hand in his.

"Lady Dara, I am pleased to see you unharmed by Scotland's barbarities. A lesser maid would be prostrate."

She stared, intrigued by his tone which held unmistakable satire rather than commonplace sympathy. "Injury is not always obvious, my lord."

He nodded and released her hand with at least the appearance of reluctance. She found herself watching him suspiciously as he deftly guided their table conversation to tales and gossip of

182

London, carefully avoiding all mention of Margaret and her Scottish betrothed. Dara ate little and drank less, but refused to succumb to painful memories of her last dinner at this table, Kerwin at her side.

Merlion was reassured of her strong spirit, while Brann felt a stubborn pride in his contumacious sister.

Her true thoughts were masked and mercifully so. She made every effort at forgetting, but at any unguarded moment, the MacAmlaid was with her, his image as unrelenting as reality.

Morning found her again testing her wits with a man hourly more determined to wed her. He had followed her to the garden where the sun was shining with a brilliance rare for December. Its heat was near to melting the crust of ice and snow beneath her soft-booted feet. Her cape was of somber woolen, blending well with the lifeless shades of tree and bush, but her hair would not be confined to the folds of her hood and escaped in lively color.

She did not see him. She was looking into another garden, a summer one alive with color and scent. Laughter bubbled from young throats, and a half-grown hound, sleekly white, bounded just out of reach. A spasm of pain gripped her heart. She had not expected all of Chilton to be haunted.

Merlion stepped forward, and she started. "Lord Blaecdene, I thought myself alone."

He ignored the lack of welcome in her greeting. "So you were, until this moment. Alone and in another space of time, I'd warrant."

She eyed him consideringly. "A happier time."

As she walked on, he fell into step beside her. "Brooding serves no purpose."

She rejected that charge with a quick motion. "The past is always with us. It cannot be ignored or forgotten."

"It can be overcome. I lost a dear-loved wife, and for a long time, thoughts of her were sore painful. Now, she is a sweet memory."

"You are fortunate," she answered drily, whereupon he took her arm and brought her about to face him.

"You mislike that I have spoken my desire to wed you."

"I mislike that you and Brann would seek to force me to wed. I'd have my marriage based upon more than my brother's ties of loyalty to a friend."

"I make no claim to an attachment, Lady Dara, but my choice is no whim, nor is it blindly made. Brann is not so doting a brother as to ignore your failings, and these as well as your virtues he has recounted to me. A certain obstinacy of temperament is not to be disdained. My first wife did not lack for spirit, I would choose another with her strength."

Dara fought to bridle her temper at this calculated reasoning. "That deals nicely with your requirements, but what of mine? I will wed to please myself and no other. You would do well to heed me, my lord."

He did not appear angered nor even disturbed by her frank declining of his suit. "I am pos-

sessed of a magnitude of patience and persist-
ence."

"They will be of no avail."

"If you are so certain of your decision and so
firm in your answer, my attempts will be no
hindrance."

"Nay, but an annoyance."

Merlion merely laughed at her tartness, but
Brann found no amusement in this defiance.
Their subsequent encounters were turbulent
ones. He felt bounded by his pledge to Merlion
and grew ever more certain that in this union lay
Dara's surest security and peace of mind.
Merlion's home lay far to the south, far from the
bloody borders. Brann seized every moment to
press his argument, entreating then exhorting
her to obedience. And Mildraed was his steady
advocate.

Dara had longed for Chilton, but now it was no
more of a haven than Athdair had ever been. She
felt alienated from all who professed only love
and concern for her, and, in this alienation, she
suffered. Striving to be the dutiful sister, she
failed. She had been too long dependent upon
her own wits and found she could not submit to
his authority. They quarreled, were contrite, and
quarreled again. She made no struggle against
Merlion's efforts to engage her affections, for
none was needed. Indeed, she could feel nothing
more for him than an uneasy friendship. His
cynical frankness somehow compared unfavorably to a well-remembered, more brutal honesty.
She did not seek to make comparisons, but they
proved inevitable.

Several evenings after her return, Mildraed stood brushing Dara's hair in long strokes from crown to waist and chastising her in the same vein as on previous evenings. She made no attempt to disguise her disapproval of Dara's resistance to Brann's wishes.

"You try your brother sorely, and give him pain. Years gone saw you loyal to any who bore the name Ryland. Where lie your loyalties now?"

Dara flushed with anger as her eyes met Mildraed's in the mirror of polished silver. "My loyalties need not be questioned. Brann has given his to Lord Blaecdene. And where are yours, Mildraed? Not with me!"

Her bitterness was wrenching, and Mildraed sighed. "Only love for you guides me. Believe it, child, for 'tis truth. You have ever had a dear, loving nature, Dara. Forget it not now, when the need is the greatest."

"I forget nothing, nor is it I who have turned my heart from what the past has treasured!"

Mildraed had no reply. She could see all facets of the contention between brother and sister and grieved for both. And, selfishly, she knew, for herself. Dara was no longer a child to accept unquestioned her guidance, and Brann grew impatient with an old woman's struggle to retain authority.

Mildraed finished brushing Dara's hair and bound it in plaits around her head before seeing her gowned for bed and tucked warmly into thick coverlets. She blew the flames from the candles and moved towards the door. "Sleep well, child. The days will brighten."

Despite Dara's unvoiced doubts, that prediction proved accurate. The tension between herself and Brann eased slightly, and Dara acknowledged that it was due to his backing away. Thus when he came into her morning room where she had withdrawn for an afternoon, she was able to greet him with something of their old closeness.

Glancing round at the satin daybed and delicate chairs, he seized an embroidered cushion and tossed it near her feet. He smiled at the silk-threaded needle and square of linen in her idle hands.

"If I remember aright, you mislike the tedium of needlework."

"It disguises my laziness with an appearance of industry that I must confess is false."

"Mildraed would be pleased to see you so posed. I remember too well her scolds when Kerwin and I allowed you to ride and hunt and hawk with us."

"Allowed me to share your scrapes and your punishments," she corrected.

"Father never punished his favorite."

"I was favored only when father deigned to notice us at all, which was seldom. It was Mildraed who meted all penalties, and her softness was for ne'er-do-well brothers!"

"May you be plagued with sons of a like nature!" he teased before moving from jest to seriousness with a rapidity that took her unaware. "Have you no wish for children, Dara, for a husband? You are close of an age for marriage,

and Chilton Castle cannot be all your life. Nor
can I."

"I grieve yet for Kerwin—and for others."
She did not keep reproach from her answer.

"My authority is absolute, and I know best for
your future." He stared into the fire, avoiding
her eyes.

"You would force me to compliance?"

He looked up quickly, disturbed by what he
heard in her voice. "Never. I ask only that you
give me opportunity to prove the merit of my
choice."

"I have no objection to persuasion, Brann, 'tis
force I cannot stomach."

Having gained that much, he put forth the
initial reason for seeking her presence. "Merlion
must return home to attend to matters concerning his country estate. He wishes us to accompany him for a visit of a fortnight or two."

"Leave Chilton?" Her voice alone was protest.

"For no more than a visit," he assured her. "I
would enjoy the hunting, for he extolls the
plentitude of his game forest, but I will not leave
you so soon. I go only if we go together."

"Lord Blaecdene is little more than a stranger
to me."

"It need not be so. He has been a true and
loyal friend."

"I go on this condition, Brann. When I wish to
return home, whether it be in a fortnight, a
week, or a day, there will be no hindrance to my
departure."

"Agreed. You have my word on it."

He left her then, and she sat attempting to

overcome a deep reluctance to leave Chilton. It was home and dear to her even though it had not proved the haven she had once thought it. In honesty, she admitted that this was not entirely Brann's fault nor Mildraed's nor even Merlion's. The restlessness was within her, and she feared it would be with her always.

With an unwilling heart, she at last rose and climbed slowly to her bedchamber to begin preparing for an extended visit. She would have none accuse her of unfairness. She would go with at least the intention of remaining the full fortnight. Whether she did or not would depend much upon her host and his manner towards her.

Within the hour, Mildraed joined her. She knew of the proposed journey and was obviously pleased. Dara's heart hardened to her. She shared no confidences and revealed no distress to the woman who recognized regretfully the unbridgeable gulf between them. Still, Mildraed served as best she knew, packing and sorting gowns for the hardships of travel, mending and altering where necessary or desired.

They were to leave the next morning, and Dara awoke with a sense of loss. She had scarcely been home a week, and she was again to leave unwillingly. Deep within her a voice reminded with painful repetition that each mile from Chilton was also a mile farther from Scotland, and from Laochlain. She felt an empty desolation at the thought, and this feeling confused and frightened her. Her ultimate defense was anger, sheer and simple. She cursed her brother,

her lover, and her suitor equally and felt better for it.

It was this anger that stiffened her to the final packing, anger that nerved her to bathe and dress with special care. Determined to outface misery, she donned a fine woolen gown of lovely midnight blue and allowed Mildraed to arrange her hair in loose piles confined with polished wooden pins. Her heavy cloak was grey velvet trimmed with squirrel, and her only ornament a pendant of beaten gold shaped to the form of a single flowering bloom. Satisfied that her mirror reflected only composure, she left the chamber and Mildraed without a backward glance.

Mildraed followed her from the room and watched in silence her graceful descent, sensing she had lost the girl forever.

Brann awaited Dara below with Merlion at hand, his fine-drawn face impassive. The vast hall was frigid, for the wide doors were continually opened to baggage-laden servants as they cleared the piles of trunks upon the floor.

Merlion drew her nearer the draught-plagued fire. "My manor will not disappoint you. Nor will I." His manner and tone were those of an accepted lover.

The smile on her lips did not deceive him, for it did not warm her eyes as she replied, "Not the greatest luxuries of your home will cause me to wed you, m'lord."

"Ah, Dara, we shall deal far better together than you now imagine."

She stared at him, feeling a strange fascination for the certainty he displayed in the face of her insistent refusal. Without arrogance or artifice, he was quietly without doubt of her final surrender.

Suddenly frightened, she turned away from him to seek Brann. He, at least, had promised she would not be forced into that which she did not desire. Without true reason, she was, in that moment, certain she could not expect the same consideration of Merlion Blaecdene.

Chapter XV

Laochlain lifted the crude earthen mug to his lips and sipped its contents without tasting the bitterness of the inferior ale. His eyes and his thoughts were on the woman who bent low over a kettle swinging slightly above the smokey fire.

"We shall be gone soon, mistress, fear not."

She straightened at the sound of his voice. Her face was thin and tense but young still. "Gone, aye, but what evil will ye leave behind?"

"Less than your lord left Athdair," he answered laconically.

She moved about setting a few pieces of earthenware on her bare table. There was no fear in her of this hard Scottish earl, for neither he nor his men had offered any harm or even incivility to her. True, they had forced their way

into her home and meant to stay until they had
ended whatever it was they had come to do, but
she felt safe enough amongst them.

They had come at sunset two evenings past.
Six of them, wary but bold. Four had quartered
themselves in the rickety shelter her husband
had long ago erected for a cow that was no more.
This man and another slept on her floor beside
the hearth. They were no charge on her meager
resources. Indeed, she ate of their food, cooking
for the lot of them. But they were Scots and
meant harm to Lord Chilton. If it were possible
to thwart them, she would, even to murder, but
she was never left unguarded, and she lived far
from her neighbors.

The crofters whose lands bordered hers were
God-worshiping, privacy-respecting people,
and, as long as her chimney yielded smoke,
visitors would not be likely. Only if her hearth
grew cold and her few goats bleated their hunger
would any feel concern for her. She regretted,
now, her dead husband's independence in
choosing his plot so far from the others, though
once she had been proud of it.

Frustrated by her helplessness, she set a bowl
of herbed stew before Laochlain with a force
that splashed the steamy gravy onto his hand.
Scowling, he put the scald to his mouth. B'God,
he thought, do all English teach their womenfolk to be so inhospitable? It was an unfortunate
thought, for it brought to mind a pridefully
defiant lass, one he had been striving to forget.

"But at least the color of her hair gave fair
warning," he muttered.

The woman started. "Ye spoke to me, m'lord?"

"Nay," he grunted and settled irritably to his meal. If he had some diversion, his mind would not turn to harassments he need no longer deal with. Dara's stubbornness was her brother's concern. Bretach should have returned ere now. There was little enough danger in his task of spying if he kept his mind to the matter. Likely he had chanced upon some comely crofter's lass and endangered them all with dalliance.

Bretach, returning at dusk with what he considered welcome news, was thus surprised to find the MacAmlaid both short-tempered and critical. Shrugging, he relayed his findings.

"Think you they will leave tonight?" Laochlain questioned.

"Nay, 'twill be morning. It's London for the earl and his sister and that London lord."

Laochlain rose smoothly. "Then we'll have an early rising. Watch the woman till I return."

Meeting fully her gaze of hatred and loathing, he nodded slightly and let himself out through the only door. The red was quickly saddled though he snorted resentfully through the proceedings. It was near feeding time, and he was less content with his stabling than was his master. The wind ripped chill despite the sheltering of trees around the makeshift enclosure.

Laochlain scouted the twistings and turnings of the rough road south. Success seemed certain when he considered his followers. He had intended none, but when he had taken leave of Niall, the five of them had been waiting within the stables, horses readied. They had been headed by Bretach who spoke for them all.

"We would go with you, m'lord. The Highlands are home, and you will need loyal men at your side there."

"I go first to England," he warned.

"Aye," Bretach answered, "we've a stake in it."

"Does Niall know?"

"He knows."

That was three days ago. They had followed him unquestioningly to England and waited without complaint for his command. Now it was given. Dawn would see a reward to patience.

It was a grey, gusty dawn, denying the bright days before it. In the opened doorway, Laochlain pondered the disposal of the woman who had sheltered them, albeit unwillingly. She could not be left unhindered to take her tale to her neighbors upon their departure, nor would he see her slain as one of his men had baldly suggested. Her contemptuous silence and straight, baleful glares bespoke no fear of his intentions nor any likelihood of a promise of silence in return for her own safety. Nor would he trust her if she did give it.

A short while later, he tested the leather thongs binding her wrists. Dispassionately, he assured her that one of the men would return to free her. "Else," he concluded, "you would freeze when your fire burned out, or the beasts would break the door to get to you."

Her eyes blazed with the curses that her gagged mouth could not speak.

Laochlain was undisturbed. His spirits were

markedly lifted as he went out into the low-skied morning. The horses were saddled and waited patiently, tails tucked against the cold wind.

Laochlain paused before mounting, and his gaze touched each of the leather-clad men in turn. "I'll have no blood shed except when needful. One man alone bears the blame for all—the rest but follow his orders. As you will follow mine or earn the consequences."

Satisfied with the straightforward looks that met his, he seized loose-hanging reins and swung neatly up into the saddle. His strategy was simple. From the fells above, he watched as the travelers crossed the open grasslands about the castle and then, with a few words, dispersed his men. Two to the fore, two to the rear, to separate the outlying guards from the main body. Bretach rode with him.

He considered their forces closely matched, for he discounted the unarmed servants and avoided the probability of Dara rashly assailing her brother's attackers. The advantage of surprise was this time to the Scots. The English would little suspect the enemy at their gates and by morning's light.

Waiting noiselessly behind the boulders littering the foot of the hills that rose sharply from the road, the two men exchanged grim but confident glances. Laochlain placed his trust in the man at his side, but Gerwalt's death was still a bitter loss. It was ironic that the man he now looked to kill had avenged that loss with Ruod's murder, avenged but not eased.

The lines about his mouth harshened as the noise of approaching riders reached them. Just now should they find themselves amidst the enemy.

Angry shouts and frantic neighing drew Laochlain and Bretach from their waiting places. Laochlain found himself face to face with an Englishman whose resemblance to Dara could not be denied or ignored.

"So, Lord Chilton, we meet once more."

Fury etched Brann's face. "Scots bastard! You dare too much. We are not unarmed."

"Perhaps not." The MacAmlaid glanced at his men holding the English guards at bay. "But your arms are amply occupied. It is you and I now, Ryland. How stands your courage?"

"In better stead than yours, MacAmlaid."

Brann swung from his saddle, ignoring Dara's sharp protest.

Laochlain's eyes sought hers, a mocking anger in their grey depths. A bitter smile twisted his lips as he nodded his head. His silence was almost an insult of itself.

The blade of Bretach's broadsword held Merlion cursing to his saddle as Laochlain dismounted. It was a claymore the MacAmlaid lifted high above his head, and "For Duncan!" was his only challenge as they engaged.

Brann pressed hard and unfalteringly. He felt a hatred beyond any emotion he had yet known. His blade eagerly sought the Scotsman who had held his sister, used her, and then dared to trespass on Ryland lands. Malevolence was in his glittering eyes, in his bared teeth. But at each thrust, his sword encountered not flesh but metal. The MacAmlaid stepped back unscathed from each vicious swing, a triumphant gloating upon his face that taunted Brann to careless attempts. His hatred numbed him to all but a desire to kill.

Dara's anguish grew with each rash lunge that brought death closer. The men about her, watching and waiting, were almost unbelievably silent. A smothered sobbing came from one maidservant, and the sound, though stifled, was abnormally loud in accompaniment of the battling men's labored grunts and the clashing of their blades.

Her knuckles went to her mouth as those blades met and held midair. She bit her own flesh as muscles strained against any yielding.

With a mighty force, Laochlain thrust Brann backwards and then waited until he had regained his footing.

Desperate for blood, Brann lunged prematurely. His footing was awkward, and as he searched for a hold, he slipped on a treacherous stone, slipped beneath the MacAmlaid's blade. The Scotsman poised above him, tense before the final thrust.

"Laochlain!"

Dara's scream cut through the horrified silence. She could see no mercy on that vengeful face, and she did not plead further. She had averted him from the heat of bloodlust but knew the choice was his.

Laochlain looked back down into the blazing eyes of his defeated enemy. Hazel eyes. He stepped back and lowered his claymore.

"Rylands do not beg for mercy," Brann spat at him, fingers still clenching the hilt of his sword. "If you would have slain me, do so now."

Laochlain shook his head. "I have brought you to the point of death, and I deem vengeance served by your downfall. With each rising sun, remember you live because of a Scotsman's mercy."

A stifled protest at his words drew his attention to Dara. He ignored the man still outstretched at his feet.

"Did you find contentment at Chilton, lass?" His very tone was a gentle torture.

She shook her head slowly. "You destroyed my peace forever, MacAmlaid."

"Nay," he denied compellingly, "'tis not destroyed but only for you to seek."

Drawn despite her will, she nudged the mare forward, halting only inches from him.

Unheeded, Brann got to his feet. He stared disbelievingly at the sister he thought delivered from this rogue. Her hand was outstretched, touching the Scotsman's face almost tenderly.

"Dara." Brann's voice was ugly. "Stand away."

Slipping to the ground, she faced him from the side of the dark-browed Scot. She was pale, her expression anguished as she pleaded for his understanding.

"Forgive me, Brann. This is my choice. I could not abide by yours. He is Scottish, aye, but his hands bear no bloodstains of any Ryland. 'Tis time to put away the murdering that Kerwin began."

Brann started forward but found, suddenly, the flat side of the MacAmlaid's claymore barring his way. They exchanged murderous glances.

"You brought her to this, you devil! Take her from here and there will be no return for her!"

Laochlain stood silent, grimly poised.

Brann did not look at Dara again, though she spoke his name with tears in her voice.

Angry that she suffered, Laochlain lifted her to her saddle, and himself remounted. He glared at the Englishman.

"Throw your weapons to the ground."

Bretach's blade pointed deeply into Merlion's side, and his pained grunt underlined Laochlain's demand. The fury of the Londoner's eyes equaled Brann's, but he slowly complied as did the others.

Laochlain caught Brann's attention with a look of contempt before touching Dara's arm commandingly. He wheeled the red away at a gallop, not looking back to see if she followed, though there was a kind of terror within him as he strained to distinguish the sound of her horse's hooves from the red's.

After only the barest moment's hesitation, Dara sent her grey mare thundering after him. She did not look back, not at her brother nor at the man who had sought to wed her. By her own choice, and at her own peril, she had taken Scotland for her home and a Scotsman for her life. To look back would be futile.

Almost at once, they were joined by the remainder of the Scots, and one edged close to Laochlain, shouting above the wind and thundering hooves.

"They will not give chase, my lord. The Ryland halted those who would."

Laochlain glanced over his shoulder and then,

frowning, at Dara. She met his look squarely, masking her pain, but he was not deceived. His signal halted the band.

"Bretach." The clansman drew near. "Ride ahead, all of you, for the border, but slowly. Do not draw needless attention."

Reluctantly, the borderers obeyed and were joined in the distance by the man chosen to release their unwilling hostess.

Dara held her mare steady, unable to look at Laochlain until his voice compelled her to do so.

"Lass, I'd not have you blind to what we face. The Highlands will be our home, and Gallhiel will hold no comfort or ease. Nor will there be safety until my claim is met, challenged, and proved. If you would return to your brother, do so."

There was nothing in this speech to betray his feelings or what he would have her do.

"I am not afraid of my decision," she answered simply.

He stared at her searchingly, as if by his very gaze he could discern her deepest emotions. She wondered if he would have understood them any more than she if he had been able to read them. At last he nodded, satisfied, and they quickly regained the others.

Chapter XVI

Laochlain held them to a steady pace through the morning, neither tiringly swift nor frustratingly slow. The countryside was little changing around them. In warmer months the moors were mossy, boggy, and the forests thick hindrances, but now the ground was hard and the woods shorn of leaf and underbrush. They passed easily through moor and timber.

Dara could not keep her eyes from his lean face but learned nothing from it. Neither of them spoke beyond necessity.

At dusk they stopped within a hamlet, little more than a cluster of dwellings lining a common withered to brown in January's cold. There was a tavern, a single room with dark walls and low, smoke-blackened ceiling.

Dara sat at a small table bare of aught but

stains and scars. The fire in the narrow hearth smoked vilely, and the smoke burned her eyes.

Laochlain argued with the tavernkeeper, or rather he overrode the man's wretched protests.

"My lady and I will need a room in your home. My men will sleep here. They are honest and will take nothing—and you will be paid for your generosity."

"M'lord, I have no room but that which I share with my dame. The bairns sleep in the parlor."

"Then," Laochlain replied evenly, "you and your wife can join them. My lady cannot be expected to sleep here, can she?"

"N-no, m'lord," was the stammered reply, a thin gleam of sweat beginning across the man's forehead. "With your leave, I will inform Dame Bailfour. Take what you wish. I will return shortly."

Laochlain turned to find Dara fighting a smile. "You frightened him, it was unjust."

He moved to join her, taking a chair at her side. His head tilted slightly as he studied her. "I had little hoped to see you smile again."

She shrugged. "An unlikely prospect in my circumstance, was it not?"

He nodded and settled back into the hard chair, his legs sprawled almost to the next table. His broad fingers idly tapped the tabletop. "Are we done with fighting, Dara?"

Her eyes widened. "I warrant, my lord, that we have scarce begun."

He grinned, disarming her. It was a rare enough expression for his hard features. A draught swept down through the chimney, billowing soot and sparks into the already stifling room. Dara coughed and hid her face in the hood of her cloak until the fumes settled.

Grimacing, she rubbed her reddened eyes. "I would mislike the ruin of these clothes. I have no more." She paused before adding, almost challenging, "I've come to you with nothing."

"A second time," he reminded.

"Not willingly the first," she countered.

"And now?"

She eyed him warily, apparently reluctant to answer. When she did, it had no relation to his question. "You told the tavernkeeper that I was your lady. Your men know different."

"They know you are what I claim for you."

"Their loyalty to you is great," she said angrily, feeling a frustration she could not explain.

For him the matter was settled, Dara was less sure. Further conversation was prevented by the reappearance of their reluctant host. His genial smile was false, for his dame had misliked the news and it had been no easy task to soothe her.

Laochlain stood and drew Dara to her feet beside him. She pulled her hand from his, and though he frowned at the action, he spoke only to Bailfour.

"Is a chamber prepared for us?"

"Indeed, and my dame is most pleased," the man lied.

As they left the tavern, Laochlain spoke low and briefly to Bretach. Whatever the words, they were not overheard by either the tavernkeeper or Dara, who stood in the open doorway. She preferred the frigid, inhospitable wind to the stale air behind her and hoped the man's home was fresher than his business.

It was. The front room was neat and clean and smelled of polishing wax. Bailfour was pleased and relieved to see his two youngsters tucked to bed in one corner, their eyes peeping inquisitively but unobtrusively over the coverlets. From the kitchen came the sound of cooking and the stomach-stirring smell of roast fowl. Only Bailfour appeared to notice the inordinate volume of noise his normally quiet dame was producing. He blanched at this wordless proclamation of her annoyance.

Resigned to his fate, he led his unwanted guests through the parlor to the single bedchamber his home possessed. It boasted no hearth, but the furniture was solid and gleamed of polishing. A diminutive table, definitely out of place, stood in the crowded space at the foot of the bed. It was laid with pewter, and two backless stools edged it.

Satisfied with the arrangements, Laochlain drew his purse and paid the man in coin.

Bailfour stammered his thanks and left the room, glad that here, at least, was something to appease his goodwife.

Laochlain closed the door and turned to watch as Dara nervously paced about the chamber's narrow confines. He scowled. "A caged beast is more restful."

Dara stopped, resting a hand lightly upon a carved bedpost. She was at a loss for conversation, an unusual occurrence for her. A knock reprieved her, and she sighed in relief.

Dame Bailfour set a full-laden tray upon the table before turning piercing eyes upon her intruders—that was what she considered them, nobility or not. Laochlain lifted a brow quellingly at her stare, but Dara's eyes flashed quick resentment. Dame Bailfour did not linger.

The supper was a plain but lightly browned moorfowl served with chunks of tender vegetables and dark wine. Dara sat opposite Laochlain, and they helped themselves to the food.

"'Tis their own meal," Dara remarked guiltily as she accepted a fleshy drumstick from Laochlain.

"Our need was greater."

Philosophically and hungrily, Dara decided to accept his rationalization and set her teeth neatly into the fowl. Conversation went lacking as they yielded to their appetite's demands. Empty as she certainly was, Dara nonetheless found herself satisfied before Laochlain, and she fell idle, watching him.

"Will your men fare as well?"

"They are not ones to suffer," he answered and pushed away the remainder of the meal. It was not much.

Relaxing, he refilled his goblet and drank slowly. And stared at Dara until she was hard put to endure it longer. As the amount of wine remaining diminished, she grew ever more nervous. At last he rose and left her to assure himself that his men lacked for nothing. Within moments, Dame Bailfour brought in a kettle of water for the deep washbasin, and before Laochlain's return, Dara was bathed and her gown carefully refastened.

Stripping to the waist, Laochlain washed.

Dara stared in fascination at his muscled back, for it was marred many times over. She tentatively touched one of the scars.

"You have been oft wounded, my lord."

"Aye." His answer was muffled in the towel. "Some from boyhood brawls and scrapes, more from Jamie's war."

Turning, he drew his dirk from the belt of his leather breeks and slid it beneath a pillow.

"I'll not rest easy sharing a bed with that," she protested.

"But I'll rest the easier for it, and so should you."

She stared. "Surely you expect no danger from Master Bailfour?"

"Nay—more likely from his dame." He dismissed the matter lightly. He had other things to think on just now.

He lifted his hand to her hair and twined his fingers in its silkiness. She stood her ground though she could not still her trembling. His hands left her hair and slid around her back, clasping her to him so hard that for a moment she thought she could not breathe. "I thought you lost to me forever, lass." His words brought tears to her eyes, but she blinked them away.

Her lips were soft and warm and sweet as they lifted to his. His hands were clumsy at her hooks, but then her gown was parted and she was free of it as he drew it from her shoulders. He touched her breasts lightly. It was a searing pleasure, and she strained to his touch. He lifted her, placing her on the bed to await him, and with half-veiled eyes, dark and dreaming, she watched as he came to her.

Dawn caught them sleeping. Laochlain woke first and dressed quietly. He stood near the bed a long moment, watching the peace of Dara's expression. He had seldom seen her so untroubled, and it worried him that he might not keep her so. He bent to kiss her lightly, and she stirred in her sleep, murmuring his name but not fully awakening. He felt a surge of protectiveness that, even sleeping, her mind was upon him and not upon the sorrow behind or the danger ahead.

When at last Dara opened sleepy eyes, the table held their breakfast, generous amounts of porridge and bread and honey.

Laochlain stood at the opened window, his back to her, but he turned at the sound of her rising. She hesitated uncertainly and then stooped to gather her clothes. The graceful movement teased Laochlain's desire, but he stood motionless as she shook her gown and spread it upon the bed. She struggled into her shift, arms above her head, breasts arched tautly, and he abandoned the window.

She drew the thin garment downward, settling it about her body. Her attention was caught by his approach, and she waited with racing pulse as he crossed the room to her. His hands cupped her barely covered breasts as he bent to kiss her, and the demandingly possessive touch filled her with fire. He released her with a reluctance that matched her own as noises beyond their door reminded them of the family stirring there.

The day began auspiciously. The sky had cleared and warmed, and Dara did not encounter the difficulty she expected in facing Laochlain's men after willingly leaving her brother's protection to share his bed. There were no covert looks or speculative stares. Their greetings were friendly, and their attitudes such as if she were in truth Countess of Athdair and Gallhiel.

They rode now with their backs to the moors; before them were rich hills. They kept to open road and chanced upon slightly more travelers, but none gave them pause. For the most part the folk they passed were honest burghers about their business, and if any were not, they were no threat to a band of such number.

On the outskirts of one fair-sized burgh, they passed a church built on lines of strength with tall pillars, vaulted roofs, and little decoration. Dara, riding at Laochlain's side, regarded it thoughtfully.

"Are there churches in your Highland?"

Laochlain looked surprised, and then his mouth quirked in amusement. "We are barbarians, perhaps, but not heathens."

"I never saw a priest at Athdair."

His eyes narrowed. "Priests are not requisite for worship."

"A strange reasoning, surely."

He refuted her statement. "Priests are corrupt, they live on the poor and grow rich on lands they have gathered from honest folk. They own the choicest fields and school their illegitimate offspring at the expense of their communicants."

Dara was disturbed. "I argue not that the

priests are fallible, 'tis what they represent of God that we are to worship!''

"Such are not the teachings of Rome! We are to believe the Pope immutable, and his emissaries unassailable. Only a fool would believe it!''

Dara's grip tightened upon the reins, and her grey mare danced in protest. She relaxed her grip, but her temper flared. "A fool I may be, but my soul is not damned by rape and murder!''

"If I am damned, my lady, no puling priest can deliver me!''

They were silent thereafter.

There were numerous streams to forewarn of the River Clyde, thin rills of silver that the horses splashed through without demur. The countryside was lovely even in its winter death. The villages they passed were neatly enclosed, the outlying fields waiting for spring. Symmetrical orchards abounded. Bothwell Castle, proud and confident, loomed, guardian of the border. The Clyde, curved about its wideflung gardens, glinted bronze in the midday sun.

Dara stared, realizing that this fastness housed one of England's most hated foes, the Hepburn, Earl of Bothwell.

They crossed the river by Bothwell Bridge, its old stone arches spanning the untroubled waters. Dark found them crossing another river, the Forth, in a rising wind. Missing the sun, Dara pulled her cloak tighter, a movement Laochlain did not miss. They took shelter in the next small village.

Lying next to Laochlain in the dark, her body still aching from the passion he evoked and then

211

satisfied, she wondered if she would ever understand him. It was an unlikely prospect. The past, his past, had molded him with experiences she could never comprehend. She could only begin and continue with what he now was, not ponder over what he once had been or might have become. With his hand possessively warm on her hip and the hard lines of his body pressed to her, she was content that it should be so.

The weather changed as abruptly as the land. Beneath a brooding sky, villages and burghs dwindled and the roads connecting them roughened considerably. Worse than a nuisance, the stony ground proved a hazard. Dara's mare was lamed.

Laochlain straightened from his inspection of the hoof in disgust. "She'd best not be ridden for a day or so." He glanced at Dara who was holding the mare's head firmly. "You'll ride pillion with me." He looked back at his men. "Crieff!"

A smooth-faced lad leapt agilely from his horse and came forward. "Aye, my lord?"

"Lead my lady's horse. We will ride slowly to favor the leg."

On a makeshift pillion, Dara rested her cheek against Laochlain's back. Her arms clasped his hard middle, and she found the position quite pleasant. "You block the wind, m'lord."

She felt rather than heard his chuckle and settled contentedly to the movement of his great red stallion. The day grew darker with each mile, and Dara began to wonder if it were not snow that hung in the ominous clouds above them. Within the hour, a downpour of rain proved that it was not. There was no shelter from the torrent in the rocky hills, and the riders hunched their shoulders against the biting pelts of rain and continued on. Dara was grateful for her hooded cloak and Laochlain's broad back as she pressed closer to him for warmth.

The first and only refuge they encountered was a Pictish broch overlooking a narrow estuary. Dara watched from the single entry as the horses were unsaddled and tethered between the circular tower of stone and an outlying cluster of huts, abandoned and crumbling. Many of the roofs had collapsed, and more than a few walls had buckled beneath that sagging weight. Dara backed away from the doorway as the men raced for shelter. They smelled overpoweringly of wet wool and leather.

"What is this place?" she asked Laochlain as he shook water from his hair.

"A broch," he answered, looking about the confined space in which they stood. "Come."

He grabbed her hand and drew her with him to the winding staircase centering the room. The tower was double-walled, with windows cut into the inner walls revealing the space between. At each landing the windows were cut into both walls to permit an unhindered view of the countryside and sea loch. No lime or mortar had been used in the setting of the stones. They did not stop until they reached the final landing. The vista was dizzying.

"'Tis a peel tower?" Dara frowned in puzzlement, picturing the watch towers along the border.

"Of a sort. These were built centuries ago by

the Picts. When the dwellings below were inhabited by fishermen and crofters, the tower was used for haven in case of attack."

Dara looked down at the desolate hovels. "They are so lorn. Where did the people go, and why did they leave?"

Laochlain shrugged. "Mayhap attack, mayhap sickness. Or it could be they tired of a land that feeds few and leaves too many to starve."

Dara shivered in a sweep of wind, and he moved closer. "Come, 'tis warmer below."

It was indeed warmer below, for Tamnais, the eldest of the men, had succeeded in starting a flame with peat and wood gathered from within the huts where the rain had not reached.

"God save your quick wits, man, a welcome sight, this." Laochlain looked about the room. "Where is Neacail?"

"With luck, he is fetching fresh game for our supper, though he may drown in the cursed rain," Tamnais pronounced gloomily.

The odor of wet leather pervaded, for the saddles and trappings had been brought inside and lined against the walls. Relaxing in the growing warmth, Dara prowled about their quarters and soon found there was little to investigate. When she settled at last onto a spot near the fire where Crieff had spread blankets upon the dirt floor, Laochlain joined her.

"We will remain here until morning. 'Tis near nightfall now, and this rain will not abate before dark.

Dara leaned against his shoulder and nodded silently. His breath was warm against her head, and in a drowsing joy, she knew she had never been so content and never would be again away from him. All the wealth and comfort of England could not buy for her the tremulous excitement and warm security he gave her with his presence alone. Now were the long days and lonely nights of Chilton explained.

The wild boar Neacail slew was tough and gamy, but not even Dara disdained its meat, for it was long in cooking and she was half-starved before it was done. All the while she was eating, she felt Laochlain's gaze touching her hair, her face, felt his arm against her back where he braced himself on the hard ground behind her.

Sighing and declaring herself overfull, Dara got to her feet. The air was choked with smoke, and she thought longingly of fresh, sharp breezes.

As she moved away from Laochlain towards the stout wooden door that defended the old tower, he watched the swing of her hips and was drawn to follow.

The clouds had separated in places to reveal a glittering of stars, but the moon remained obscured. A steady wind blew in from the water, unhindered by the barren hills surrounding the loch. Dara perceived a beauty in the very poverty of those cold and bleak and desolate hills. She shivered and suddenly found Laochlain's arms around her, his body shielding hers. She could feel his heart beat, and she smiled.

"I did not hear you, m'lord. How much longer before we reach Gallhiel?"

He smiled into the night at her English accent

215

upon the beloved name. "Another day, though it could depend upon your mare and if she is even fit for riding upon the morrow. We could free her here and save a later hindrance should she go lame again."

"Nay! Haefen was a gift from Thayne, my father, and all I have of him now."

Laochlain shrugged, biting his tongue. He would prefer she had nothing of her family or of England. She sensed his annoyance and turned from the subject.

"Have you not once returned to Gallhiel in all these years?"

"Never." It was not an encouraging response.

"And if someone has claimed the keep, what then?"

"No one has the right! I am Chief of the MacAmlaids by my father's death, and Earl of Gallhiel by Jamie's decree."

"I have heard the Highlanders rule by their own laws, acknowledging no sovereign's right to interfere."

"Aye," he admitted, "it is so. But James earned my respect and my loyalty, and I pledged faith to him. A MacAmlaid's pledge is not broken. I will strengthen Gallhiel, gather its people and make them prosperous—and loyal to James. And if I must fight to do so, then so be it."

Wanting something far more than conversation of her, he silenced any further comment with his lips on hers. It began as a gentle, questing kiss but hardened with desire as his body hardened to hers. The ferocity of his hunger left her breathless, and the lingering caress of his hands soon had her limp in his embrace. With arms encircling his neck, she surrendered to hands which slowly unhooked her bodice and slipped inside. His fingers were cool against her flesh, beginning beneath her breasts and gliding upward to touch lightly, tormentingly, their dark, tender tips again and again until they tautened with desire. He bent to kiss her parted lips and then her nipples as she lay helplessly in his arms.

She was dazed when he withdrew from her. "There is no place here, sweetheart, no privacy."

Shamed by her own frustrated longing and dismay, she felt tears sting her eyes. She whirled from him and refastened her gown with a clumsiness that drove her to muttered curses.

Laochlain was amused at the violence of her reaction and stepped round before her. His fingers gently lifted her chin. "We've nights ahead without end, lass, though I am no less regretful than you that we must stop now."

She gasped. He thought her disappointed rather than humiliated! She jerked her chin from his light touch. "Do not think I desire you, m'lord, you but inconvenience me!"

He seized her arm as she would have fled. His grip was hard. "Shall I prove your desire, Dara?"

His voice was soft, but his eyes bored without mercy into hers. She shook her head angrily, glaring at him through the brightness of tears.

"I should have accepted Lord Blaecdene's proposal. Bold though he was, he was not insufferable as you are wont to be!"

217

"You refer to the Englishman who looked so deadly when you chose to ride with me?" The question was a lazy drawl not requiring an answer. "He would not have suited you, lass. He would have been ice to your fire by the look of him, nor could he have been too ardent a suitor to lose you so easily."

He was enraged at the image of her in the Londoner's embrace, but Dara saw only a sardonic calm mocking her.

"He was ruled by a code you'd not understand, MacAmlaid! That of a gentleman!"

"Nay, I am no gentleman, my lady, but I can tame your fury—or match it with my own." He pulled her roughly into his arms and kissed her hard and savagely.

She was forced to admit the truth of his words. She could not resist him or herself, for there burned a flame between them that no denial could extinguish. Still, she clenched her teeth against the admission, though her body proved it.

The men inside the broch had already settled for sleep when Dara and Laochlain reentered. She felt uncomfortable in sharing his blanket so near them, though she lay down fully clothed. Laochlain appeared to delight in her embarrassment, and she retaliated by rolling as far from him as the length of the blanket allowed. Perversely, his strong arms pulled her back to him, and she found herself pinned tight against his chest.

"Those without breeding make their own rules," he said softly in her ear.

"'Tis as well you make no claim to breeding, my lord." She whispered the words fiercely to him before relaxing, contrarily, into the warm shelter of his embrace.

Daybreak was luminescent above the charcoal of the earth's silhouette. The wind had blown the sky free of clouds before dying, and countless fading stars were visible. No move was made to light the fire, and a cold breakfast was nothing to linger over.

The morning was pleasant. Dara again rode behind Laochlain, her arms clasped about his waist. Their pace was easy to favor Haefen, who followed one of the men at rope's length. Laochlain had not mentioned again the possibility of leaving the mare behind. The sun was warm upon their backs, and as the wind had not freshened, the cold was more bearable.

Scotland was most beautiful in its Highlands, even in the midst of winter. The stark, cragged mountains were riddled with burns whose rushing, crystal waters gave welcome to travelers. And in glens undisturbed by man, deep and secretive lochs nurtured verdant glades. Cairns rose unexpectedly, landmarks of imperishable stone placed by mortals long dead, while mountain evergreens blued the horizon for leagues ahead.

The men, too long in the border, felt their spirits rise with each mile traveled, and though Dara felt pricked by the distance gaining between England and herself, the feeling was surmounted by a buoyant optimism. Whatever ghosts might haunt Gallhiel would hold no terrors for her, and those she had left behind her could not follow to this wild, lovely land of mountains and glens and dangerous gorges.

Chapter XVII

Gallhiel was below them where the towering mountains fell away to a wide, hill-dipped valley. Skies of wintry silver touched the crenellated turrets of the castle and reflected upon the still waters of the loch beyond. The fortress had been built of grey Scots stone and was meant only for the defense of those it housed. With tall parapet and small, defensible slits for windows, it had a closed, daunting look about it. A keep that rejected and warned but did not welcome. If there was beauty, it was in the eye of the beholder. Dara found none.

The narrow trail down the mountainside was precarious, and horses were allowed to set their own pace. On either side were slopes of evergreens with the wind caught moaning in the branches. Dara knew an intense relief when the ground finally leveled and they were trodding frosty white fields.

As they neared the castle, Laochlain grew wary and watchful, but not a soul ventured forth from the crofts they passed, neither for greeting nor challenge. The long, low huts had window-less walls of stone and pebbles and mud and thatched heather roofs without chimneys to emit the peatsmoke that choked such dwellings. The fields were imbedded with stone, but High-land crops were as adept at sprouting amidst boulder-strewn furrows as they were at clinging to steep hillsides. Abundant springs fed the valley, while thick woods gained most benefit from them. Nor could these thieves of sunlight and moisture be sacrificed to the axes for the sake of the fields. Their harvest of game was necessary for survival when storms devastated the crops in the fields or when raiders from other glens set torch to them in the dry heat of summer.

Dara, mounted once again on Haefen, rode quietly at Bretach's side. Laochlain had bidden her fall behind him lest they be approaching danger. She was dismayed by the barren look of the hillside fields, but it was the lack of beasts about the crofts that struck her most forcibly.

"Have these people no animals for meat, no cows or goats for cream and butter?"

Bretach grinned broadly. "Aye, but winter is no safe time for beasties in these mountains, too many hungry wolves and mountain cats. The crofters take their few stock into their dwellings for safekeeping."

Her eyes slanted in disbelief as she turned to stare at the windowless, chimneyless hovels. They could be naught but unbearable with the odor of animals added to the choking smoke of peat.

"You make sport of me, Bretach!"

"No, m'lady, I swear 'tis true. They save the droppings until spring to be spread upon their fields, though to little good. The soil here is thin and sour and produces little."

"Then why do they not leave to seek more fertile grounds?"

"They are Highlanders, my'lady."

She was slowly beginning to realize the vastness that one word encompassed. Highlanders, Gaels, a breed and a law unto themselves, allowing no betrayal of their king and of their ways. How would they greet Laochlain, one who had turned away from them in youth only to return a man, and their chief?

The outer walls of the castle, unscathed by the passage of time, were merely weathered by bitter Highland winds as the mountains were weathered, to an invincible strength. Stout wooden gates barred their entry but yielded scrapingly to Tamnais' sinewed thrust. The courtyard within was laid with huge, irregular stones and strewn with debris. The horses danced nervously in the musty, alien air.

Dara, drawn away from the others, was frozen by a snarling from within the gaping dark of the guardhouse door. A bitchhound with the wild and slavering look of a starved wolf lunged, sending Haefen plunging away in panic.

Laochlain whirled in the direction of danger,

leaving Dara's safety in the hands of his men. It was Crieff who grasped Haefen's reins and forced her to a halt as his chief flung himself upon the snapping, snarling beast. His dagger found the jugular, surging deep until blood gushed from the wound and the animal's un-blinking eyes glazed in death.

The scene did not long hold all attention, for in the doorway from which the dog had leapt emerged an unkempt, maniacally howling fig-ure. A claymore was gripped between grimed fists, and black eyes glittered wildly from be-neath matted tangles of hair. He spewed fury and hatred in a language Dara could not com-prehend.

Laochlain answered swiftly and strongly in the Gaelic. His words were few and simple, but their effect was forceful.

The crazed warrior lowered his weapon and peered at the MacAmlaid. "Ye are chieftain?"

"Aye, Duncan was my sire."

This the man understood, dim though his mind had grown. A chieftain's authority was unassailable, the rights passed from father to son. With slow deliberation, the ancient's loyal-ties were transferred from the chief he had not laid eyes upon in long years to the figure before him. At long last his task was fulfilled, he could deliver Gallhiel into its master's keeping.

Now, with single-minded attention, he cast down his claymore and stepped forward to lift the slain bitchhound in his arms. His face twisted in grief as he carried her back into the guardhouse at the foot of the tower.

Bretach sheathed the blade he had palmed in

readiness, and Neacail removed his hand from the hilt of his sword. Their eyes met in unfeigned relief while Tamnais, dourly counting himself less gullible, followed the old man to ensure he was as harmless as he appeared.

The men dismounted, and Crieff hurried round to Dara's side only to find her alighting without need of assistance. Laochlain scowled slightly at his crestfallen look before turning to Neacail.

"Go among the crofters, state my needs, and obtain them—with payment of coin if freely offered. If any deny me, they forfeit payment and risk retribution. We need food for ourselves and the horses, and women for cleaning. I would have the keep habitable by nightfall."

Neacail nodded and swung back into his saddle, beckoning Crieff as he did so. The lad followed eagerly. Neacail was strong and sagacious, worthy of respect—but not so awesome as the MacAmlaid oft appeared. Aye, he was a likely man to follow and to emulate.

Laochlain gave his stallion into Sim's keeping. Their horses were more valuable than gold in the mountains, for they could not be readily replaced. Mountain stock was sturdy and indomitable but lacked the magnificence of southern-bred mounts.

Such a look of grimness hung about Laochlain's face as they neared the keep that Dara sensed there was as much pain as joy in this homecoming.

The shelter of Gallhiel's great hall differed from the courtyard only in that it placed a roof over their heads. The walls and floors of stone were as bare as the parapet and flagstones. A cavernous fireplace, long in disuse, bore only the bleakest remembrance of flame in its soot-blackened hearth.

Laochlain came to rest at the long, planked table, touching the gouges marring its rough surface. "Duncan's meals would have sat him better could they have been taken from this table in the long years past."

"It was bitterness and choler that soured your sire's food," Dara discounted, remembering too well the old man's cruel temper, "not nostalgia."

Her regret at speaking at all was instantaneous, for Laochlain turned a narrow, glaring look upon her.

"You find it easy to disdain that which you have not suffered."

"Have I not! He found it easy enough to taunt an English hostage, sorrowing and alone! His exile, at least, was freely chosen."

"As yours is now."

"Aye," she agreed, less impassionedly, "and I do not regret it, but do not ask me to feel compassion for a man who felt none for others."

Laochlain smiled grimly. "I've asked little of you, lass. Thus far."

With that warning hanging between them, he turned from her to Bretach. "I commend Lady Dara to your care. I would see to Gallhiel's boundaries and will return at nightfall. I trust you to ensure that my orders are carried forth and that my lady lacks for nothing."

Without another word or look for Dara, he

strode from the hall. With an effort, she forced her eyes from the door that swung shut behind him and found Bretach eyeing her cautiously. She smiled somewhat ruefully.

"I will never learn to guard my tongue or heed the warning of his frown, Bretach, but he provokes me to my tempers."

"He could never abide a pliant lass," Bretach assured her even as he wondered what would come of this union of two iron-willed temperaments.

The sweep of the valley and the rise of the mountains encircling it had lost none of the beauty and pull that Laochlain had known as a youth. Swift and sure, his stallion trod the age-old paths skirting the mountains and fording the burns. An ancient stone bridge spanned the narrow finger of the loch that opened into the sea beyond the mountains. Across the bridge lay the valley's second passage, leading deeper into the mountains. From there would come the raiders of neighboring clans when Gallhiel regained its wealth. And it would regain the wealth and power that the past had known, Laochlain swore. Wealth would never come from the arable crops the peasants toiled over. It must be cattle, an undertaking much more suited to the poor, rocky soil. Scottish cattle were highly prized in England for their flavor, and in them the clan would prosper. The main hazard to such a gamble were the vicious winters of the storm-wracked slopes, but Gallhiel's valley was a shelter that many holdings lacked.

As Laochlain formulated the plans he had long held in his mind, the afternoon slipped away. The sun ridged the mountains as he rode among the crofts nearest the fortress. When it dropped, the darkness would be abrupt and complete, but for the moment the scattered, heavy clouds burned a fiery orange. With knitted brows, he noted that if those clouds gathered and lowered through the days ahead, they would bring snow. Not the light, wind-whipped flakes of the border, but a harsh, driving, smothering snowfall.

Dara had no time to study the horizon or brood upon the future. Her hands were too full with the present. The women from the croft had arrived with their menfolk just as she was coping with her dismay at her inspection of the keep.

She had begun with the long gallery beyond the hall which, if it had once held furniture, did so no longer. The salon opening off from it fared little better. What pieces there were proved irredeemable. The MacAmlaid would have to begin anew if he hoped to live in comfort, and, surveying the draughty rooms and damp, de-nuded walls, she feared it would be a spartan comfort at best. The bedchambers on the floor above disclosed rather better conditions. The furnishings were adequate, some pieces even lovely beneath a layer of dirt. The rooms were enormous and many. That long-ago unfortunate victim of the Norseman's avarice must have envisioned a mighty host of descendants, but the fates had decreed the Norseman's offspring to be Lord of Gallhiel and founder of its clan.

In all her explorations, it was the vast kitchen that Dara most deplored. With rock walls and earthen floor, it had little equipment and no provisions. The black-beamed ceiling might once have been hung with flitches of bacon, dried herring, and great hams, but no more. Tall cupboards of stone were bare of all but the crudest cutlery and tableware. The fireplaces alone appeared adequate. One was fitted with hooks and cranes on which hung huge pots. The other was set with spits and iron pikes, awaiting a burden of fresh game or beef or pork.

The first difficulty encountered with her help from the crofts was one of language. Dara could speak no Gaelic, the women nothing else. Dara needed Neacail's aid to instruct them in their tasks. She directed half the women to the cleaning of the kitchen, and the other half to dusting furniture and airing beds whose damp mustiness threatened permanence. When the tempest began, the men fled the hall and were seen no more until eventide promised supper. Similar tasks awaited them within guardhouse and stable. Built of stone, these had remained solid through the years, but fresh bedding was required for stalls raked free of molding hay. The bedding of the guardhouse was beyond salvation, for what had not rotted had been shredded into nests for hosts of rodents.

The ancient who had been the lone inhabitant of these premises had lived unfazed by the deterioration, and he watched suspiciously as his home was invaded. The reawakening of his beloved fortress was both a disturbance and a joy. He had served Duncan from his youngest days. He had been a warrior and received a warrior's wounds, but his greatest suffering had come in Gallhiel's wasted years, in seeing the clan disperse with no authority to bond it.

Laochlain was pleased to find the initial steps so smoothly executed, for he knew the difficulties would increase with the progress made. Satisfied with this beginning, he bedded his horse in a freshly hayed stall and crossed a courtyard as dark as the cloud-covered heavens.

The blazing hearth in the hall dispelled the shadows that had long lain over the keep like the mists upon the loch. Dara stood at the foot of the long, curving stairs. She wore a country woman's gown of coarse woolen whose bulk could not disguise her slender curves. Her hair was caught up in a cloth at the nape of her neck, but silky strands escaped with her every movement as she attempted by gestures to direct a young girl in her work. Laochlain was more interested in Dara's allure than in her dilemma until she beseeched him with a despairing look.

"I doubt not that she cannot understand my speech, but surely she can see that these stairs are desperate for cleaning!"

Laochlain strode forward to instruct the blushing, awestruck girl and watched as she fled to the kitchen for lye soap and water. His eyes glinted with humor as they returned to Dara.

"They are but crofters, and unfamiliar with the mime of court players. Have patience, m'lady."

"I've patience, Laochlain, but 'tis not boundless! An interpreter would not be amiss, for I've

230

doubts that any of them have wits enough to learn a civilized tongue."

"Have you wits enough to learn theirs?" She glared at him furiously, but with his next words he dismissed the subject. "Soon I will send Bretach to purchase Gallhiel's needs and yours." He touched the woolen gown she wore. "I delight to see you in silks."

Not yet forgiving, she retorted, "I thought your delight was rather in their absence!"

He grinned. "That, too, my love." He bent and kissed her hungrily, as if the privacy of their bedchamber enclosed them.

Her resistance was brief. Melting, she clung to him, her lips parting beneath the force of his. When he finally released her, glancing over her shoulder, she whirled to find the girl returned, a basin in her hands and a wondering look upon her face.

Blushing, Dara started up the stairs and found Laochlain barring her way, his expression quietly urgent. "When I lived within the border lands, I found it necessary to put aside things Gaelic— or be forever defeated by my own obstinance."

He stepped aside then, and she fled, but the comparison was taken.

Supper that night was a simple meal. Spitted beef, vegetables, and cold loaves of oatbread. Dara had already determined that Gallhiel's cook should learn a greater variety of dishes than these Highlanders employed. For now, however, the plain dishes before her were more than satisfying. The day had been long in terms of struggle and accomplishment, and she longed only for the comfort of a bath. She escaped to the bedchamber as quickly as she could.

Once there, she shed her clothing and stepped into the iron bathing tub. The water was deliciously hot, for it had been heated in a heavy iron kettle in the chamber hearth, thus not cooling in being carried through draughty halls. After it was poured, she had sent the servant away and prepared for thorough enjoyment of the moment. As she soaked, she eyed the immense master chamber. The walls boasted thick skins taken in hunts long forgotten, but the rushes on the floor were dust now. And, like all of the keep, it was a room absolutely bare of adornment. Tamnais had placed rushlights, rushes soaked in sheep grease and then dried, into the wooden holders on the walls, but there were no candelabra or tapers to fill them. The laver on the washstand was of tarnished pewter, reminding her that polishing was yet another task for the morrow.

Laochlain entered the chamber as she combed her hair, drawn forward over her shoulder, with his comb. She had none of her own, nor a mirror to guide her efforts. As she sat on the edge of the bed, clad only in her shift, her neck and shoulders were tinted by the flames that warmed the room. He came to sit behind her and pulled her back into his arms. His lips moved slowly over her neck, sending chills down her arms. She leaned back against him, and the comb fell unheeded into her lap.

A while later, his eyes roved the room, and his thoughts were much the same as Dara's earlier ones. "Gallhiel was never elegant, but in my mother's time it gleamed of polished silver, and the rushes were never allowed to stale."

"Silver, my lord?" Dara's voice was doubting.

"Aye, there was silver here once, and carpets and tapestries, but all was sold when the third James needed funds. Gallhiel was impoverished by a hopeless cause, and I have brought you to its poverty."

"I did not leave England and Brann for your possessions, Laochlain," she said quietly, "but for you."

His hands caressed her arms. "You would have pleased my mother. She was a Camdene, a fierce lot but loyal and true to their kin. Bretach is a Camdene. His father was a cousin of my mother's and we are distantly so."

She twisted to face him, her eyes alight with humor. "I'd swear you bloodkin to the last of your men, my lord. A multitude claim it."

"'Twould be difficult and foolish to disclaim it. MacAmlaids have ever been free with the wenches, and many of their bairns bear the blood of the MacAmlaids."

"As free with servants as with hostages?" she questioned tartly and then blushed at his laughter.

"Less pleasantly so, lass. Fear not, none have held the place you hold now. When my place here is secure, we will leave long enough to seek a priest, since you set such store by the blessings of the church. I'll wed you rightly. Gallhiel's last chatelaine was Iseabal, and Duncan ruled this fastness and the clan." His eyes darkened. "My wealth and my border powers will have little scope in binding the people to me. It will be a legacy of my ancestors that affords me greatest power."

Aye, Dara thought, a legacy of boldness and harsh courage. A legacy of warriors.

But it was not a conquest of warriors that would rebuild Gallhiel. The Highlanders were suspicious of this man who had deserted his birthright only to return with an English maid at his side. They remembered well the old chief, and they remembered his curses when his heir had gone from the mountains. They returned, Duncan's clansmen, but slowly, drawn by the promise of fair authority, fleeing untenable lands and poverty. Some returned to the crofts they had abandoned in favor of land protected by other clan chieftains, but many more chose to fill the ranks of Gallhiel's men-at-arms. The MacAmlaid was reputed a fierce warrior and a valorous one. A chief to whom any man would be proud to swear fealty, and these men valued courage and loyalty above all else. And, in the end, the conquest was one of patience.

Among the first to seek Gallhiel, now it once more housed the chief, was Dunstan MacAmlaid. He came with his family amidst the snowstorm that Laochlain had foreseen. Bretach, accompanied by Sim and Crieff, had left two hours earlier, before the first flurries, with a list of Gallhiel's needs. Bidding the travelers Godspeed, Dara had taken note of the clouds piling heavily together on the low horizon and had felt an apprehension. Later, when the winds whipped the snow into the valley, she feared for their safety and stood several times at a window embrasure looking out into the fury. Thus was she watching when a crude cart entered the courtyard and muffled shapes struggled towards the shelter of the hall. Calling for Laochlain, she rushed to throw wide the door.

A man, slightly more than middle-aged, bearing a child too bundled for Dara to perceive its gender, thrust a woman and a near-grown youth into the hall before him. Dara took the child from his arms and urged mother and son nearer the hearth while Laochlain greeted his kinsman. Then, gravely, Laochlain told the man of Gerwalt's death, for this red-haired titan was Gerwalt's brother.

Dara felt a twist of pain at hearing the horrors of that day retold and was relieved when they finally passed on to other matters. Cradling the child before the hearth, she smiled at Dunstan's wife, Lady Garda. "You chose a most inclement weather for travel, mistress. Have you come far?"

"Not in miles, but far indeed in difficulties. Had my husband not our son at his side, he would have had far less chance of bringing us all to safety. Our retainer was lost to the loch at the storm's beginning."

The boy smiled briefly at his mother's praise but quickly recomposed himself to sobriety. Dara would soon learn it was a trait gained of his father, a good man but one of rare smiles and rarer jests. For now, she saw only his likeness to his mother, for he had inherited her coloring, and so, Dara soon discovered, had his sister.

Growing warm and curious, the girl emerged from her blankets like a butterfly from a cocoon. She was five, perhaps six, quite certainly no older. Her skin was creamy with the rose touch of childhood, and her hair hung in loose honey-brown curls to her shoulders. She had her mother's looks, but her eyes were the startling blue of her father's and Gerwalt's.

Those bright, inquisitive eyes were staring now in candid fascination. "Mama, she is like the portrait in the gallery of Airdsgainne, only she looks not so wicked as the lady in green!"

Before Garda could respond, her son admonished the child with the gentle insults of a lad to a troublesome but still young sister and finished gravely to Dara, "Mairi meant no harm, m'lady."

The little girl raised her eyes earnestly to Dara. "The Green Lady is beautiful . . . and I was not rude, Parlan!" The last was flung vindictively at her brother.

The advent of a quarrel was broken by the serving of hot spiced cider, and even Mairi's ready temper was not proof against the enticement.

"Airdsgainne?" Dara tested the name on her tongue. "You come from there?"

"Aye." Garda looked momentarily subdued. "'Tis Kiarr's fastness. He is Duncan's only living brother, and I fear the years rob him of reason though he is still young in body."

There appeared no answer to that, and Dara was not sorry when Laochlain and Dunstan joined them.

"Lady Garda, 'tis long since I've seen you. You

had but the boy clinging to your skirts then. Now I find a lovely lass to replace him, and he has taken his place at his father's side."

"And we were pleased, my lord, to learn you had returned to Gallhiel. These mountains have sore missed the chief of the MacAmlaids."

His eyes narrowed. "I know Kiarr, and my curiosity is great that I did not return to find this keep and my rights to it claimed by him. I anticipated fighting to reclaim them."

Dunstan answered, and it was what Laochlain expected. "The people would not have him while Duncan lived."

"And now," Laochlain said slowly, "it is the son who bars his way."

"Aye, and he likes it not. Had he learned of Duncan's death before your arrival, he would have made his claim then."

Mairi was growing restless, and Garda's weariness was obvious. Reluctantly, Dara led them to a comfortable chamber, leaving the men to their discussion though she would have preferred to remain and listen. She chose a large chamber with an adjoining room where Parlan would sleep for the nonce. Garda predicted despairingly and somewhat worriedly that the youth would soon wish to remove to the guardhouse. His greatest ambition since learning of the MacAmlaid's arrival had been to serve him in a man's capacity.

Dara left briefly to direct the removal of their belongings from their cart to their rooms abovestairs. She returned with a perplexed look upon her face.

"From what direction did you come? I've seen naught but mountains that no cart could traverse!"

"We ferried upon the estuary. Airdsgainne is set into a mountain not so very many miles from here. The loch is narrow where it passes, but affords passage for small conveyances."

She watched in silence as Dara directed the maidservants and listened without surprise to her few halting words of Gaelic. When they were alone again, she commiserated; "'Tis a difficult language for one not born to it. If I can aid you, please permit me to do so."

Dara was grateful for her offer and did not disdain it for pride's sake. And although she learned with an adeptness that pleased them both, she was delighted to have another female in the keep who shared her own language. They swiftly bridged the gulfs of heritage and age to friendship. Mairi gave to the keep something it desperately needed, the unashamed joy and laughter of childhood, while Parlan attached himself to the men and fitted well amongst them. He was quick-witted, keeping his own counsel but not forgetting his duties to his mother and extending them to Dara, also. He, like his parents, soon forgot or chose to ignore that she was not in truth their lady.

It was a clear, cold day when Bretach and Crieff and Sim returned, leading horses packed with necessities and luxuries. Dara greeted them with pleasure and relief, and not for the sake of their purchases. She had grown to care for each of the men who had so carefully watched over her on the journey from all she had known. Watched over and accepted her, a gift of themselves she valued highly.

Among their burdens was a chest purchased at Laochlain's bidding filled with lovely cloths. In their chamber, she stroked the fabrics delightedly, envisioning the gowns that would come from them. She was sitting on the rushes examining a forest green velvet when Laochlain's shadow fell over it and her.

"You're pleased?"

She smiled up at him in undisguised pleasure. "Indeed, but with more than you are considering. Gallhiel itself pleases me, though I did not think it would from my first look at it. I am content here."

He reached down and lifted her to her feet and, taking the length of velvet, draped it across her shoulders where her hair touched against it like bright fire.

"And you please me, lass." His lips brushed across hers, and his hands slid caressingly down her sides to settle at her waist.

She yielded gladly to their pressure, leaning in to him. With a quick movement, he toppled her to the bed, pinning her beneath him, the velvet entangling them. Laochlain smiled down at her as she struggled playfully. Her laughter died as he unfastened her gown and pulled the bodice free of her. He explored with gentle fire, and soon she felt the warmth beginning, curling through her body from its center. Their clothing was soon tumbled upon the floor.

Sunlight slipped in through the cracks of the

shutter, illuminating Dara's face and playing, unseen, on the dark Scot's scarred, iron-muscled back and the discarded bedclothes.

When they finally lay side by side, skin touching skin, Dara smiled into his eyes. "Are you content, Laochlain?"

He drew her near so that his answer was muffled into her hair. "Never more so. I love you, Dara Ryland."

The sun withdrew slowly from the room, appearingly reluctant to leave the lovers' company. Laochlain slept lightly, but Dara lay wakeful, awash with happiness at hearing his love for her spoken.

It was a happiness soon shadowed, for with the hope of spring came Leslie.

Chapter XVIII

Kiarr MacAmlaid's daughter arrived on a day that dawned in indecision, a mid-March day that entertained notions of spring with a fragile warmth but retained a solid hold on winter with a wind both sharp and chilling.

There was nothing of indecision about Leslie MacAmlaid. She rode boldly through gates flung open at her command. Her mount was a small, fierce stallion, and two burly men rode at her side.

Dara, coming from a morning's ride with Laochlain, had left him in the fields with Neacail, now steward of Gallhiel. She stood poised on the wide, shallow steps leading up to the hall and watched as the girl leapt agilely from her saddle. Her gown was the color of the rowanberry, and her stride was lithe and graceful.

"I seek the MacAmlaid, he that is chief. I am Leslie, daughter of his uncle."

She spoke in purest English, but Dara did not need her words to know she shared Laochlain's blood, and closely. She bore his features, arranged to femininity but not softness. Her hair was silkily dark and plaited about her fine forehead. Her lips reflected the color of her dress, and her eyes were darkly blue.

"Laochlain will return soon. I am Dara. Will you not enter and await him?"

Dara's composure hid a multitude of tensions, for the MacAmlaid's wild and lovely young cousin appraised her with an insulting coolness before turning to give orders concerning the care of her horse. Almost carelessly, she accepted Dara's offer and followed her through the great hall and into the salon. Dara felt more at ease here for it had been furnished to her bidding and she spent much of her time here.

A maidservant entered before they were settled to learn Dara's wishes. Leslie did not relax into a chair but paced the room, noting its renewal with speculative eyes.

"When last I was here, these rooms were bare."

Dara unconsciously touched the folds of her chamois riding skirt as she replied, "Laochlain has done much for Gallhiel."

"He owes it much!"

There was a glittering in blue eyes quickly veiled by sweeping black lashes. Dara wondered if it was animosity. Were the closest of the MacAmlaid's kin to be the least forgiving?

The servant entered bearing brandywine and sugared cakes on a silver tray. Leslie accepted a goblet in her gloved hand and lifted it towards the motto etched in stone above the doorway.

"'Strength prevails,'" she translated. "Have you been told already the watchword of the MacAmlaids?" Her dark eyes were very still and very watchful.

"No, but I deem it appropriate."

"You are English, I have heard. Did my cousin abduct you? My own mother was abducted from her very bed."

Dara stiffened, hoping her shrinking was only inward. She had no intention of responding to such bold, rude questioning. Her own questions remained unspoken. Why a girl of Leslie's youth should travel unaccompanied but by servants. And why she had come at all.

Garda's sudden entrance was a relief, as was her casual acceptance of an unexpected guest.

"Leslie, I was told you were here. You look well, I hope your parents are equally so."

"Garda," the girl replied in greeting. "Gallhiel contents you. 'Tis in your face. I've been making the acquaintance of Lady Dara, who performs the duties of hostess with ease . . . as if they were hers by right."

Garda's calm features tightened. "Do not mistake the matter, Leslie, the right is truly hers. She is Laochlain's lady."

"Aye, every keep in the mountain talks of it."

Dara was more than dismayed now, she was angered at the open insult of Leslie's tone and at being spoken of as if she were incapable of replying for herself. Her eyes flashed with the

243

vehemence of her feelings. "It is to be hoped that the topic profits them. Truly, life must be dull through long winter months if my presence at Gallhiel can be of such interest."

"The matter of interest is in your . . . protector. My cousin has made a reputation for himself over which men have fought, for his honor or in the belief that he has none. You are but another example that the MacAmlaid is a law unto himself."

"Leslie!" Garda was enraged by her kinswoman, but Dara cut silkily into her rebuke.

"Compose yourself, Garda. Perhaps Lady Leslie's manners will improve when she has rested. Please show her to a chamber where she may do so."

And Dara watched, every inch the chatelaine of the keep, as the Scottish girl strode angrily from the room. Dara had touched the nerve she sought. Without a doubt, Leslie had thought to step into a role already filled. Gallhiel would not have two mistresses, and Dara would not step down. Nor did she intend to be thrust down.

Her preparations for supper that evening were unobtrusive but effective. She spoke first with the cook, stating her wishes with tactful authority. She gave further instructions to the maidservants in the hall and then retired to her chambers for the remainder of the day. Leslie would be unable to find cause for complaint in the running of the clan keep.

Garda sought her a short while later, entering without knocking for her hands were full. "You ate none of what you had served to Leslie, and your breakfast was hours ago. We will have a wee meal now, and mayhap there will be things you are wanting to ask about Laochlain's brash young cousin."

Dara was grateful indeed. Garda had brought no light sweets to unsettle a nerve-tensed stomach, only bread and cheese and cold meat with a pitcher of fresh cream. They faced one another across the corner table and ate in companionable silence. It was Garda who began to talk of Leslie and Kiarr and Airdsgainne.

"She was the only one of their many bairns to survive infancy, and for the nineteen years of her life she has had no denial from her parents. She rides the mountains at whim, always accompanied by two of Kiarr's fiercest fighters. With any other parents, she might have been pampered into helplessness. Instead, she has been taught the skills and abilities of a lad. Her suitors are without number—all disdained for their shortcomings whether real or imagined. Cairistiona has fostered her daughter's pride, and Kiarr her boldness, perhaps to their eventual regret."

Garda paused, and Dara voiced the inevitable question. "What does she want here?"

Garda shrugged. "Not even Leslie knows her own mind. Perhaps 'tis to satisfy her curiosity, or perhaps she is the first tentacle of Kiarr's grasping. Kiarr wants Gallhiel—not the keep itself, but all that it entails, the power, the wealth, the chieftaincy. He would pledge his soul to Satan for it."

"Does Laochlain know this?"

"Aye, yon lad is no fool, but the first move

must be Kiarr's. When he leaves that foul-mooded mountain keep, then Laochlain must look to his defenses."

"But if the clan would not accept him before, why does he think they would now?"

"Their loyalty was to Duncan, a chief who led them bravely into battle—for all they were defeated. For these many years they have thought on Laochlain as traitor, and there is no worse blame for a Highlander. He has made a beginning in regaining their faith, a strong beginning, and I do not know what Kiarr could do to his discredit. I do know that a crueler, more devious man does not live. Laochlain must be wary indeed."

"And Kiarr's lady, is she of his nature?"

"In a far more subtle manner," Garda paused to seek words in explanation. "When enraged, Kiarr is like a bull, blind to all but the object of his anger. Cairistiona is like the serpent, she may remain poised for what seems an endless passage of time, but when she strikes, she is swift and deadly. Leslie has combined traits of both, mayhap the worst of both. Beware her, my lady, she is capable of much evil."

Garda left her with much food for thought, though her warnings only emphasized Dara's own intuitive recoiling. Emphasized and broadened, for Leslie as her father's emissary might mean harm not to Dara alone, but to Gallhiel, and, far worse, to Laochlain. Dara vowed that Leslie would have no moment unobserved but those spent in the chamber assigned her. Leslie would find either Garda or herself a constant companion, unpleasant though the task would be.

When Dara emerged from her bedchamber at eventide, there was no startling change in her, but her hair was newly washed and hung loosely to her waist, its color that of a turning autumn leaf, and the fragrance of her bath soap floated lightly about her. The gown she wore was of the forest green velvet, emphasizing her slender form. A ribbon cut from the same cloth was threaded through her curls.

Laochlain had returned home expecting the smooth comfort Dara created in Gallhiel and found instead tension and hostility. The source was apparent and, yet again, indiscernible. Dara presented Leslie to him calmly, and Kiarr's daughter found her cousin's amazement quite pleasing.

"No doubt, Laochlain, you remember me with too long legs and an awkward frankness."

"I would not have known you, Leslie," he admitted lazily as his eyes followed Dara's graceful movements as she brimmed his cup with ale and brought it to him.

Leslie spoke again, returning his attention to her. "I'm no longer the pixie without grace, but I'm still uncomfortably frank—or so Garda would claim." Her look met the older woman's challengingly, but Garda said nothing.

Laochlain ignored the exchange of hostile glances. "And how fares Kiarr?"

Leslie shrugged. "My father makes his own disposition for good or ill. At the moment, he is restless and torments Mother to death with his vile moods, but his health is good."

"Cairistiona is more than his match. Will Gallhiel see them soon?"

She smiled. "Of a certainty, Cousin."

Dunstan drew her attention then with questions of others of the clan. He had parted with some of those he asked about only short weeks earlier, but life moves quickly and dangerously for Highlanders. Dunstan was not alone in his interest in her tales of birth and death.

Later, over a repast of hot venison pasties and wild fowl, Laochlain had opportunity to study the veiled animosity between Dara and Leslie. Their words were too courteous by far for the dagger thrusts subtly exchanged by flashing eyes. He had no doubt that Leslie was the instigator. Her comments hid razor probes of curiosity, tactics learned from Cairistiona. Kiarr's methods were more brutal. His temperament as well as his name came from the clan's Norse ancestry. His family had long since perfected the ability of evading his temper or skillfully turning it upon another.

Once, Leslie probed too incautiously, remarking that Dara's family could not have accepted her choice of Scotland over England with any ease.

Dara dealt with her presumption quietly but firmly. "I chose the man, not the country, and I owe explanations to none. If your curiosity pains you, question Bretach or any of those who rode from Athdair, they know the tale—if you dare not question Laochlain."

Leslie flushed to meet her cousin's grimly amused glance. He knew as well as she that no questions would be forthcoming. He would ruthlessly quell any such impertinence did she dare, as would any of his men.

He drained his cup and stood, a signal for all to disperse to their beds. Giving his arm to Dara, he bade Leslie a peaceful sleep. She did not rise, but her eyes followed them from the room. Slowly, she tipped her goblet and sipped wine of the same warm shade as her mouth. Servants hovered in the background, waiting to clear away the remains of the meal, but she ignored them. A frown marred her forehead, and she moved her fingers unconsciously across the embossings of her empty goblet.

Kiarr had stressed the simplicities of his plan; now she faced its difficulties. Her cousin's attachment to his English mistress was not as light as they had judged it, and she would be removed with difficulty for she was accepted fully by his people. There was no indication of the resentment and dissatisfaction that Kiarr had told her to use to her advantage. Those of the clan who had returned thus far were without complaint, and they had closed ranks about their chief. Leslie had not been unaware of the suspicious glances cast her way, secretive though they were.

Her face was set in an expression of grim stubbornness as she pushed away from the table and rose to leave the hall.

The door to the great master chamber was solidly closed, and in the quiet, warm privacy behind it, Dara had shed to her shift. Her usual chatter was stilled, and Laochlain watched cautiously as she washed in the laver upon the washstand.

"You dislike Leslie."

"'Tis your cousin who dislikes me, though not so much as she resents my presence here," she answered without turning.

He made an impatient gesture she could not see. "Leslie is no more than an unruly child."

Dara turned, quickly masking the effect of Garda's remembered words. She found Laochlain close upon her.

"She's no child, and I fear she reflects your uncle's views. How would he regard me, my lord. As your pretty English whore?"

He gripped her shoulders tightly, angered by her choice of words. "He would name you so at great risk!"

"He will wish a Scottish lass for Gallhiel," she persisted. "A Gaelic lass."

His eyes were dark and narrowed as they met her troubled look. Her eyes were very green and soft, and he knew himself bedeviled. He drew her close.

"Damn Kiarr and Leslie and any lass but you, Dara Ryland, English and Scottish alike. No other exists for me."

They sank as one to the fur pelts beneath their feet. He slipped her shift from her shoulders and kissed the curves to which it clung. Her hands touched his hair, then entwined in it as he pulled the shift free of her and plundered the loveliness revealed. When he withdrew to discard his own clothing, her body ached for his return. His hands, so strong and hard, were tormentingly tender as he stroked her breasts, her belly, and the insides of her thighs until she burned with the fire he kindled so effortlessly within her.

They kissed and touched and explored until they were driven to the limits of endurance. Their bodies merged in ageless rhythm before he drew her hard against him and she clung, exalted.

The morning sun pried at the shutters, but the room was still in shadows when Dara woke. She did not stir, for they had slept entwined and were so yet. The room lightened slowly, but her boding thoughts did not, for even thus, cradled in Laochlain's arms, her fears were inescapable. Leslie had brought disquiet to the keep, and it would remain as long as she did.

Dara knew when Laochlain awakened, for his arms tightened about her and his lips moved gently on her bare shoulder where only his breath had stirred a moment before. She turned her body welcomingly to his and was in some manner reassured.

Rising brought a more cheerful aspect as she washed and dressed swiftly, looking ahead to the most pleasurable part of her day, her morning ride with Laochlain. The winds were strong across the valley, but winter's promised end had made them less biting. The fields were dew-dampened, and the highest branches of the trees slowly awakened to the sun.

Dara had come to know many of the crofters by name, for, no matter how early they rode, the tenants were in their fields. With each day, Laochlain's wishes progressed. Stones were routed completely from those sections of land set aside for food crops. That space was then bounded by fences of stone and mud. The remainder of the valley would be given over to grasslands for the herd as yet only envisioned.

On this morning, as they spurred their horses into a gallop away from the castle, Dara glanced at Laochlain, strong and tall beside her. Before too many months, she would have to suspend the daily pleasures of these rides, for her contradictorily hopeful and apprehensive suspicions were slowly giving way to certainty. She feared Laochlain's reaction. Would he feel pride and pleasure, or would he liken the babe to Ruod, another nameless bairn born to the clan?

Their headlong gallop chased her fears, flinging them as her hair was flung, outward upon the wind. The sun was full and warm above them when they finally halted to speak with the men in the fields.

Broad, muscle-strained backs bent to the task of tearing great rocks from the earth and setting them firmly, one upon the other. The rocks were layered with mud, mixed with great joy by several youths. When dried by the sun, the mud would bond the fence as solid and indomitable as the hills themselves.

The man closest to them paused in his labors. His clothes of homespun woolen were as mud-daubed as the stones, and the hand he lifted in greeting was calloused and grimed, but his back was straight, and his eyes met the MacAmlaid's in a look that gave respect but no servility. He nodded politely to Dara before speaking to Laochlain.

"A heartbreaking task it is you've set us, MacAmlaid."

"Aye, but rock does not spring anew from the ground. Once done, this land will be open to all you would sow." He nodded towards the others. "It nears completion?"

"It does, and a mercy 'tis so. The soil is easy now, but when the rains commence, there will be little enough we can do."

"Are any among you dissatisfied?"

"Nay. What you propose will aid us all with less hardship and more gain. But even were it not so, you are chief. There'll be no word against you."

Laochlain felt a sweep of pleasure at his success with his people. His hopes had been for willing compliance rather than forced submission, though he had been resigned to at least a token resistance. To see his behests carried forth without rancor was the fulfillment of those hopes.

The pounding of hooves broke the peace of the morning, and they turned to its source. Expressions of bewilderment, wonder, and finally admiration chased across the crofter's face while Dara's heart sank in recognition of Leslie. She did not look at Laochlain as she schooled her face to a composure only she knew was false.

Leslie halted her stallion only inches from Haefen. Her expression was patently displeased as her gaze moved from Dara to Laochlain. "You rise early, my lord."

"My day begins early."

"I had thought to ride with you. I have not explored the valley for some years."

"You are welcome to ride with us any morning," he offered with a negligence that Dara knew his kinswoman would not find pleasing.

She smiled inwardly as Leslie swept her crop imperiously before her. "What is being done here?"

Laochlain half smiled. "My orders are being followed in matters that could not be of interest to you."

"All of Gallhiel interests me!"

"I doubt it not," he said drily, and Leslie flushed.

Prompted by a demon, Dara said, too sweetly, "Surely, there's no harm in Lady Leslie knowing Gallhiel's future. She is your cousin, Laochlain."

Her condescension was rewarded by a poisonous glare from Leslie, the first acknowledgment that her presence was noted.

Laochlain was openly amused. "No harm," he agreed, "but I've not the time." He turned to Leslie. "Will you return with us or finish your ride?"

"I'm done," she said sullenly. She had not missed their shared amusement at her expense, and her temper was accordingly ill.

Leslie's rough little mountain stallion was as vicious as his mistress, flailing with teeth and hooves at every opportunity. He even dared to challenge Laochlain's red stallion, struggling with Leslie for control of his head, though the great red did not deign to notice his impertinence.

Watching the horse plunge dangerously down a narrow hillside path, Dara was forced to acknowledge his rider a daring and superb horse-woman.

She was also forced to acknowledge the success of Leslie's warfare of the next week. If Leslie's intent was to disrupt the household for the bedevilment of its mistress, she was victorious. The servants were soon confused as to whom they owed their obedience, even while struggling to serve both mistresses. That proved impossible, for Leslie's demands inevitably, and purposely, clashed with Dara's. Garda's diatribes at the girl were futile, and Dara remained silent. Pride and dignity would not permit complaint to Laochlain, neither from herself nor from Garda.

Garda pled, but Dara was adamant, and in the face of the trials besetting her, Garda had not the heart to increase them with her own disloyalty. In this instance, she turned to woman's cunning and poured her anger and worry into her husband's ear. Dunstan had no qualms about relaying the truth of the matter to Laochlain. He'd not cared overmuch for that spoiled she-devil in times past, and he cared less for her now. So, when Laochlain's comfort was overturned, he knew from whence his trouble came.

Laochlain knew he could force Leslie from Gallhiel, but, for his own purposes, he did not wish to do so. Castigating her would settle the matter but afford Dara little reassurance, and he was not unaware of her needs in that quarter. With all this in mind, he had Neacail call his household together.

They filled the great hall. His men-at-arms

lined the walls in relaxed and patient curiosity, while his retainers bunched close together, silent and uneasy, though they had known nothing but fairness from the MacAmlaid. Dara stood quiet and tense at his side, knowing without being told what was to come. Leslie perched upon the long table, unsuspecting or boldly defiant.

Laochlain's eyes traveled from one anxious or expectant face to the next. "I've had no complaints of you or from you since the day of my arrival. You have served me well, and your loyalty has not gone unnoticed. Of late, however, there has been a confusion among you and I tire of it. Whether Lady Dara's commands are mine or her own, they are to be followed. She is your mistress. No one else has claims to your obedience save those who speak on my authority. If doubts arise, you shall bring them to me or to my lady."

As he dismissed the staff, Leslie's defiance gave way to fury, for he had left no doubts and no room for sly evasion. He claimed the English bitch as his own before witnesses. There could be no uncertainty of Dara's place here, a place Leslie had been determined to secure for herself and at Kiarr's urging for the furtherance of his schemes. Venom filled her with each sidelong glance she received from the servants passing by her. She damned Laochlain in her heart and sought her chamber to nurse her hatred in solitude.

Dara caught Laochlain's eye at her passing. "You've made an open enemy of her."

"Kiarr's daughter could only be foe here, open or hidden. Her mind has been his to direct from the moment of her birth, and his hatred and derangement have been hers from that time. Do not worry more over her. She is a vexation, but a harmless one."

His arm encircled her waist, and she leaned against him, wondering how long he could continue to so underestimate his cousin.

Chapter XIX

Wanderers were rare in a land where families clung in tight-woven groups and warred insensibly upon one another. No stranger needing haven was turned away, but to be suspected a spy of another, hostile clan meant a knife in one's throat or an axe in one's head. Often had a man been given food and shelter one night only to return the next at the fore of a roving band of raiders. No keep was immune, and no clan was innocent.

It was a light, lovely afternoon that a stranger entered Gallhiel riding a neat Spanish jennet and carrying a lute before him. His moustache and straight, shoulder-touching hair were of pale, gleaming gold, and he was dressed in costly fashion. He was a minstrel, and his name was Banain.

259

Leslie was alone in the hall, prowling its emptiness in bored frustration. She had just decided to ride out in search of Laochlain when Crieff entered with the stranger.

Banain knew the history of the keep but few of its clan. When Crieff presented him to Lady Leslie MacAmlaid, he made but one assumption, the wrong one. He swept a practiced bow.

"Banain, my lady, for your pleasure."

"A pleasure in truth." She inclined her head. "My lord is busy, but he would not deny us the joy of company and music. From where have you come?"

"Dunkeith, my lady."

Her face lit. "You must tell me of its news. Come! I shall show you to a chamber myself so that we might talk privately. I long for diversion."

Banain's attention was wholly caught or he might have noticed and wondered at Crieff's expression of angry disgust.

Leslie saw it but dared to ignore it, for she saw in this another means of humiliating Dara. She could scarcely wait for supper when the minstrel would greet her as chatelaine of Gallhiel before all its household—and Dara. It mattered not to her that Crieff realized her aim.

The open space of the courtyard was filled with men, wrestling, spear throwing, and sword fighting. Such games, frequently and enthusiastically initiated, were an idle warrior's means of maintaining his strength and skill for battle. Raiding was another method. Both were entertainments thoroughly enjoyed and heavily wagered upon.

Tamnais and a taller man of leaner proportions stood abreast surrounded by a circle of onlookers. They hefted unwieldy spears in hard fists, their tensed forearms bulging with muscle, as they awaited the roared command of a companion appointed mediator. When it came, the spears were released in a surge of power and sped to a target of tightly bound rushes several feet in width and thickness. Tamnais' spear reached the target first, edging the mark, but his fellow's spear, only seconds behind, centered the mark.

When those two men were replaced by two more, Crieff sought Tamnais and drew him beyond the crowd. His face was so grim, and his grip on the other's arm so tight that Tamnais was moved to protest.

"Faith, man! I am not so disgraced by my miss that I must flee!"

Crieff looked at him blankly before shaking his head impatiently. "Kiarr has made a kailwife of his daughter."

Tamnais chuckled his disgust. "Some are blinded by other considerations. You are not?"

"Nay, the wench undermines her own appeal. I took yon minstrel to greet the mistress and make his petition for lodging, but 'twas Leslie of the black locks and blacker heart who greeted him. My tongue is slow, and he thought her the mistress. She knew his mistake and aided it. Another trial for our lady when the tale is bandied about as it will be."

"Why did you not speak then, lad, art dimwitted?"

"I could but thwart her in this and leave her

261

unscathed to try again. I would give her a lesson she would long think on. She must be made to see that Lady Dara does not stand alone."

"And what lesson would you teach?"

Crieff looked disgusted. "Did I know, I would have said at the start. I've no plan. You are a man of little speech, but 'tis agreed you've a canny mind."

Tamnais peered at him, enlightened. "So the problem is to be laid on me, and I'll warrant I'm to reap the harvest if it should prove blighted."

He rubbed his hand against his jaw, leather against leather, while Crieff waited in expectant silence. Patience was needed, for Tamnais' renowned canniness lay mainly in the caution of his thinking. He drew himself up, having settled upon a profitable scheme and one least likely to involve him.

"Who has shown himself least averse to the wench?"

"Neacail." Crieff's tone proclaimed his view of the man's weakness. "He sniffs after her like a bear to honey, though you'd think him too wise for that snare."

Tamnais grunted. "The bear knows the bee will sting, and yet he will steal the honey." And with that, he began to disclose his plan for the downfall of Leslie MacAmlaid.

Night fell ever more softly and ever more slowly with the advent of spring. There was a barely apricot glow across the sky when a demanding knock brought Leslie to her door. She was half-clothed, but, expecting only a serving wench or perhaps Garda, she made no move to cover herself more modestly when she opened it. Her gasp was a mixture of startlement and rage as Neacail thrust his way past her into the room.

His smile was one of pure devilish enjoyment, and none can give the devil his due as can a Highlander, nor enjoy so thoroughly a woman streaked with cruelty.

At his careless stance, Leslie snapped, "What do you here besides gape, dolt?"

She made no move to cover the area revealed above her bust, and he made no effort to redirect his gaze.

"Why, mistress, that is a better reason for being here than the one that did bring me."

"And that was?"

"To ensure your wickedness without fruit." At her waiting stare, he added, "The minstrel, Banain."

Crieff had likened Neacail truly. He was as the bear, strong, direct, and fearless. He relied seldom on craft or cunning, but success was generally his by virtue of sheer, unwavering determination. Guile was foreign to him, and so also was the ability to recognize it in others. And Leslie was nothing if not guileful.

She wet her lips and widened her eyes. "What is your intent?"

"To keep you here until the evening is done."

"I cannot appeal to you."

"Ah, lass, but you do." He was laughing at her.

She flushed and tossed her head, the action tousling her hair in conscious provocation. "It seems Laochlain's mistress lacks not for knights errant. Or perhaps she lacks not for lovers!"

Neacail's grip was surprisingly swift and cruel. "Lady Dara is as true a maid as you are false."

Leslie cried out in genuine distress, for his fingers bit deeply into her bare shoulder. The tears, however, and the soft look of pleading were wholly contrived. She raised a slender hand in supplication, a fair hand whose soft look belied its strength.

Her prey's reaction was immediate and gratifying. His fingers eased their painful pressure and slipped to her back.

In drawing her near, he unleashed her powers.

There was little enough that separated them. Her scanty undergarment was quickly discarded, and his plaid easily lifted. Not a man of refinement, Neacail saw no need for complete divesting, and Leslie soon discovered that that fact far from limited her pleasure. This was a man, virile and satisfying. Not her first, but the first to reduce her to trembling, physical need. Always before, that power had been hers, not now. Only afterwards, when her damp body stretched limply beneath his, did Leslie experience a resurgence of self-preservation.

She wriggled to gain freedom from his embrace and rolled clear. "I must go now. I will be missed. But I shall soon return—you need not rise."

"I need not, and you will not."

His flat tone caught her unaware, and she stared at him in disbelief. "I have lain with you,

264

and still you would keep me here against my wishes?''

"The one has naught to do with the other.''

How often had she seen her sire treating her mother with equally casual disdain. Instinctively, she reacted as Cairistiona would have, with raging, voluble violence. Her hands became claws, and her mouth spouted obscenities.

Neacail merely laughed at the she-devil in his arms and subdued her with cuffs that set her ears ringing.

Tamnais' scheme, once set in motion, did not falter. The unwitting minstrel abetted by descending the stairs with perfect timing, and Crieff was there to greet him and whisper a word of warning as they neared the lengthy table.

"My lord," Crieff's voice was casual. "We have entertainment.''

Hastily prepared, Banain executed a low bow before the imposing figure of the earl and the graceful one of his lady.

Laochlain was rarely surprised by the contrivances of his household, and he smiled slightly as his glance encountered the lute Banain held with possessive care.

"You are welcome here. I favor the lute nearly as much as does Jamie. Have you played for His Grace?''

"Not for a twelvemonth, my lord. The lowlands profited me little. In these mountains, my talents are more a rarity, and the welcome increases.''

As the two talked, Crieff grew more at ease. He had ignored the enquiry of Dara's raised brows, and thus far the MacAmlaid seemed incurious as to Banain's unexplained presence. He was less easy when Banain left them at his host's invitation to sup, and Laochlain's gaze turned upon him questioningly.

"'Tis odd my lady did not tell me of our guest."

"I knew of none," Dara murmured.

"You've a look of a cat in the cream, Crieff."

"Have I, my lord?"

"We would share your enjoyment."

"It was Lady Leslie." Crieff shifted uncomfortably. "She greeted Banain when I brought him to the keep."

"I see nothing in that to pleasure you." Laochlain's eyes swept the assembly. "Leslie has not yet joined us. Will she?"

Crieff shifted again. "No, my lord."

Laochlain sighed at his slow progress. "Are you responsible for her absence?"

"Aye, my lord, but she presumed!" Crieff looked startled at his own outburst.

Laochlain looked interested. "Leslie always presumes." At his man's continued silence, he sighed. "Crieff, we will discuss it later."

"Aye, my lord."

Crieff's relief was so exaggerated as to be comic. Dara watched him hurry away.

"I trust I will hear the tale from your lips, Laochlain. He seemed loath to speak of the matter on my account. And all know how Lady Leslie's intrigues interest me," she added wryly.

They supped on fish and fowl freshly caught, and Dara made no pretense to a dainty appetite.

She had discovered she could eat far more comfortably by night than by morn and was duly obedient to the dictates of nature. When she had swallowed the last mouthful of fowl her stomach could accept, she raised her cup for a servant to fill. Laochlain was watching her, and she smiled uncertainly at him.

"'Tis an amazement to me, lass, that you remain light enough for my arms."

"I soon will not be." She shut her mouth and stared in her cup. She had planned a better moment than this to tell him.

"Do you think my strength not equal to your weight and a wee bairn's?"

Her eyes widened. "You know?"

"Should I not?" He looked surprised and slightly amused. "Your body is no secret to me."

"I feared to tell you."

He frowned. "You should fear nothing where I am concerned. I love you, and I will love our child. Mayhap you carry my heir, no man would find that displeasing." Something in her look enlightened him. "The babe will have my name, lass, from the moment of birth. We will not delay wedding any longer."

A weight of worry lifted from her heart. The past weeks had been agonizing ones for her with the image of Ruod ever before her. She would have left Gallhiel and Laochlain before allowing her child to be raised as he had, a bastard living on charity.

It was growing late when Laochlain bade her retire alone, and Crieff was ready for his summons. Having worded his explanation mentally throughout the evening, Crieff was fluent in his account.

Scarcely ten minutes later, Laochlain knocked upon the door of Leslie's chambers.

After a long moment, Neacail opened it and grew uneasy when he saw Laochlain.

Laochlain grinned. "Have you enjoyed this extra bit of night watch, Neacail?" His eyes went beyond him to where Leslie was huddled in the bed, noticeably furious.

"Night watch? Aye, my lord, I have indeed." Neacail was also grinning now.

"You watch is ended, man. Begone whilst I have a word with the lady." He opened the door for Neacail to move past him before he entered the room and closed the door again.

Leslie lifted a hand to her breast and dropped it again. She rose in one fluid movement and twisted the sheet neatly about her. She had been revealed completely for a moment, but Laochlain evinced no interest. His gaze rested pointedly on her bruised and swollen lips, and he smiled.

"You've had your reckoning, lass. I need not further it. My men guard my own. Do not forget it, again."

"How could you bring her here! An English whore, far worse, even, than a Scottish border wench! She has no place here. It is mine!"

"Nay," he returned furiously. "It has never been yours, nor will it be! Kiarr has poisoned you with his own greed and promised that which was not his to give. I have been forbearing with you until now, but you shall not malign my wife.

You will leave by morning's light."

She whitened. "You dare not! My father has a stronger claim to Gallhiel than a traitor. You fought with James against your own blood. Had I been a man and older, I'd ha' skewered you! Yours was a betrayal, Laochlain MacAmlaid, and none forget!"

"If 'tis not forgotten, 'tis because Kiarr breathes fresh life into the tale whene'er it falters. Does he think me witless? I mark his intent, but all of his scheming will avail him nothing."

Her eyes were wide and glittering, her mouth twisted. "And all your wit and wealth will avail you nothing. Kiarr will triumph!"

"Many men have coveted that which I hold, and one by one they have met defeat or death. I do not fear my uncle. You will tell him so on your return."

Leslie had a sudden and terrible vision of returning to Airdsgainne in disgrace, her defeat bandied about on crude tongues. Her fears evoked a transformation. From stone, she warmed to supple flesh, wriggling from the sheet that clung to her. She swayed before him, her body pale and perfect from pointed breasts to tapering thighs. She lifted her arms.

"Nay, Laochlain, do not banish me from Gallhiel. No English wench could match the pleasures I offer."

His expression did not alter as he turned from her. "I will send Neacail to you. His heat matches your own."

Staring blindly at the doorway he left gaping,

she sank slowly to her knees. Crouched naked upon the rushes, she bit her lip through and tasted blood. She had been foiled, but Kiarr's daughter would not, dare not, fail. Gallhiel would see her again.

The morning sun hesitated upon the ridge, daunted by the shadowing clouds. The light it cast was pale and without warmth. The air was mist-laden. Leslie watched wordlessly as her stallion was led forward. She had pulled the hood of her cape far forward, shielding her face, but Laochlain's terse orders had been emphatic and there were few about to observe and comment upon the manner of her leaving. Her retainer stepped forward hurriedly to assist her. She placed her booted foot into his cupped hand and sprang lightly to her horse's back. Without a glance backward, she brought her riding crop down viciously across the stallion's gleaming rump. He leapt forward, and men fled from his path.

Dara turned away from the window and moved back to the bed and the lean, hard form reclining there.

"She is gone," she said unnecessarily.

Laochlain raised his brows. "Aye. She had no choice."

She watched him lean back and close his eyes. His lack of concern was almost unnerving. Slowly she fastened the intricate hooks of her gown, brushed her hair, and secured it with ribbons. When she was done, Laochlain still had not moved.

"I do not trust her, my lord."

"Nor do I. MacAmlaids have been an unlucky lot in matters of family loyalty."

"Your uncle will be enraged by this."

"Kiarr?" He finally looked at her through half-opened eyes. "He is never pleased. Lass, do not worry so."

"There is that about Leslie that stirs my fear. Not her childish jealousy of me, but something deeper. She is like a piece of fruit whose skin gleams over a putrid heart. I do not fear the girl, only the harm she may do to you."

"Have you the sight, lass?"

She looked at him sharply and realized he was teasing her. She shook her head. "If I had, I would pray it be taken from me."

"Those born with the sight soon find they cannot escape it." He teased no longer.

"Will she return, do you think?"

He rose in a swift but unhurried motion. "Aye, but not alone."

Watching him pleat his plaid and belt it at the hips, she wondered if the power of premonition might not be more a thing to desire than to fear—if it could give the power to alter an ill-fated destiny.

Chapter XX

There was little beauty to be found within any burgh of barony, but viewed from the distant fells, Cienness had a certain comeliness. The wall encircling the town was softened by spring grasses feathering outward from between lichenous stone. The rooflines of the buildings within were without symmetry, but the distance mellowed their sharpest affront to the eye. The outlying fields were willow green, and the hedges bounding them were strong and thick.

Within the gates, beauty was rarer still. The dwellings were humble timber and crowded one upon another. Mean closes and narrow streets were always dirty from the middens piled at every door.

The parish church of Cienness had been built

two centuries earlier, an unpretentious building with plain walls and pillars of solid stone. The arched doorway and tiny, rounded windows admitted the only gleam of gold the church could boast, the golden glow of sunlight gleaned from the fading afternoon rays. The nave and chancel were undersized, but the eastern apse had an airy vaulted roof.

From the chancel came a quiet intonation of Latin, answered by a second voice, and then a third.

Dara kept her eyes downcast, away from the priest's stern visage. He made her uneasy. Almost he had refused to perform a ceremony binding a powerful Scottish earl and an English maid. Her plea of the babe had wavered his refusal, almost more so than the royal permission signed with a flourish and sealed by Jamie's own hand.

The priest was suddenly silent, and she realized they were wed.

Laochlain paid God's dour servant no further heed. "Art beautiful, Lady Gallhiel."

She smiled radiantly. What matter a frowning priest's disapproval? She was the bride of the MacAmlaid by all the laws of God and man. Laochlain took her arm, and they left the church.

Bretach waited in the street with their mounts, and a grin creased his face at the sight of them. Dara placed her foot in his hand and returned his smile gaily before bounding into the saddle. The setting sun haloed her chestnut coils and brushed a peach glow across her face and neck. Her eyes reflected her joy.

And she was beautiful. Her gown, the blue violet of the hyacinths growing wild upon the hillside, nestled snugly at her waist before swirling in satin folds. The neckline bared her collarbone where lay a chain of soft filigreed gold studded with pearls. Laochlain had placed it about her neck that very morning.

The burgh's single inn where they had taken a room was small and poorly tended, but Laochlain's lordly manner, or perhaps his costly raiment, garnered them satisfactory service. They were served without delay in a tiny, private dining room. Bretach was ill at ease and would have preferred to eat in the common room. Gaiety prevailed throughout the meal, however, and he had no qualms of intrusion by the time the fowl was a cleaned framework of bones and the vegetable tureen held no more than a seasoned, buttery liquid.

When the last of the wine was gone, Bretach rose self-consciously.

"I will attend the horses and seek my pallet belowstairs." He bowed low over Dara's hand and reddened at Laochlain's quizzing look.

As they walked down the hall to their room, Laochlain leaned close to Dara. "Bretach granted us our privacy, but I fear the lad would have preferred to perform my part this night."

"My lord!" Dara blushed a deeper shade than the wine she had drank.

"Do you not admit to lust in a man?"

"Your example leaves me no choice." She tossed the pert answer over her shoulder as she stepped through the doorway before him.

He barred it behind him and turned. At his expression, she retreated. He advanced as rapidly, angling towards her, edging her towards his destination. She felt the bed at her back and gave him an accusing look. He laughed deeply and took her in his arms. His kiss was rough and firing, and her lips parted at his insistence. He undressed her slowly, arousing her further with every provocative look and touch. She responded unhesitatingly, drawing him with her as he eased her to the bed. This man, her husband, knew tender as well as fierce passion—and plied them both. This, her wedding night, would be treasured forever.

Morning caught them lazy and disinclined to rise. Dara curled against her husband's side, and his fingers played among her soft curls.

"I wish I need have no fear for Gallhiel. I would take you to Stirling, Jamie is there now. Would you like to meet Scotland's king and his most powerful nobles?"

"Aye, but would your James care to meet me?" She laughed at him. "My reception might be the oubliette. I have deprived Scotland's fairest maids of their greatest treasure."

"Art certain, minx?" he teased.

"Most certain! I will not share my lord's affections, but will you really take me to Stirling, someday?"

"Aye, or to Edinburgh or Lieth or Scone or where you will. Scotland is yours."

"My lord is generous. But, Laochlain," she spoke seriously, "I would not go now even were you able. We must remain at Gallhiel until I am delivered. Our child must be born there.''

His expression told her he was pleased, for no part of Scotland could be so desired by him as Gallhiel. He had spent far too many years away from it. In future years, he might leave for a day or a week or a month, but the call homeward would be too strong for refusal. And he would want his children to grow with that same love and longing burning within their souls so that they would always come back to their beginnings.

Dara vowed it would be so. He must never know disappointment in the fruit of his loins and her womb.

Gladly did the travelers turn their backs to Cienness and their hearts and horses homeward. The crofts outside the town walls were in the midst of the morning's labors. In one field, an ox pulled mightily at the titan stones to which he was bound by stout rope, in another, a ploughman labored with his caschrom. The single curved blade at the end of its shaft of wood pulled slowly through the rocky soil, propelled by the man's foot pressing the pedal above the blade.

Beyond the cultivated fields on the sloping fells were carpets of pale primroses and wild strawberries, a mellowing of creamy lemon and rose. In the distance, the moors rolled away towards the sea. Soon the heather would blossom in lovely, perfected shades from lavender to violet. No beauty could touch a heart as could the moors tinted with heather and darkly golden gorse. Summer would come with the magic of swampfire in the peat bogs and elffire in the hills, but the first beauty of the heath in spring would remain unsurpassed. The forests were scented with sweetbriar and thyme, and the breezes carried the scent outward.

From the wooded hills came a procession of men and kine, the looks of which drew a protest from Dara.

"The beasts look to need rest and grain. Where are they being taken?"

"To England, no doubt, where they will be fatted and placed on some fine English table." Laochlain saw her look of disbelief and chided her. "Let not their appearance deceive you. Rich lowland pastures will flesh them considerably, and our Highland cattle are much vaunted for their taste. I'll warrant you've dined on the like in England. These same are what I desire for Gallhiel. They fare better and are of greater profit than any field crop."

Dara looked anew at the scraggly, ill-favored cattle and could find no improvement in the light of these revelations. She could scarcely credit them with attaining the thick, juicy proportions of the shoulders and haunches served at Chilton.

They drew abreast of the head of the herd and reined their horses to one side, out of their path. A man afoot, lean and homely as any of his cattle, paused before them. He was astounded that a man of obvious wealth would yield the path. He removed his grimy cap. "M'lord, ye are kind to allow us passage."

"I'd not have you turn your herd aside for my sake. Whose cattle are these?"

"The MacMurray's, m'lord, from Rosshire."

"A prosperous journey, man, and my greetings to your master upon your return."

"Greetings from whom, m'lord?"

"The MacAmlaid. Earl of Gallhiel."

"Aye, m'lord. I shall." His look of respect amply described the legend that was Gallhiel.

As he left them, Dara remarked cautiously, "I thought the clans were all at odds with one another."

"Often we are, and the MacAmlaids have fought the MacMurrays in times past, but these men are herdsmen, not warriors or raiders."

"The man was certainly far from warlike."

"You sound almost disappointed. Are you restive with the ease of our journey?"

She denied it laughingly and spurred Haefen onto the path as the last of the beasties passed them by.

Tiny forget-me-nots and daisies grew profusely in the meadows edging the forest, and honeysuckle twined itself fragrantly in leafy boughs. As they entered the wood, the sun was replaced by cool shadow. Frequent use kept the path clear of bush, and the only hindrances lay in overhanging branches. They rode single file with Dara between the men. Small furry creatures darted among the trees, and once they spied a doe, maybe seeking a safe thicket in which to drop the fawn she carried so fully within her.

It was at the point where the forest opened again onto rocky hillside that they were set upon. Their attackers were three, roughly dressed and roughly mannered and so desperate that even the sinewed height of the MacAmlaid did not deter them. The brigands held off until Bretach was clear of the trees. Then they leapt howling from their hiding place in a shallow ravine. Only one was armed with a long bow, which he held on the MacAmlaid, deeming him the likeliest threat. The other two carried curving daggers with crude bone handles.

Laochlain cursed long and viciously at his lack of foresight. He should have seen the danger of the terrain. These hills afforded security for rogues leaving their winter lairs and seeking their livelihood in the most profitable, least industrious manner available.

The man with the bow spoke sharply. "For the gold ye carry, we'll grant ye safe passage. Aye, safety for yourself, yon servant, and your lady."

He barely glanced at Dara, perhaps sensing he would imperil his venture as well as his life if he showed too much interest in her. Laochlain's response verified that probability to him.

"Touch my wife, and you have earned your death."

"Easy now, me lord. All we want is your coins and jewels." He lifted his bow sharply as Bretach eased his horse next to the red stallion. "Try naught, or I'll loose me arrow in your belly!"

He had no time for further threats or for action. The red stallion heeded his master's unseen signal, and iron-shod hooves were slashing over the cowering thief. His longbow fell uselessly to the ground as he shielded his face with his arms. His skin was ashen.

"Mercy, me lord! Mercy! We'd not ha' harmed ye."

He was to his knees before Laochlain quieted his horse. A gash on the thief's forehead dripped blood onto his filthy jerkin. One of his fellows had fled, the other had fared less fortunately. He was braced against a boulder, fists clutching the hilt of Bretach's dirk. He watched in horror as his blood stained his breeks and the ground at his feet.

Dara strove to calm her frightened mare. She was stunned at the speed with which events had transpired. Scarcely had she time to become frightened before the danger was no more. Her heart still raced sickeningly, and her hands were cold upon the reins. The dying man's quavering pleas for aid sounded abnormally loud to her. She turned her face, knowing there was nothing to be done for a man whose intestines bulged at a gaping wound.

Laochlain eyed his adversary with angry disgust. "You are a foolish knave and ill-suited to your profession. We were outnumbered and outarmed. A stouter heart and a steadier hand would have seen you safe. Instead your companion dies, and the other leaves you to face justice alone."

The man stared at him wildly, fearing this hour to be his last. He had chosen a fearsome man to rob, and then had bumbled a poor piece of work. "Spare me," he pled, "I'll never thieve more!"

Bretach snorted, disbelief writ plain upon his face. "You'd have us trust a man who held a longbow to our breasts?"

The thief was terror-stricken. "By the loving grace of Mary, I'll do no more thieving. And I've ne'er slain a man!"

Dara nudged Haefen closer. She felt certain they intended to do no more than frighten the man, and they had succeeded in that long since.

"A boon, my lord."

Laochlain looked at her, frowned at her colorless cheeks and look of strain. "Anything, lass."

"I grow weary and would be gone. Do we tarry longer, dark will catch us far from Gallhiel. These men have paid for what they dared."

He glanced at the man who pled so earnestly. Already his color was returning, for he had caught a glimpse of salvation.

"Get hence, then," Laochlain ordered him curtly, "and go swiftly, lest I decide on bolder measures. My lady's intercession has saved you. Remember to whom you owe your life."

The man had no time for thanks. He fled, leaving his companion who now slumped lifelessly among the rocks.

As she rode, Dara's thoughts lingered on the incident, filling her with clammy dread. It seemed almost a portent. Dark thoughts brought darker ones. Had she brought trouble to Laochlain in wedding him? Brann would have sworn it so. It pained her anew that he had not seen her wed in joy, nor would he know when she made him an uncle. Intermingled with that pain was a sharp regret that she would never welcome his wife to Chilton, never hold his bairns—and never again feel his loving embrace. She felt bereft.

She was truly exhausted by the time Gallhiel was in sight, but her heart lifted with that first glimpse. The castle looked no more lovely and no more welcoming than when she had first seen it, but she belonged to it now as she had not before. The valley was transformed with spring. No more did the land look barren and unyielding. The grass, pale and tender, cast a glow of yellow-green upon the fells, and the trees were full of young leaves. The kine and goats and hogs were no longer granted the shelter of the hovels, and their young played or slept at their feet. It was a blossoming valley, and soon it would be a prosperous one. And in the red-hued rays of the lowering sun, it looked a serene one.

The gates opened without hesitation at their advance, and grooms appeared speedily to take their horses. There was no sign of discord, yet in tense faces and averted eyes Laochlain read danger. He gestured Bretach to his side and bade Dara seek shelter in the stables. She did not obey but followed them into the keep.

The scene that met their eyes was, at first, an affable one. Familiar, trusted figures sat around the table, eating and drinking without stint. It was the lack of sounds of merriment that first rang warning, and then, almost at the same moment, the strangers were sighted. Five, nay, half a dozen brawny, armed men. And at the head of the table, in Laochlain's rightful place, sat still another unfamiliar to Gallhiel. Dara needed no introduction to this man; she knew him by his lean, wolfish look and his piercing blue eyes so like Duncan's. This was Kiarr.

Her eyes went slowly beyond him in the interminable moment of silence that followed their entrance. Her stomach tightened in anger, every nerve screaming rage. Leslie sat next to her father, in Dara's accustomed place. On her dark rose lips was a smug, triumphant smile, and in every line of her proud body was gloating.

Kiarr rose smoothly, and Dara saw that he was a tall man, as tall as Laochlain. His hair was silver, and his face was cold and menacing though he smiled.

"Greetings, Nephew, have you no welcome for me?"

Laochlain moved easily towards the table; Bretach remained in an aggressive stance at the doorway. Behind him in the courtyard, the warriors gathered, ready to do battle for their chief.

"You are welcome here, Kiarr." Laochlain's gaze flicked contemptuously to Leslie, who lost some of her composure. "I ken you have been well treated in my absence."

Kiarr's smile was false. "I fear your men were somewhat unwilling to receive me, but Dunstan relayed your orders before I was too inconvenienced. But, Nephew, were you wise?" His taunt was smooth.

"Wise?" Laochlain shrugged. "I would not have my men slay you, but my orders were to receive you, not trust you. I'll warrant you have been amply watched."

"Every moment," Kiarr replied through gritted teeth, "though the caution was unnecessary."

"Your intent is amiable, then?"

Kiarr's face darkened as blood suffused it. "I am come to lay open claim to that which is rightfully mine. The title and keep of Gallhiel."

"By what rights do you make your claim?"

"By the rights of tanistry!"

Dara could feel the shock reverberate through the length of the room, though she did not understand the term or what it entailed. The triumph on Kiarr's face and on Leslie's spoke amply of its import.

Laochlain, however, was not disconcerted. He had expected as much. "'Tis an ancient custom, Kiarr, that a brother's claim is stronger than a son's. One I do not honor."

"You deny me!" Kiarr was enjoying his role.

"I do."

"Then I challenge you to hold your chieftaincy."

Laochlain scarcely heeded his uncle's dramatic declaration. He was thinking swiftly. Kiarr and his men were outnumbered. They could be overcome, though at great cost. He could invoke James' authority, but this he was determined not to do even if Kiarr would heed it. If he would hold the clan's faith, the victory must be his alone. Which reasoning gave but one out.

"I accept your challenge, Kiarr, but the battle shall be joined between us alone. I elect single combat."

Kiarr inclined his head. "Single combat." He signaled his men who grouped behind him. Leslie joined them as her father spoke again. "We shall await you on the fells at dawn."

"I shall come."

As Kiarr strode towards the door, he was checked by the sight of Dara poised before it. His gaze went slowly over her from the soft masses of her hair to her snug bodice to the toes of her half-boots, just visible beneath her gown. He heard his daughter's hiss as he bowed slightly.

"My lady." His tone was faintly mocking.

Dara swept him a full and graceful curtsey and returned his stare bravely. "My lord, 'tis well you are leaving us. You are not welcome here."

Kiarr flushed, knowing his men listened avidly. "I shall return."

"Gallhiel shall never be yours!"

"The morrow might not see you so haughty, lass."

"Know this, sir, that which is between you and my husband is not binding upon me. If you succeed in your aim, I'll not honor any pledge of safety to you and your followers. Treachery is not to you alone. The doors of this keep shall be barred, and its warriors' weapons held in readiness for your approach. My word shall loose the first arrow—to your heart."

She moved gracefully from his path, and his glance held a blend of anger and admiration. He went silently, and the wide doors were closed swiftly upon the heels of the last of his men.

"Will you never obey me?" She whirled to find Laochlain inches from her. "Would you not rather fight in my place? Your temper is suited for battle."

She heard pride in his voice and answered with confidence. "I will do battle if need be.

286

That arrogant Lucifer and his vixen daughter shall not have Gallhiel. If you were slain, I would hold this keep and your title for our child, our son!"

"I'll not be slain, lass. Do not fear it."

He swept her up in his arms heedless of onlookers, and his stride was as easy as if he carried naught. His arms were possessive, and she heard the pounding of his heart. She felt her pulse racing in response.

It seemed an eternity until their door was safely barred, but from that moment, time sped.

Dara lay against the pillows, her arms opened to him and her eyes invited. He came to her, feeling her thighs part and embrace him. The throbbing in his loins built into pain, and he entered her with driving force. Their rhythm was unflawed until they reached the final cadence and lay content and complete in each other's arms.

With ill timing a servant rapped at their door. "Mistress Garda bade me bring your supper, my lord."

Laochlain rolled away from Dara, cursing, and she smiled and pulled the covers up about her. She watched, amused, as he took the tray from the embarrassed maidservant and kicked the door closed again. Turning back, he echoed her smile.

"At least Garda had wits enough to realize I had no wish to leave our room this night."

"With your barbarian's tactics that was easy enough to discern."

She sat up in bed and allowed the bedclothes

to fall away, but his hungry look caused her to snatch them up again to his amusement.

They supped gaily, intent on dispelling the threats that morning would bring. Laochlain fed Dara, interspersing chunks of meat with teasing kisses.

But thoughts of the morrow could not be held at bay indefinitely, and at last Dara said with a frown, "Your aunt did not accompany Kiarr."

"My uncle trusts few, and with good reason. He would leave Cairistiona to ensure Airdsgainne unbreached."

"Yet Leslie returned."

"Kiarr's triumph would be hers as well."

"He will not triumph!" She spoke fiercely and then repeated it silently as if she could will it so. He could not triumph.

Chapter XXI

The morning came in with the mists off the loch, a thick, grey damp that disembodied voices and muffled the sounds of normalcy. There were metallic sounds from the guardhouse, the sound of weapons eagerly handled.

Dara sat up in bed watching Laochlain dress. The chamber was warm, but she felt cold and numbed.

It was scanty enough protection he chose, rejecting even the lightest mail. He donned tight-fitting breeks of strong leather and a leather jacket and wrapped a woolen cutting scarf about his neck. That plaid, in the sett of the MacAmlaids, would be his only shield against the slash of Kiarr's blade at his neck.

From the parting mists came three indistinct forms. The gates parted slightly to admit them, and they were surrounded by the MacAmlaid's men as they moved toward the hall. Laochlain waited in the doorway, his eyes narrowing as he recognized Leslie. Her face was mutinous as one of the men at her side stepped forward.

"Kiarr entrusts you with his daughter. He does not wish her to view the combat."

"My uncle is of fainter heart than this wild-cat."

Glancing back at his wrathful mistress, the man looked as if he would have liked to agree but dared not. Before he could turn away, Dara spoke from Laochlain's side where she had appeared noiselessly.

"Nay, I'll not have her here." She ignored the men's startled expressions. "Kiarr thinks to have her within should he win only to find the gates locked to him. I'll not have it." Her eyes held Leslie's. "Return to Airdsgainne. This keep shall not shelter you."

"Speak haughty, bitch." Leslie spat the words at her. "I'll have your place yet!"

"When I am dead, Leslie, only then."

Dara watched coldly as the girl turned and strode past her men, leaving them to follow as they would. Laochlain started to voice his irritation, but one glance at her face silenced him on that score.

"I'll not leave you a widow, lass."

Dara raised her face for his kiss. "I'd not forgive you if you did, my lord."

They embraced, briefly, fiercely, and he step-ped away from her. The men he had chosen to accompany him fell into step behind. They went on foot, for the battle would be joined nearby, on the open fells.

Dara did not go within nor did she anguish herself by watching him leave. The fog was dissipating, and she saw at a glance that Laochlain had left Gallhiel amply defended. It was to Tamnais that she gave her orders, and he relayed them to the lounging men with a rare grin of pride for his countess' courage. The gates clanged shut and received their iron bars. Bowmen lined the walls, and spearmen knelt at the gate. Dara watched their hurried movements with grim approval. If Laochlain left Kiarr dead, there would be no need of these measures, and if Kiarr won, a code of honor demanded that he be accepted as Gallhiel's master. But Dara damned honor. If Laochlain died this day, so then would Kiarr.

She turned slowly from the readied men and reentered the hall. The rushes whispered beneath her feet as she crossed to the stairs and climbed them thoughtfully. Garda met her in the upper corridor.

"Where are your bairns, Garda?"

The woman's face was strained. "Mairi is safe with a wench in my chamber, but Parlan is with the men in the courtyard."

"They will see he comes to no harm."

"He is a headstrong lad, that one. Much akin to his father. Dunstan has given me more than one lifetime should hold of worry. Parlan looks to do the same."

Dara gave what comfort she could, her mind all the while on the scene that must be taking place beyond the walls that held her in safety. She could see with fearful clarity the flash of the blade and the flow of blood.

It had not yet come to that. There had been no polite parrying of words at the outset. No measuring of blades for justice's sake. No laying out of rules. There was no lightness, no wagering. The battle would have but one end, and this was understood by all. It was blood against blood, nephew against uncle—and one must die.

The men fanned out on either side of the combatants. Their faces were hard and grim, and their weapons were sheathed but thrust forward upon their belts in readiness. But neither side would stir unless there was treachery. It was by chance alone that the adversaries had chosen like weapons. Not the long and cumbersome claymore but broadswords, lighter but equally deadly.

As they joined, Kiarr made the first thrust and continued aggressively, while Laochlain appeared content to deflect his thrusts. The air was damp, and the ground boggy. Their feet soon groped for more secure footing in the mud.

If the MacAmlaid's men thought their lord to have the advantage in his youth, they soon found it was no great one. Kiarr's age had not brought him to lessened strength or stamina. His body was lean, but as a sapling, not a brittle reed.

Laochlain began to press. He lunged and was parried. Kiarr made a swift riposte, and his blade encountered flesh. He drew back, his face a tight, smiling mask. Blood stained Laochlain's shirt below his shoulder. The wound was slight but draining. No sound came from the watching clansmen.

Laochlain nodded slightly, acknowledging the hit. He was unshaken. Both men had begun to tire, but Kiarr lifted his blade once again, and Laochlain's defense was quick, followed hard by attack.

Kiarr leapt away, but his instinct played him false. He deemed Laochlain harder hit than in truth he was. He moved in carelessly and met cold steel. A look of sheer astonishment crossed his face as his hand went to his doublet, over his heart. Blood pumped steadily against the palm he pressed in a futile attempt to stanch the flow. His mouth twisted viciously, but the curse that issued from it was never complete. Even death was unmerciful, coming too soon.

Leslie saw her father fall. She was on the hillside directly above them, astride her fiery stallion. Shrieking wildly, she set spurs into his side and bore down upon the clustered men.

They were transfixed by the sight and the sound of her, Kiarr's men as well as Laochlain's. They scattered as she rode them down, stopping her frenzied mount with cruel jerks of the reins. Her father lay at her feet.

Her eyes lifted from his body to Laochlain. "You will die, my lord. Not now, and not by my father's hand, but I will see you slain."

Before he could answer, she whirled her horse and fled across the hills—towards Airdsgainne where her mother awaited word of her husband.

Laochlain pulled his eyes from her dimming figure and looked over Kiarr's body to the men beyond. They waited, uneasy but not fearful.

"Further death would serve no purpose," they heard him say. "Take your master's body and return it to my aunt. Warn her that I'll brook no foolish attempts of reprisal. If any so desire, you may return to Gallhiel and my service. I shall value the loyalty you have given my uncle."

He turned away and found Bretach at his side, but rejected his supportive shoulder. His torn flesh ached damnably, and luck would be his if the muscles were not severed, but his thoughts were not on his discomfort. They had flown ahead, to Gallhiel, to Dara.

Chapter XXII

T he cry was raised in the heavy stillness of
   the summer night with crofters reaching
   for scythes and clubs while their wives and
children huddled in fear. Raiders! The curse of
every Highland holding. The clans prospered by
the gains of raiding, but the people of the land,
the crofters, suffered by it.

In this July night, the hue was up from an
outlying hovel. A man lay nourishing the ground
with his blood until it slowed of itself and he
knew he would live. The shrieks of his woman
still rang in his ears, though they were but
memory for she had been wrested from his
grasp. They had been wed scarcely more than a
year. Their infant daughter wailed from her
motionless cradle.

Word sped to the fortress from ploughman to

guard to steward to MacAmlaid. Dara lay tense and silent, watching as Laochlain arranged his plaid and chose his weapons. Her child stirred restlessly in her womb and gave meaning to her fears.

"Do you think the men are come from Airdsgainne?"

He grunted and shook his head. "To steal a wife? Nay. Cairistiona would have her men murder or burn or pillage—no less."

"Whoever they are, the villains will not await pursuit. Can there be any hopes of capturing them?"

"We can but try." He bent over her, seeing the fear in her eyes yet not knowing how to allay it. She was in her sixth month, and of late the bairn seemed almost to drain her.

"Sleep," he said, "I will be back with the dawn."

He kissed her mouth tenderly and was gone, knowing she would not sleep. Bretach met him in the corridor, and they went downstairs together.

"It begins."

"Aye," Laochlain said thoughtfully. "I had expected it earlier, but Kiarr's lady bides her time. She must think us unsuspecting by now, hoping we will leave the keep but lightly guarded."

"God help your lady if we did."

"God help Caristiona if she dared," was the grim reply.

The guardhouse was full of men, roused and readied. Some talked quietly, speculatively, amongst themselves, others waited in expectant silence. The MacAmlaid's entrance quieted them all.

His gaze went around the room, and his mind worked with intuitive swiftness. "A handful of you—you, Micheil and Pert, Alpin and Iniss— will ride with Tamnais to give chase. I do not look for success nor do I wish you to ride upon Airdsgainne, though doubtless that is where the trail will lead you. Half of those left will follow Neacail and Dunstan guarding the keep. The other half shall ride with Bretach and me." He glanced towards Bretach. "Choose your men quickly."

Within fifteen minutes, Laochlain's guard were mounted and awaiting his command. Torches brushed against the heavy dark of the night and cast a hellish light over grim brows and jaws. Their chief's voice carried easily to them.

"You will encircle the valley by pairs with no more than half a league between. You will be invisible and silent. I want no warning that we are not unprepared."

He signaled them forward, and for brief moments there was no sound but hooves tapping against flagstones. He and Bretach passed through the gates last. They parted just outside the walls at Laochlain's direction.

"The crofters are to prepare but wait within their homes. Their first care is to their family. I'll await you at the bridge."

Bretach turned to the right, Laochlain to the left. As Laochlain bade his tenants remain with-

in and look to their own protection, he regretted
the hard ride he had given the red early in the
evening. His mount was sturdy and willing but
lacked the stallion's power and stamina. Turning
away from the last crofter, fierce in his anger at
the intruders, resolute in his determination to
hold them from the valley, Laochlain headed for
the narrow neck of the loch spanned by a small
stone bridge built by some foresighted chief long
ago. Bretach was not yet there, and he awaited
him patiently.

A quarter moon revealed little of the valley
gripped by the fleeting Highland summer, but he
knew by memory that the boundary walls had
lost their harsh newness and that the crops
within promised abundance. The growing herd
of cattle had been moved from the slowly yellow-
ing valley to the fresher pastures higher in the
hills. They were well guarded, and if need be,
that guard could be increased.

Bretach came upon him noiselessly, and together they crossed the bridge. The water below
it was untroubled and lapped faintly at the stone
of the bridge and the grassy shores of the loch.
In a sheltering of boulders beyond the bridge,
they dismounted and made themselves as comfortable as possible to wait and to watch. The
likeliest path from Airdsgainne was the loch,
and the likeliest source of aggression was Airdsgainne.

The hours slipped by unmarked by any disturbance, and the men of Gallhiel silently cursed
their inactivity. The night was mild and their
watch no hardship, but they would have pre-

ferred battle to this uneventful passing of time. The only sounds were those of a restless horse, quickly quieted, and the muted voice of a summer night. A dog barked briefly, distantly, and was silent.

It was near dawn that word was brought stealthily to the chief that Tamnais' band of men had returned unmolested. The trail they followed had indeed led to Cairistiona's mountain fortress, but there was no stirring there now. With morning's first faint light lining the mountains, Laochlain acknowledged the uselessness of their watch. Caristiona waited still.

Nearing Gallhiel, Laochlain uttered an exclamation which startled the drowsing Bretach into alertness. He relaxed at Laochlain's rueful smile.

"Yonder is my lady, Bretach, watching from the battlements, and I'll wager she has been there all the night."

"I would not take your wager on a certainty. She is a bold-spirited lass. If I could find another such, I would be a bachelor no more."

"There is not another like Dara in all Christendom," Laochlain stated with conviction. "Ruod would not rest in his grave did he know the good he brought to me by one feckless move. The knowledge would be torture to him as surely as that of some poor devil put to the rack."

At their approach, Dara abandoned her watch and awaited them in the courtyard. Laochlain dismounted and gathered her in his arms, taking hungrily the lips she offered. After a while, she drew back slightly.

"My lord, your breakfast awaits you, readied and kept hot for an hour past. If you had not come soon, I vow I would have brought it to you!"

Laochlain laughed down at her before lifting his eyes to Bretach. "Not in all Christendom! I swear it!"

Her puzzlement over the comment was forgotten in her desire to have Laochlain's hunger sated that he might rest. The pleasure of food to hungry men, however, could not delay the matter of Gallhiel's protection.

"Neacail, you shall command a dozen men by day to keep watch over the valley. Bretach shall do the same by night. I will have a force ready for instant pursuit when word is given of intruders. Your men are not to leave the valley undefended. Dunstan commands the men left to the keep when I am gone. Severe punishment for any who trespass in my valley will be a warning for all."

Tamnais snorted. "Cairistiona will not be warned."

Laochlain ignored Dara's accusing frown. "Nay, but if her men fear me more than her, she will be rendered helpless."

"'Twould be ill-advised optimism to look for such a contingency." was the sour reply. "That one will never be helpless."

Talk turned then to the young crofter's wife, whether she had been kept alive and the surest means of regaining her. There was no question of whether or not the attempt should be made. That was a certainty. In return for their loyalty, a chief owed his vassals full measure of his power and forces in their behalf. And more, it was a matter of Highland pride.

It was a harried day for Dara, though Laochlain slept through most of it. The servants seemed to get little done with men striding purposely through the hall at all hours. Dara thought them much more eager than grim as she directed a wench to chase the restless, excited hounds from the hall and another to fling their bones after them. All the while her mind was on Laochlain, for he would go at dusk to confront Cairistiona in her own lair.

In the afternoon hour in which he had directed her to awaken him, she went to their room, bearing food and drink. A strong lad of some twelve years followed at her heels with weighty cans of hot water. Dara placed Laochlain's supper on the table and watched as the boy filled the tub. When he was gone, she moved close to the bed. Laochlain slept lightly, easily as he ever did, and she knew she had but to touch him or whisper his name to waken him. She was loath to do either. In this moment he belonged to her alone; when he woke, his responsibilities would claim him.

She studied him with loving eyes. The lines about his eyes had deepened in the months since they had come to Gallhiel, but his smiles and laughter were much more frequent now than when first she had known him. Hard as the life was here, great as its difficulties and dangers, he was content. And so was she, save for her fear of Cairistiona. If Laochlain were taken from her, not even his child could ease her pain.

Slowly she reached out a hand to touch it to his lips. His eyes opened, and his mouth lifted to a grin beneath her fingers.

"Have you come to join me, love?"

"If I could hold you here in safety."

"Would you have me turn from my responsibilities, from a man who frets for his wife and a babe for its mother?"

"No," she sighed. "I would have you aid them, but have a care that your own wife and child are not left fretting for you."

While he bathed, she stood at the opened window and stared out across the valley. The stifling stillness of the day before had given way to cool, damp winds. Heavy clouds darkened the sky and threw purple shadows over the fells below. The distant green of tree and bush bowed spasmodically under sudden gusts, and sheep milled nervously in their enclosures.

"It will be vile riding this night," she remarked.

"Mayhap to our advantage. There will be few eager to share the storm with us, and Airdsgainne's guard might well have their attention focused on their discomfort rather than the probability of intruders."

He had risen from the tub and was vigorously toweling himself. Dara bit her lips against an anxious rejoinder and was smiling as she turned and offered him wine. He took the cup and drank deeply before tearing into the tender, roasted duck. She could eat nothing, for her emptiness was not from hunger. It would be dark in so few hours, and the clouds would hasten that dark.

Her face was calm as she descended the stairs at his side. The effort of serenity was needful, for her sake and his. She would have him go with ease of mind, not carrying her fear as an added burden.

The great hall was the scene of a low-toned but vigorous battle. Parlan faced his mother with set face and braced torso. Garda's stance was just as firm, but while the son's expression held excitement and anticipation, the mother's was filled with anguish.

"Nay, Parlan," she said sharply. "What you ask of me is too much."

"I do not ask, Mother. 'Tis for children to seek permission."

She stared at him, stunned, and then whirled to face Dunstan who had, thus far, said nothing. Her eyes were frenzied. "This is your doing. You have made him believe he is a man grown, and now you watch idly as he denies his mother!"

"Nay, mistress, 'tis you who deny your son. Parlan is boy no longer. It is a man you see before you with a man's strength and judgment. I would willingly take the responsibility you lay on me, but it would have been so regardless."

"Through long years I have waited in fear for you to return from each foray—or for your body to be laid at my feet. Do you condemn me to do so for my only son as well?"

By this time, all had become aware of the MacAmlaid's entrance. His frown silenced them, and his slow gaze studied Parlan's broad shoulders and strong limbs before lifting to meet his clear, forthright look.

"You count yourself fully a man, Parlan?"

"Aye, my lord, by your teachings and my father's."

Laochlain nodded, keeping his smile inward. It was a wise answer. "Dunstan, I wish a further guard on the kine—they are our future. Place Parlan amongst that guard."

Dunstan laid a hand on his son's shoulder. "Come with me."

Neither dared look back at Garda who swayed wordlessly. Dara led her to a chair. "'Tis the way of men, Garda, whatever their age." But the stricken mother only shook her head, refusing to be comforted.

Their approach was too easy by far. No outlying guards challenged them as they left their boat tied at the bank of the loch and climbed the stony face of the cliff to Airdsgainne. The men-at-arms along the walls were far from Airdsgainne's best and were easily overpowered. Gallhiel's force entered the fortress with little hindrance and less bloodshed and made their way to the guardhouse. It was empty. So was the great hall. The walls there were stained with centuries-old moisture, and the rushes were strewn with filth. The gaping pit in the center of the floor smoked acridly with little flickerings of fire licking over the spitted carcass of a half-stripped boar. Fat hissed into the dying fire.

Laochlain, with Tamnais at his back, climbed the steep stairs. He wondered if he would find even womenfolk at home this night. The keep had an air and appearance of abandonment.

Cairistiona was in her chamber, surrounded by her ladies. Her carriage and shape were still youthful, and she was garbed far more regally than her surroundings, which could boast only threadbare hangings. She was no longer lovely, though it was not age that had marred her looks so much as it was the evil and hatred that peered out of silvery blue eyes and smiled with full, cruel lips. She heard Laochlain's voice calling to her, and all of the hatred within her rose up to meet him. Her answer was mocking as she denied him entrance.

As the door to her room splintered beneath powerful shoulders, she gestured her ladies away and stood alone. The door gave way almost eagerly.

As the intruders righted themselves, she sneered. "Art come to claim this pitiable keep, oh murderer of my husband?"

"Nay, I would not have taken it from Kiarr, and I will not from you. Your death will be soon enough for my possession or that of my heir."

"Then why are you so unwelcomely come?"

"To retrieve what was taken from me as ever I will, be it beast, man—or woman."

"And if I refuse?" Cairistiona made no attempt at dissembling.

"I do not grant you the choice."

Her fingers curled at her side. She longed to rake out the eyes that had looked upon her dying mate and looked on her now so confidently. How she hated him!

"My lord MacAmlaid?" The call came questioningly from the corridor.

"Here." Tamnais' voice guided.

Two men that Laochlain had set to searching the keep entered with the proof of their success. The woman's eyes were red-rimmed and the marks of the chains that had bound her were raw, angry bracelets about her wrists. She had not yielded easily to captivity, and Cairistiona had delighted in subduing her—after her men had had their fill of her. The pleasure would have been far greater if she could have seen Laochlain's countess spread-eagled and writhing as one grunting, sweating man after another had emptied himself between her pinioned legs. Far greater indeed.

The released captive ignored her tormentor. Her eyes were for the MacAmlaid. "Pray thee, m'lord, my husband and my bairn, they are safe?" There was terror in her voice.

"They are unharmed and waiting for you."

He gestured to his men, and they led her out. Laochlain once more turned his attention to Kiarr's widow. "It is well for you that she lives. My anger is less for it."

"Your anger affrights me none!"

His eyes narrowed. "You dare to be bold when you are ill-guarded. Where are your men?"

"I am left with few enough."

"But more than are here," he answered suspiciously and repeated, "Where are they? And where is Leslie?"

Cairistiona's slow smile was all the answer he needed. With his curses a terrible thing to hear, he gathered his men to him and left the keep. Cairistiona's laughter rang through the hall as she followed, exulting at the mischance that had brought him from his fastness in the same hour that her men were riding towards it.

Chapter XXIII

The brewing storm was now in full power. Rain was swept on biting winds that threatened to fling the party from the cliff to the churning waters below. The single woman in the group clinging to the mountainside showed no more fear than any of the men, for with heart and soul she strove to regain her home and daughter and husband. No force of nature would keep her from them.

The loch raged against its banks, making negotiation of its waters a dangerous and difficult task. Laochlain cursed the haste that had sent him by boat rather than circling around by horseback. Words were useless as communication, for the same wind that pelted them with icy drops whipped the sound of their voices from hearing. Before their rain-stung eyes, lightning rent a tree on the slopes above, and they watched briefly as the downpour dashed the first leaping flames.

The horses huddled by the stone bridge were a welcome sight, and they quit the boat with relief. They were landsmen all, not seamen. The lad that had kept watch over their horses greeted them with white face and faltering courage. He was soon left behind with one horse and the crofter's wife, but, leading the animal with the woman on its back, he followed hastily in their path.

The rain-slurred scene that greeted Laochlain's eyes was what he had feared. Nature's battle was little alongside that which raged on a sloping hillside. Men fought afoot and astride with dagger and claymore and battleaxe. The MacAmlaids were not yet in force because those left to defend the fortress were held there by a small band. Several bodies lay between the shielded huddle of marauders and the parapets of the fortress.

Even as Laochlain watched, men poured from the gates, outnumbering and overpowering the few who had delayed them. He turned his efforts to repelling those at hand.

His crofters had been devastated. Their gardens had been trampled purposely, much of their stock lay slaughtered. One hovel lay in ashes and another had been gutted by flames before the rains had come. The slackening of the torrent was now a further relief. The MacAmlaid's lifted voice rallied his men to greater courage and strength and gave hope to his beleaguered tenants. Wielding his blade with violent rage, he defended his own and cried vengeance for those fallen. Where he went, so went victory.

When the last of the reivers were routed, Laochlain sped towards the fortress. His pulse quickened as he recalled Dara's unaccustomed frailty of late. Dread gripped him.

He reckoned without the strength of his wife's temperament. Her fears and anxieties she channeled to useful purpose, forcing her servants to obey her willy-nilly. She ignored their terror and overrode their reluctance to stir from secure crevices. When hungry men and wounded men returned to the castle, there were hot food and healing poultices and clean bandages for their comfort.

She flew to Laochlain's side as he entered the door, and joy blazed in her at seeing him walk upright and unaided. Even in the privacy of their chamber where she bathed and tended a gash in his thigh and a long but shallow cut on his forearm, that joy did not abate. It was well hidden, however, when she spoke sharply in bidding him sit quiet beneath her attentions. Her bottom lip was caught between her teeth as she pulled shreds of leather from the wound on his leg.

Laochlain eyed her blanched countenance. "Garda could tend this, or Bretach."

"Not so carefully as I," she averred.

"I've survived years of combat and numerous wounds without your aid heretofore, my lady."

"You shall not survive this if you speak or move again, my lord!"

He snorted disdain at the threat but did not

stir or speak more until she at last wrapped a bandage snugly around his leg.

"I am not helpless, lass. I could yet punish your insolence."

His voice and face were grim, and she eyed him warily, backing away. Her answer came saucily enough, however. "You would need two sound legs to catch me, my lord."

"And if I commanded you to come to me?"

"Commands are for those who can enforce them!"

With a speed she did not expect, he lurched forward and seized her with ease, ignoring the jar to his injured thigh. No punishment was forthcoming, however. Dara's arms slipped around his neck and locked tight. She laid her head against his shoulder and sighed.

"Ah, Laochlain, I feared so for you. Do not be reckless in battle, for your death would be mine also."

Clumsily he sought to comfort her, but his reassurances could not still her inner trepidation. She could not but wonder what deity had gifted her with such treasure, and, more fearfully, what mischance might yet wrench it from her.

The summer storm had renewed itself and, with frenzied urgency, swept over the hills and dashed against the unyielding mountains. Though the crofters huddled miserably in their hovels, they preferred the violence of nature to that of man. Their losses had been extensive in beasts and crops, but they looked to the MacAmlaid to succor them.

The loss to the clan had been slight. Laochlain

sat at the head of the long table as one after another of his captains gave an accounting of his men. Neacail had lost one man, with two injured. Bretach named another dead. Dunstan had no losses but one man maimed to uselessness. One of those dead was Crieff.

There were yet no tidings of the cattle guard, and Garda waited in agony, her eyes fixed accusingly upon Dunstan. Two crofters had been slain in the fray, a woman and a brave young man, and each left a mate and young bairns.

At last Laochlain demanded an explanation. "So then, Bretach, 'twas you and your men who were to keep reivers from the valley. How did you fail?"

"Through lack of wit. A herdsman approached us with the news that the kine had been attacked. We followed to find all peaceful and none injured, though spears and arrows had been loosed upon the encampment. It took but a glance to realize our folly. We returned to the valley, but the enemy were there before us. Your anger and Gallheil's losses must lie with me. The blame is mine."

Laochlain shook his head. "You did what expedience demanded. There is no blame. We've lost men, and a number of the crofters have lost home and livelihood, but many more are untouched, those who lay out of the path of destruction. None will suffer a lack of food or shelter."

When all was done that could be, orders given for the care of his people and the bolstering of the valley's defenses, Laochlain yielded to Dara's urging and sought his bed. She would come in a while, but, for now, Garda needed her companionship. Dunstan had ridden up into the hills to ascertain for himself that the cattle and their guard had remained unmolested. Garda would not rest until Parlan's safety was assured.

"Word would have come swiftly if there had been danger," Dara comforted. "Those are good men that my lord has set to watch the beasts."

"Parlan is but a boy."

"And closely watched by his companions, I am sure. Place not so little faith in Laochlain's judgment and even in your son's ability. And in Dunstan. What father would send a boy to a man's task, knowing that boy unprepared. Nay, do not distrust them all."

"Forsooth, my lady, words of confidence come readily to a woman whose bairn is safe in her womb. When your child first begins to elude your grasp, you will speak with less certainty and far more fear."

Ignoring her bitterness and speaking honestly, Dara denied the charge. "Not if it were to their father's care that I relinquished my children. If I died in childbed, I would regret not knowing my child, but never would I doubt Laochlain's care for its future."

Garda was horrified. "Do not even hint on that possibility. No harm shall attend the birth!" Garda was less confident inwardly, for she had delivered more babes than one, and stillborn infants and fever-ridden mothers were too common by far.

Dara was calm. "I am not fearful, I merely made an example."

"An ill one!"

"Art superstitious, Garda? I have anxieties no less than any woman, but not for myself. They are all for my child and Laochlain."

"My lord MacAmlaid is without weakness."

Now it was for Dara to feel a chill, though she refused to voice it. Nor could she have in the sudden thundering that shook the great outer doors. At her sharp command, a servant rushed to open them. Two men with a third figure carried limply between stumbled through. They were surrounded by Gallhiel's guards. The men were strangers to her, but her attention focused upon the burden they held. Ignoring the strangers, she lifted her eyes to her husband's men.

"Explain."

One man stepped forward and dropped to his knee. "They came alone and begged sanctuary. They yielded their arms willingly."

"You did rightly." She glanced towards the objects of their conversation. "What need have you of sanctuary?"

Even as she spoke, they laid their burden on the rushes. The cape shielding the still form fell away with the action, and Dara flinched. Dark lashes lay against white cheeks, hiding blue-black eyes. Dark hair streamed wetly against sodden clothing.

"Our lady was thrown at the height of the storm; we hid with her until the valley was quieted. She is ill and injured, Lady Gallhiel."

"And what did she in our valley?" Dara's voice came harshly through the pressure in her constricted throat. Her eyes glittered angrily as she was answered by the cautious exchange of looks. "So, she led her men against Gallhiel, murdering and burning, and you cry mercy for her!"

"She is helpless enough now, my lady."

"From a fall? I doubt that as much as I doubt that any horse—or man—could loose her hold to rid himself of her."

Another exchange of looks. "My lady, she was weak from loss of blood when her stallion was frightened by a bolt of lightning that tore huge rocks in twain. 'Tis the loss of blood more than the fall that endangers her."

"She was wounded? How so? In bearing arms against us?" By their faces, she knew that it was so. "How dare you, then, bring her here? Gallhiel will not succor its enemy. Take her from here!"

Into the incredulous silence that followed her command came an unexpected countermand.

"Hold."

Dara whirled to see Laochlain at the head of the stairs, dressed only in his breeks. The servant who had wakened him, fearing danger to his lady, hovered in the shadows of the upper hall.

Laochlain came down to them swiftly and directed his questions to Leslie's men. "She looks more corpse than aught else. Are you certain your lady lives?"

"She does, my lord, but she would die long before we could reach Airdsgainne."

"And if she is tended here?"

"Lady Leslie is strong of body and will. She would survive."

Dara stared at Laochlain. "You will surely not

have her within these walls. Remember her treachery—and her father's."

He frowned. "I do not forget, but she is helpless as she is."

"But she will recover, and she is capable of great evil. Do not think yourself infallible. Will you place us all in jeopardy for pride's sake?"

Laochlain eyed her coldly, angry that she should question him in front of his men. "The decision is made. Leslie will remain—but alone. Her men will return to Airdsgainne with my assurances of her safety."

And what assurances have we of ours? Dara longed to fling the words at him, but she dared not.

Instead, angry and humiliated, she held her tongue and swept him a low, mockingly servile curtsey. Under his gathering scowl, she made her way up the stairs, cursing the moment she had first encountered this family of stubborn Scots. Who but a man, a MacAmlaid, insufferable and self-assured, would clasp a traitor to the heart of his keep? She scarcely dared believe he did not mean to shelter Leslie's retainers as well. What fools were men!

Laochlain felt the prick of anger but did not build upon it. He loved Dara as much as a man could love a maid, but none save he ruled Gallhiel. Mayhap he had been overlenient with her, but theirs had been such a stormy union throughout that he had hoped to ease the pain she had felt at losing all ties with England and her brother. In recalling the past, he softened somewhat, but he left her to her sulks while he directed a young kinswoman to the care of Leslie. Ailis was a fair girl and not yet mated. He had thought to make a match between her and Crieff, but he would have to seek elsewhere for her settlement now. She was an obedient lass and reliable, and Leslie would fare well in her care.

Laochlain relented, but Dara did not. Rather she bolstered her anger through the long day in dreary, self-imposed solitude. Her wrath grew apace with the time she had to dwell on the reason for it. When at last Laochlain retired, she needed no more than his light rebuke over her failure to eat to send her into a rage.

"What care you, my lord, should I eat or starve when your fair cousin is like to slit my throat as I lie sleeping? What matter, then, if my belly be full or empty?"

His little patience vanished completely as he surveyed her sparkling eyes and flushed cheeks. She stood before him with fists on her hips and chin thrust mulishly foward. There was defiance in every inch of her.

"Allow me wits to protect my own, Dara, and the power to punish those who defy me! I will not have my word questioned by you or any other!"

"Aye, then! Class me with servants and guards and humble relations. You care no more for me than that!"

"I care so for you that I show restraint in your handling," he gritted. "I care so for you that I will not banish you from my chamber to await my pleasure in some less pleasant surroundings."

"Banish me! Nay, then, there is no need. 'Tis your pleasure that must await me!"

With a swirl of skirts, she left the room, letting the door fly with thunderous punctuation to her exit. He started forward, planning instant discipline, when he was recalled of her situation. Snarling, he sat on the bed and removed his boots with vicious grunts. Without removing his breeks, he stretched upon the bed and consigned his disobedient wife to the devil.

Chapter XXIV

If Laochlain chafed at the distance their disagreement set between them, he was yet content to leave the cause of their contention bide within his reach. Though Ailis declared her recovered and Garda concurred, he did not bid her go, nor did it seem that she desired it, though she was bidden to keep to her room. A guard was not placed at her door, for even did she wander freely about the castle there was little harm she, a lone girl among his people, could do. Confining her to her room was for Dara's peace of mind, not for his.

Since the night of the storm, Cairistiona had held her hand, nor, he was certain, would she attack the valley or fortress again until her daughter was returned to her. He was not disturbed, even, that Leslie's men refused to depart but camped stoically just outside the gate. They hindered no one and made no trouble. When questioned, they replied that they did not leave their mistress.

His feelings towards Dara were complex. His own loneliness coupled with her bitter silence fed his anger, but he could not bring himself to chasten her. She looked less well with each passing day, for constant and unalleviated resentment must take its toll. When at last he confronted her, difficult because she slept and even ate apart from him, he met with no success.

Chancing to be leaving his chamber as she passed in the corridor, he laid his hand on her arm. She shook it off but did not move away. There was a long, uncomfortable silence before he spoke.

"Lass," he began haltingly, "you are foolish to punish us both. Your fears will come to naught. Leslie has done us no harm nor will she."

It was not a speech apt to please her. Perhaps if he had expressed his longing for her or the pleasure the sight of her, graceful and growing with his child, gave to him, her reaction might have been a relenting one. To take her to task was the worst he could have done. Not even anger and shouting on his part would have brought all her resentments to the fore as did this gentle chiding as if she were a child.

"You are a witless, suckling babe if you think Cairistiona or her wanton daughter are done with us. Art blind that you do not realize it? You call me fool because I am wary, but I do not forget whose blade slew Kiarr."

"A fortnight is gone, and Cairistiona is quiet. I realize her men will come again and at her command, but it will not be while Leslie's life is in my hands. I do not trust my aunt, but I know her. They three were like vicious beasts, a den of wolves, but their loyalties are human. Kiarr's death but strengthened that loyalty between the two who remain."

Dara's face was without color save for that of her eyes. Her hands trembled at her side, no longer in anger but in fear. Laying her pride aside, she pled with him.

"Laochlain, it is not for myself that I am fighting but for you and our child. Truly you do not see how totally evil a woman can be, nor how devious. You look for honor and loyalty where none abide. Mother and daughter would each destroy the other if doing so would destroy you. Close your mind to your pride and heed me—I beg you!"

She knew final defeat when he shook his head. "Can you not trust me now as you have been wont to do?"

"Not while vainglory blinds you to the danger I fear," she replied quietly, despairingly.

He did not try to stop her as she moved away. She longed for him to call her name and give her reason to turn back. Pride was both their enemies.

On the first morning of August, before dawn had gained dominance over the sky, Leslie rose from her narrow bed and dressed in total darkness. It was no new skill for her and was swiftly accomplished. None of her belongings had been removed, neither her clothing nor her boots with the sharply honed dirk concealed in the soft leather of one of them. She tucked the dirk into her waistband where the handle nudged her breast with welcome familiarity. She ran her hand over the edge of her washstand. Sixteen notches cut into the smooth wood. Sixteen days. It was time.

The servants had risen and removed their pallets from the floor of the hall. They stared curiously as Leslie trod amongst them, but none dared speak to her or attempt to stay her until Ailis met her near the door.

"Where do you go?"

Leslie's eyes narrowed. "I am recovered. My men await me."

"You were recovered long since and bided till now. Why?"

"It pleased me," Leslie snarled. "Now it pleases me to go."

She pushed past the girl roughly and gained the door. The courtyard was still in predawn darkness.

Ailis wasted precious moments in staring at the door, wondering if she should risk the Mac-Amlaid's wrath in awakening him or if that wrath would be greater if he did not. She wasted another precious few in standing outside his door, her hand raised to knock but her mind still undecided. He had been ill of mood and short of temper since the Lady Dara had taken a room apart from him.

By the time Laochlain at last heard her tidings, Leslie had reached the gate. The guard eyed her warily but admiringly as she swayed forward to stand before him.

"I wish to rejoin my men and depart."

"Has the MacAmlaid permitted it?"

"Has he forbidden it?" she countered.

The guard looked dubious. "No, Lady Leslie, but . . ."

Whatever his thoughts, they were forever silenced as a cry was raised from beyond the gate and answered with savage joy by Leslie. The guard whirled to give warning, and Leslie's dirk slid beneath his light mail. It found its mark, and blood spurted darkly. The indrawn breath that would have lifted his voice to his fellows was expelled in a death sigh.

Leslie strained to unbolt the gate, hearing shouts from behind her. She succeeded as the first man drew near. The forces of Airdsgainne and Gallhiel met under the arches, and Leslie slipped away unscathed.

Dara's window, open to the summer's warm, fresh air, caught also the first sounds of the disturbance. She fled into the corridor and Laochlain's path. He gripped her arm.

"Stay within your chamber and bar the door until my return."

She stared at him for one brief moment before saying flatly, " 'Tis Leslie's doing, is it not? Leslie, to whom you gave aid and shelter."

He turned away without waiting to see her safe, and her accusation hung on the sounds of men fighting and men dying.

The heat of battle soon drove away all considerations save survival and success. His battleaxe slashed, struck flesh and bone, was withdrawn and slashed again. The enemy fell away beneath his furious attack. When he found himself separated and fighting more men than caution advised, his call brought his men running to back him. He did not escape unscathed, but his wounds were superficial ones. Wresting his blade from a fallen opponent, he glanced around to see where the need was greatest. His gaze encountered a sight to induce terror.

Tamnais alone, one arm pressed uselessly to his side, held the stairs against three who would press above. Dara poised at the landing above, her hand gripping the cornerstone, her eyes searching the fury for Laochlain. He gained Tamnais' side, and there was no time or breath for bidding her to seek safety. Forgetting all but the enemy, he beat them back with Tamnais' awkward aid. When a space presented itself, he leapt clear, intending to drag Dara forcibly to her chamber.

Anger and fear gripped him. She was no longer frozen into immobility. She had begun to descend the stairs, a torch seized from the wall gripped menacingly in one hand, the weapon she would bring to her lord's aid.

"Stay, Dara!"

His call startled her for her mind was intent on anger and hatred for the intruders who threatened her husband. She faltered, lost her balance and fell.

It seemed to Laochlain an agonizing eternity before he reached her, halted her torturous descent. He lifted her awkwardly sprawled body

326

and carried her back up the stairs.

Garda and Ailis, huddled in the hallway, followed him to his chamber and watched as he placed her carefully on the bed. They did not speak to him as he left the room, for his face had the look of one demented.

The fearlessness and apparent invincibility of the Earl of Gallhiel in that battle was captured in song and legend to be sung and retold through countless generations of MacAmlaids. So also was his harsh justice. 'Twas Cairistiona who led her men in attack on Gallhiel, and 'twas Cairistiona who urged them on when they would have faltered.

She knew no fear until a dark form towered above her, shadowing her. Then she knew terror, but it was brief. Her fear, her breath, her life were inexorably squeezed from her by merciless black-gauntleted fists. When at last Laochlain looked on her distorted, lifeless face, he felt no pity, but his rage died with her.

It was a sad count taken when the battle was done. Few enough of Airdsgainne's men lived to flee the castle, but Gallhiel's losses were also great. The toll was twenty-odd men, two wenches—and the tiny infant that was to have been Gallhiel's heir.

Laochlain heard Garda's words at the door of his chamber, saw her pitying look. His mind burned, but his face was expressionless.

"Dara?"

Garda wanted to weep at his flat tone, recalling Dara's struggle to keep the child, her anguish when the pains ripped it from her.

"She will recover, even inwardly, if you go to her now and comfort her. She has need of you."

"Had she obeyed me there would be no need of comfort for either of us. I have nothing for her." He was unaware of the irony of fears allayed, then turned to rage by his relief.

Through the opened door, Dara heard his words and his tone and turned her face towards the wall.

She slept, and she dreamed. Beauty turned to horror, and sweet dreams to nightmares. She woke to the soothing ministrations of gentle hands, was comforted by a calm voice, and slept again. Through it all, through pain and fever and desolation, she knew that he did not come. Garda fed her, bathed her, changed her linens, but there were no strong arms to hold her, no unfailing strength to sustain her.

On the second morning, she woke clear-eyed and met Garda's compassionate gaze.

"You will grow stronger, now. The worst is past."

Dara nodded listlessly, her fingers twisting and untwisting the edge of her sheet. "My son . . . was he buried?"

"By his father's own hands."

Remembering his words through a haze, Dara was silent.

"He allowed no one to help him or even to go with him."

"The MacAmlaid seeks no comfort and gives none," Dara answered bitterly.

"He grieves, Dara."

"As do I!"

Fearing the effect of Dara's agitation on her recovery, Garda merely nodded as she prepared another soothing mixture of herbs. It was this that had given Dara the healing sleep, but now she refused it.

"Nay, sleep will not return my son to me."

"It will give a measure of time for your recovery," Garda urged.

Dara paled. "Was the damage such that I will bear no more children?"

"Nay, I referred to a different manner of recovery. There was no damage to you or even the bairn. He would have lived could he have drawn breath, but his body was too tiny. He never did."

Dara knew he had not, for she had seen Garda holding her son, sobbing aloud as his tiny body turned blue and his struggle for life slowly ceased. Pain assailed her at the memory, pain such as no woman should be made to bear.

"I am not unmindful of my debt to you, Garda, but I have no more need of nursing. I do have need of solitude. My heart will heal less quickly than my body."

She would have taken solace of her husband, but what he denied her, she would not seek of others.

Glancing back from the doorway, Garda saw that she had averted her face and was staring through the opened window. The morning beyond was cruelly clear and glorious in the sun's golden warmth.

Laochlain was seated at the table in the great hall. His clothes were battle-torn and blood-

stained, the same he had worn two days past. He
had not bathed, nor had his several wounds been
tended. Luckily, they were without depth and
had crusted over of themselves. A goblet stood at
his elbow, filled with the last yieldings of a keg
he had tossed heedlessly to the rushes at his feet.
The servants avoided the hall and his temper.
Garda did not.

She chose a seat opposite him and studied his
drawn, haggard face and his eyes, blurred with
drink and exhaustion.

"Have you eaten?"

He looked at her blankly, and then a hard light
of suspicion dawned in his eyes. "Are you come
to chastise me on my neglect of Dara?"

"No."

"Will you not belittle my cruelty, scorn my
need for drink?" he pressed still, half-angry.
When she merely shook her head, he slumped.
"Then you are the only one who does not."

"And are you not the worst of those who do?"

"Aye," he acknowledged grimly. "For I might
have killed her with my pride. I could not admit
the truth of her arguments."

She bit her tongue against words of commiseration, he would not welcome them. She stood. "I
will fetch something that will sit lightly on your
stomach, and then I will have a bath poured for
you."

"Not in my chamber," he requested wearily.

"No," she agreed. "Not there."

He ate, but did not taste, bathed, but found no
relaxation to wearied muscles. Fresh clothes
were brought him, and he donned them. With-

out grumbling, he allowed himself to be shaved and his hair to be trimmed, but when all was done, he sent the servants from the room. Dara awaited him, and he knew not what to say to her.

Words were not given him by his first look into her face. It was closed and wary, her eyes without trust. He was somewhat surprised to find her gowned and seated in a chair. The cost of the effort she carefully hid from his gaze as he entered the room and sat near her.

Speech between them was slow and difficult. Laochlain enquired of her health and did not doubt her quiet lie that she was entirely well, for, seated as she was, her weakness was not apparent and nervousness had given abnormal color to her pallor.

"I feared I had lost you, lass," he said at last.

"Perhaps you would have preferred the loss."

"No."

Her lips twisted disbelievingly. "Though I murdered your son?"

"Dara," he began hesitantly, "my words were not meant for you to hear. I was fair out of my head. I feared damnably for you, and when I found you were safe, I found, also, that our child would never live. I did not realize how much I had anticipated the bairn's coming."

"Until my disobedience destroyed it all," she finished, throwing his words back at him.

He stared at her in silence, not knowing how to explain his sudden, unreasonable, unlasting rage against her.

She took his silence for accusation and retaliated. "What of your blame, my lord? I did not open this fortress to the enemy. 'Twas you who bade Leslie enter and then left her free to do her worst, and that worst cost me my child! Do you think you grieve?'' she spat. "I grieve! I, who carried the bairn, felt his movements within me, felt it wrenched from my womb, because, foolishly, I feared for you and looked to aid you. I shall carry my guilt through all this life, but yours I will not bear!" She ended on a sob and clenched her eyes against the tears that would undermine her control.

This was not what she desired. She wanted Laochlain's arms about her, her head against his breast. She wanted to give solace and to receive it, not fling accusations at him. She opened her eyes, thinking to start anew.

It was too late. He had gone, and she was alone.

Chapter XXV

A brisk wind rustled through the tall, sun-
dried grasses and the young mare sidestepped nervously, tossing her head. Dara
tucked the reins a bit to control her and laughed
softly at the display of pretended fear. It was her
first laughter in many long weeks.

She lifted her eyes to the harvesters busy on
the next rise. The early weeks of September had
produced a sky of unclouded saffron, but now
the increasing heaviness presaged disaster if the
crops were not swiftly gathered. Too frequently
the merciless gales of autumn destroyed the
yield of long labor, that which was to be the
succor of winter months. Through steady vigilance, the MacAmlaid had kept the valley safe
from raiding clans, but that same vigilance
could not be applied to nature. It was the

harvesters' turn to cheat the foe.

September now. Soon October. A year of fleeting joy and lingering pain come full circle. So, too, had her relationship with Laochlain. They were strangers again, but too aware of one another to be indifferent.

She had left the castle before dawn, fleeing a night riddled with troubled dreams and long periods of wakefulness. By midday, hunger forced her return. A stableboy met her in the courtyard and grasped the reins she flung to him while his superior made a cup of his hands for her feet as she dismounted.

"Did my lady enjoy her ride?"

Dara rewarded his anxious inquiry with an assuring smile. "Indeed, but mind her feet. I fear she is near to losing a shoe."

"Aye, my lady, I'll see to it myself."

Her step slowed as she neared the hall doors, but her chin remained lifted and her shoulders straight.

Laochlain was in the hall with Bretach and Neacail and a stranger. Dara was curious and oddly, unexplainably apprehensive, but she was aware that Laochlain had ceased speaking as she entered and that his eyes followed her. She did not pause, but went immediately to her room.

Breakfast as well as dinner had passed without her, but at her entrance one maidservant followed her up to her room to pour a can of hot water into her laver, and another entered soon after with food ample for several persons. As she ate, she put Laochlain and the stranger from her mind and concentrated, instead, on the length of fine arras covering the tapestry frame. During her days of apathy, when she could be induced to take interest in very little, Garda had produced the heavy woven cloth and a suggestion as to its use.

Brilliant threads depicted the initial scene that was near completion. A longship of detailed splendor breasted the seas in proud paganism as it neared a rugged shore where waves splashed against boulders and sprayed upward in foaming white. The oars of the ship were lifted in preparation of beaching. One man stood at the prow, and his handsome, imperious stance left no doubt as to his identity. His likeness was patterned after his descendant. She planned other scenes. The slaying of the first lord of Gallhiel. The taking of his daughter in marriage. The final scene would be the Norseman's leaving, his eldest son at his side and, watching from the shore, his lady and second son, from whom the line of MacAmlaid chiefs had descended.

Her concentration was broken by a knock upon her door. Before she could answer, the door opened and Laochlain entered. She stood, filled with tingling anticipation. This was his chamber, but he had not set foot inside its door since the night of Cairistiona's death and defeat, the night their son was lost. She wondered if his presence here had aught to do with the stranger.

He gestured towards the table. "Continue. I do not wish to disturb you."

His tone was chill and distant, and Dara answered in kind. "I am finished. Did you wish something of me?"

"Are you strong enough for rides that encompass all the morning hours?" he asked unexpectedly.

She could have smiled. He was aware of her movements and not so indifferent as she feared.

"Quite strong enough, I assure you."

"I would prefer you rode with a groom."

"I prefer to ride alone."

She chided herself for the disappointment she felt when he did not press his concern. He was glancing about as if seeking further reason for conversation when his gaze lit on the tapestry.

"This is how you spend your hours? I had wondered what kept you closeted here for such lengths of time."

"Would that I could spend them tending my son." Her voice was brittle, her manner defensive.

He regarded her with narrowed eyes. "No more than I."

There seemed to her a challenge in that, for their last, bitter argument still rankled, unforgiven. She realized she was trembling, and tears blurred her vision. Hateful weakness! She whirled so that he saw only her rigid back and slightly bowed head. "Please," she pled, "please leave me now."

The long quiet was deadly. "Aye," came the slow, considering reply. "I will leave you. Have a care, my lady, that you do not regret your request."

When she heard the door thunder shut behind her, she sank to the floor and wept, but her tears were not from the anger that had swept her so briefly. She wept in pain for the all-consuming love that burned more fiercely than ever for this man, this stranger who was her husband. When exhaustion overtook her, she slept, still crumpled upon the floor.

Hours later, she dressed in hard-won composure. With an ungiving, analytical scrutiny, she studied her reflection in the mirror. She had lost the pallor of her illness, and her hair had regained its luster. Her gown molded a body as slenderly promising as ever, though perhaps with hollower curves now. She no longer had the look of reckless innocence that she had had when first Laochlain met her, but surely she was no less comely. Mayhap, though, she had lost the power to move him with her lost naivety. Her chin came up. If she was no longer possessed of the artless youth of a year ago, it was also true that she was a woman of greater resolution than many a man had known.

She left her chamber with these thoughts foremost in her mind. Garda was in the hallway ahead of her, and Dara bade her wait.

Garda smiled as she approached. "Good evening, Dara. You look more rested than when I saw you this morn."

"I slept after midday," Dara replied. "There was a man with Laochlain when I returned from my ride. He was unknown to me. Who is he, and what does he here?"

"Why, 'tis a royal messenger—from James. I do not know why he is come nor what message he bears." They moved on towards the stairs, Garda matching her steps to Dara's as she continued, "No doubt we will soon learn why he is here."

"It may be that his tidings are brought in confidence."

" 'Twould take much to keep aught secret in this keep."

Dara's first glimpse of Laochlain, already at table as were most of the household, brought a familiar pang. She had to suppress a desire to touch the dark, springy hair curled against his neck as she passed behind him. She took her place, and all conversation lulled as the piper began to play. After he had gone, Dara had missed Banain, the minstrel, but in a transition that had taken her unaware, the bagpipes had come to be a sound of beauty to her ears.

As she ate, a plan came to her, a plan that would not be dismissed though it risked much. Mayhap it would regain for her all that she had lost, but mayhap it would leave her with nothing. She bided her time through the dining and drinking and dicing, saying little but listening much. When the hour was late and much of the keep abed, she again left her room. She had not disrobed, but her hair fell heavily to her waist.

The hall torches were extinguished, and the candle she carried did no more than threaten, without result, the black veil of night. Laochlain opened his door quickly at her knock. His room was well lit, and a chair, pushed back from the table, awaited his return. It was not accounts nor correspondence which kept him so late. The small table was bare save for a slim, elegantly bound volume of poetry. A bed and a washstand comprised the remainder of the furnishings. It might have been a servant's cheerless quarters. Certainly it was not fitted to the Chief of the MacAmlaids.

He was looking down at her, frowning slightly. She forced her eyes to meet his.

"Must I stand in your doorway, my lord?"

He stepped aside, and she entered with pounding heart. It was difficult for her to begin, and she feared she did so badly.

"I could not but hear at the table that James will wed Margaret of England by proxy this January to come. The Earl of Bothwell is to be his proxy?"

Laochlain nodded. "That is what has been arranged."

He seemed suddenly much too near. She crossed to the open window, more to place a distance between them than to breathe of the fresh night air that entered on a breeze. She turned her back to it. Watching his face, she gave him the means whereby he might be free of her or, as she prayed, might be made to realize his need of her.

"I have thought often of Chilton these past weeks, of Brann. I would heal the breach between us."

"You think it possible? I remember your parting."

"If I could see him, all would be well. I know it." His frown had deepened to a scowl, and something akin a growl forced its way from his chest, but she plunged ahead. "There is peace along the borders now, and Gallhiel is no longer so threatened that an escort could not be spared me. I would require only Ailis to tend me. Your comfort would not be disturbed. I would go now—before the winter storms begin."

"You shall not go now or ever," he ground out. "Do you think you would be allowed to return? Your brother is my enemy still. Or perhaps it is this you seek?"

She did not deny his accusation. "Would you be so distressed at my loss?"

"You are the wife of a MacAmlaid chief. They are not easily relinquished." His eyes were like the loch, flat, icy grey. "If you desire only to escape my presence, be easy. I will yield to James' urging and join his winter court at Edinburgh. There are to be great festivities honoring his marriage." He paused. "You need not fear my return before spring."

Dara was stunned. She had had the reaction she desired but not the consequences. Far from forcing him to acknowledge his feelings for her, she had driven a further wedge between them. She gathered the support of her pride and curtsied briefly.

"I will bid you good night, then, my lord, for I fear we have no more to say to each other. Please do not delay for my sake. I wish you safe journey."

Dara had cause to regret those prideful words, for morning dawned on the preparations for his going, and by midday he was gone—and with no further farewell sought from her.

The days seemed slower to pass after that for they were not marked by his coming and going.

The hours stretched endlessly through daylight and dark, unbroken by any excitement and little pleasure. Dara did not pine, she was too strong, too filled with the spirit of the Rylands for that kind of weakness, but she did suffer.

It was the busy harvest season that lent its aid. She worked long with her household as the rents of the crofters were brought in kind. There were vegetables and fruits to be sorted, perhaps dried, and stored. Some fruits were preserved with sugar or syrup. There was a constant need for barley, which was most carefully hoarded. She even oversaw the garnering of fodder for the beasts and the curing of beef and mutton and fish from the loch. The sight of her, skirts kilted up out of the way, astride Haefen or the younger, less tractable mare she often rode, soon became an accustomed one.

She might be found anywhere by day, kitchens, cellars, buttery, brewery, bakehouse, or field. By night, she kept to her rooms and worked upon her tapestry. Only those who cared particularly for her knew there was pain beneath her industry, and when they dared speak of it, she shrank within herself.

For days Garda refrained from comment, but there came a time when she could no longer. She had brought a tray to Dara's room, for Dara had been away from the keep at mealtime as she often was. Her lips were pursed disapprovingly as she entered to find her lady bent over a ledger of accounts.

"Dara," she began in a tone that was a warning of her mood, "there will be little gained if

Laochlain returns to find you a frame of bones. The press of harvesting is past now. There is no need for you to continue at such a pace. And, even so, Gallhiel has more than enough servants to deal with the tasks you take upon yourself."

"Work eases my restlessness."

"And your hunger, too, it would seem," Garda returned sharply, indicating the tray barely touched. "What good can come of neglecting yourself?"

"I do not do so intentionally." Dara surveyed her hands ruefully, short, rough nails, skin no longer smooth and white. "Has the rest of my appearance fared as ill?"

Dunstan's judicious wife surveyed her countess. Her gown was becoming but well worn, and her hair was confined to a careless knot at the nape of her neck. These things, however, were scarce to be noticed alongside bright, lively eyes and cheeks chafed by the wind to a lingering rose. "You are as lovely as ever," she finally answered truthfully, "but 'tis apparent you care little for that."

"What need?" was the short reply.

"Will you leave him go so easily?"

Dara stared at her almost angrily. "What choice have I? He is gone."

Garda gave her a curious, probing look. "When were you ever one to accept defeat? And with so little attempt to gain victory? He is gone, aye, but not lost. Not while you have your beauty and your wits and your will."

No more was said, but that brief conversation lay at the surface of Dara's mind, far from forgotten. And in the beauty of a crisp October morn, the day upon which, a year earlier, she had first seen the MacAmlaid of Athdair, it reaped the harvest that Garda had desired. Nay! She would not be so easily defeated. Laochlain would not find her so willing to be thrust aside!

Her preparations were hasty, but careful. That very eve she gathered the mainstay of Gallhiel's defenses in the great hall. A fire, one of the first of the season, was a glowing background for the scene.

Dara's glance encompassed them all before she began. "It is my intention to follow my husband to Edinburgh. I realize he placed every faith in your obedience and ability to follow his wishes, and I do the same. However, before I could leave with ease of mind, I must be certain that all will be well until his return. Tamnais," she captured his gaze firmly, ignoring his evident disapproval, "are your men satisfied, without complaint of any kind?"

"They best be," he retorted, "I'll have no malcontents."

"Very well," she said calmly. "Neacail, you are factor here, but I know as well as you that the land and the people are secure in their provisions for the winter. I am, however, uncertain as to the disposition of the cattle. Are any to be sold this year?"

"Nay, they have been brought from the hills and are safe until spring. A year hence, in the fall, they will be driven south to the markets."

Dara came now to the greatest threat Gallhiel had known, one she feared still. "All is well within, but Kiarr's daughter still broods upon her mountain. Her sire and her mother were slain by your lord. 'Tis necessary to know if she plots further evil. Dunstan, you must determine the best means of discovering this."

He nodded, and she spoke the conclusion of her thoughts. "If she gives us no need to fear, then I will leave in four days. I wish you to accompany me, Neacail, with four men of your choosing."

"My lady, four guards will scarcely be sufficient," he protested. "You will make your own protection an impossibility."

Dara shook her head. "There will be little enough to protect. I shall take only Ailis to attend me, and one beast will be sufficient to carry my baggage. We shall not form an impressive entourage, but a swift one."

And an unsuitable one for a countess, she knew most of them would be thinking. It was Garda who protested the arrangements as she and Dara and Ailis sat at the tapestry, sewing and planning.

"I doubt not that four men will be ample protection, for Neacail will choose wisely, but a single beast of burden cannot possibly carry all that will be necessary for a court season!"

"I am not overburdened with possessions. Of jewelry, I have only the chain of pearls Laochlain gave to me on our wedding day and my ring, and my gowns are few that would be presentable in fine company."

"We have cloths to contrive more."

Dara shook her head stubbornly. "Even were I

inclined to delay for their making, I will not go among the fine ladies of King James' court and find myself clothed out of fashion. I will be dressed in Edinburgh, and my lord will find my tastes quite extravagant!''

They laughed together at the thought, and no more arguments were put forth.

With a reason for renewed hope, Dara regained her peace of mind. She no longer felt driven to seek that peace in exhaustion. Her appetite returned with startling rapidity, and that night she slept without waking at every hour that passed. Nor did she feel the need for constant labor. The next morning found her playing contentedly with Mairi in the salon.

Neacail sought audience with her there, and his tidings were wholly unexpected.

"My lady, you've no need to fear further. Lady Leslie can do no more harm. She is quite mad.''

"Mad?'' Dara repeated disbelievingly. "Are you certain?''

"Dunstan and I have seen her. Her men have deserted her save for a loyal few. Her women are with her still, but she knows none of them. She wanders the fortress, at times raving without meaning, at others conversing with those slain. Her servants dare not let her leave the walls of Airdsgainne for fear she will come to harm.''

Dara was silent, trying to imagine that loveliness destroyed by insanity. Dark blue eyes staring out from a tortured mind, that strong, young body never to know the joy of a husband and babies. The thought came to her that Leslie's insanity had begun years ago and found its outlet with her loss. Dara shuddered and was recalled to Neacail only by his speaking again.

"I have made every preparation possible for your comfort, my lady, but it shall be far from that, I fear. If we travel so lightly escorted, we must avoid the main roads, for they are the territory of thieves. Laochlain would have my soul if I allowed aught to befall you."

"Nothing shall." She smiled suddenly, brilliantly. " 'Tis well, however, that you do not seek to dissuade me."

His grin was wry as he admitted, "I'd not even try."

Nor did anyone else, and on the day and in the manner she had chosen, they left Gallhiel. It was a grey dawning with the brilliance of autumn blurred to winter's beginning. They were warmly dressed but without any of the richness that would have been an attraction for brigands. Ailis rode Haefen for she was not an accomplished rider, and the mare, grey as the sky, was to be trusted in any circumstances. Dara rode the mettlesome bay filly she favored of late.

Neacail led the way, with his men at the sides and rear of the group. In the center rode Dara, Ailis, and a boy approaching maturity who would tend the horses and perform menial tasks. The sturdy horse that carried the baggage was tied to his saddle.

The roads they traveled were little more than rutted trails, and the waters they crossed were seldom bridged. Sometimes there were ferries of dubious safety to take them across, but much more frequently they forded on horseback. Fortunately, the burns and rivers were not rain-swollen, and at times they were able to cross without getting wet at all.

Dara found that Neacail had indeed planned carefully for her comfort. The days were broken by meals taken in agreeable taverns in burghs along the way, and they slept snugly at night in lodgings bespoke by the man Neacail had sent ahead. Dara never met their forerunner, but she had reason to be grateful to him. He executed his commission thoroughly.

They did not pass every night at taverns. Twice they stayed with kin of the MacAmlaid in manor houses that Neacail informed her were properties of her husband and whose rents helped fill his coffers. Their journey was delayed at one of these holdings by a gale that raged with icy fury for two days. Dara found her surroundings satisfactory but was disconcerted by her hosts' manner. They were unresponsive without being openly surly, nor was it her imagination. Ailis commented on it, and Neacail was as glad as they to depart. He promised himself that Laochlain would hear of the grudgingness of their hospitality to his lady—his English lady. It might well be that they would soon find themselves in no position to dispense of even the meanest hospitality, abiding in no place fitting for travelers to seek it!

Edinburgh received them with icy dampness. A seeping fog veiled stars and earth, masking the city's perpetual filth. Dara clung to her saddle, fighting cold and exhaustion for they had ridden since dawn. As the sun had begun to lower,

Neacail had put it to her whether they should stop for the night or press on. She could not bear the thought of delaying when another few hours would see her with Laochlain.

She could see little of the city and gained only an impression of tall, narrow houses of stone. The meaner sections were distinguishable by the foul odor of middens and slops. Near Castle Hill, in the finer residences, shutters withheld the golden light of tapers and torches but could not entirely muffle the sounds of merriment that poured forth when a door opened to emit an elegant guest. On these fashionable streets, lords and ladies traveled to and fro, well guarded by burly henchmen. The night was young and lively, but Dara felt as if dawn should be breaking, so weary was she.

If possible, Neacail was even more anxious than she to reach Edinburgh Castle. He was not particularly weary, nor did the cold bother him, but the responsibility of his lady's safety was a heavy burden. As long as they traveled country paths through woods and meadow, hill and moor, he had felt fully confident. It was around the habitat of men that brigands did abound.

Dara spoke once to Ailis as they started up the esplanade to the castle. There was a moment's silence, and then Neacail's deep voice answered.

"She is asleep."

Dara was startled by a hint of tenderness in his voice. Had she truly been so blind, or was she now imagining things? She stared through the fog. Nay. There was Neacail at Ailis' side, his broad shoulder supporting her as she slept.

Their entrance to the castle was a confusion of challenge, answer, and admission. The royal steward arrived and displayed every respect due the wife of one of the king's most loyal and favored earls.

Dara requested that she be shown to the chamber allotted her husband, though she was informed the court was still attendant upon his royal majesty at table. "I do not desire that my husband be informed of my arrival," was her last instruction before she was left with Neacail and Ailis in Laochlain's apartments.

She felt a sudden apprehension and quickly thrust it from her. "Neacail, what arrangements will be made for your comfort? Ailis will remain here with me, but . . ."

"Be easy, my lady. I will do well enough. I'm no stranger to the castle." He shrugged inwardly at the knowledge of a pallet on a cold, hard floor with snoring, loutish servants for bedmates.

Dara saw the way in which his eyes strayed to Ailis as he spoke, and, with a murmur of weariness, she withdrew from the anteroom to the bedchamber beyond. Let them have their moment of privacy. If Laochlain did not approve the match, they would have little enough time together.

It was a brief interlude. Ailis joined her swiftly, her eyes bright and her skin flushed with the look of one kissed and embraced.

Dara bathed in the cold water upon the washstand, refusing Ailis' desire to harry the castle servants to her attendance. "I would be asleep before you could return," she said honestly. "If

you will but comb the tangles from my hair, I
will require nothing more."

The slow pull of the brush through her curls
was soothing, and when Ailis was done, she did
no more than remove her gown and slip beneath
the heavy bedclothes. The room was agreeably
warmed by a fire blazing in the ample hearth.
Her eyelids drooped, and she was scarcely aware
of Ailis straightening her discarded gown and
snuffing the tapers. She was asleep before Ailis
left the room.

Chapter XXVI

Laochlain should have been warned by the absence of light in his chamber. The candelabra were always left burning for his return. Unfortunately, his attention had already been claimed by the willing beauty in his arms. If he thought at all about the darkness as they entered, it was with a resigned shrug for the laxness of the castle servants. He was not drunk, but the wine he had consumed coursed warmly through his veins, and it was that which had ignited the fire he had long held in control. In truth, no woman had held any lasting allure for him as long as Dara's image was vivid—and taunting—in his mind.

This night he had firmly set all thought of her from him, determined to allow the Lady Liane her seduction. Wife of the French ambassador,

she had made it plain from the moment she was
first introduced to the grim, handsome Highland
lord that she must have him. Tonight, she was
sure, ambition would be fulfilled.

Unfortunately, her soft giggles as he drew her
through the shadowed anteroom into his chamber, lit only by the low-burning fire, were con-
trasting unpleasantly with his memories of Dara.
He felt a strong regret for what he had begun
and an equally strong urge to end it prematurely.

It was as he neared the hearth to stir the fire to
fresh life that his senses alerted him. He felt a
prickle along his spine and turned slowly towards the bed. Even before he saw her, he heard
her voice, splintered ice ripping the silence.

"How delightful. Must I leave your bed so that
your whore may serve you?" She paid no attention whatsoever to the outraged gasp of his
companion, but she had a burning impression of
honey blond hair, heavy perfume, and a shock-
ingly low-cut gown.

Laochlain stepped swiftly between them, for
the Lady Liane looked poised to strike. She was
no gentlewoman despite her breeding, and it
was her fire, akin to Dara's, that had first attracted him. That and her obvious desire for
him. He addressed her lightly. "I regret, love,
that you must seek your own bed this night. My
time looks to be wholly engaged."

Her eyes flashed across his shoulder to Dara
and swept over her insultingly. "Do you really
think so?" It was Dara's turn to gasp angrily, but
Lady Liane merely shrugged. "Ah, very well,
there will be other nights."

His gaze followed her swaying walk to the doorway where it encountered Ailis' shocked and disgusted face. She sidestepped with a contemptuous movement to allow the French woman to pass.

"Leave us, Ailis, your mistress will not need you further this night."

"Stay, Ailis!" Dara contradicted him imperiously.

Laochlain smiled grimly and moved towards the door. Ailis retreated into the anteroom, and he slammed the door shut and barred it.

Dara flinched as he turned back to her. She had risen from the bed with only a blanket twisted about her nakedness. Her hair was tumbled in disarray.

He stifled lust and forced contempt into his narrow gaze. "You chose an ill moment, my lady, to play the wife and seek your husband's bed."

"Bastard! I did but delay here on my way to Chilton. I knew not that your bed would be too busily occupied to grant me sleep." His face had darkened at her lie, but she continued rashly. "I want no more of you or Scotland. Let me but dress, and you may recall your French whore."

He moved closer. "An English one will serve. You've the language for it."

Her eyes widened, and the color left her face. Without conscious volition, she drew her hand back and struck him, hard. She would not have stopped there had he not seized both her wrists, the angry force of his grip threatening to snap her bones. She bit her lips against the pain. The blanket slipped to the floor, and her body, glowing in the firelight, drew his gaze. She read lust in it and shrank away.

"Nay," she gasped. "I would despise your touch."

He pulled her up close so that she felt as well as saw his desire. His breath was hot against her ear. "Do you think it would matter now, lass? I could beat you . . . but I will not."

"I would prefer that," she cried despairingly as his hands released her wrists to move searchingly down her body. She hammered at him as she felt a familiar heat scorch her veins. Her struggles to retain her fury were in vain as were her efforts to free herself from his grip. Helplessly, she felt him lower her to the bed, her protests silenced by his lips.

At last she lay quiescent, sobbing involuntarily at her own weakness as he left no part of her inviolate. He caressed her side, kissed her quivering belly and gently parted her thighs. Leaving her briefly to disrobe, he soon returned to kiss her deeply, searchingly as he entered her. With a soft cry of surrender, she moved to meet him.

He thrust slowly, sweetly until her hands dug into his back and she arched upward against him. She called his name softly as the exquisite torture of need tore through her and was met and satisfied.

Into the silence and calm that washed over her came bewilderment and faint disquiet. Laochlain left her without a word and, after washing briefly, dressed in the same clothes he had discarded. He lit the candles and opened the door. Ailis came at his first call.

"Aye, my lord?"

"Help your mistress to dress."

He did not look again at Dara though she watched him warily as he left the room. She considered refusing to dress but could think of no good reason for further incurring his wrath —save for a genuine need for sleep. She flung back the covers and sat up. If she had little energy for dressing, she had less for further battle—at least until she knew why and for what she battled.

Ailis brought hot water for her bath, and she washed thoroughly before dressing. Uncertain of Laochlain's intentions, she donned a simple gown of golden brown silk. Ailis arranged her curls loosely and laced them through with ribbons the same cream color as the lace trim of her gown.

She had not long to wait before Laochlain returned. Bretach and Neacail accompanied him. Both men avoided looking at her as Laochlain sat before a well supplied desk and wrote swiftly. He rolled the paper and sealed it before handing it to Bretach.

"This is for James. When you are granted audience and it is delivered, you shall join me at Athdair. I leave all matters here in your hands."

He took Dara's arm and drew her from the room. Just outside the door, she hung back. "We are going now? My things aren't packed."

"Ailis will tend to them," he said shortly.

"She does not go with us?" Dara was becoming more bewildered, but he pulled her along with him.

"We go alone."

Their horses were saddled and awaiting them in the stable. When Dara saw that Haefen had been prepared for her, she wondered how Ailis would fare on the lively bay. She considered protesting, but something in Laochlain's face made her deem that an unwise move. No doubt Neacail would see that Ailis came to no harm.

The morning was still and fresh and crisply cool. The fog had lifted save for lingering wisps that swirled about the horses' feet as they left the city.

It was a stranger journey than any she had yet taken, for it was accomplished in almost total silence. They stopped at midday to eat, but their conversation was confined to essentials, Dara following Laochlain's lead in this, though truly her own inclinations did not lead her to seek idle talk.

That night they slept in a tiny lowland burgh, and again Laochlain made love to her, roughly at first but then with an all-encompassing tenderness. Uncertain of this mood that had taken hold of him, Dara responded with all of the passion he aroused in her. She spoke no words of love, though she ached with them, for he did not. Again they rose early and rode at dawn.

Before the sun reached its highest point, they halted on a barren moor buffeted by unhindered winds. Laochlain's eyes were bleak, his face devoid of any expression as he held her gaze.

"Along that path lies Athdair. That way," he gestured at an angle away from the trail, "that way lies England—and Chilton."

Dara's heart felt cold and weighted within her. Her head spun. Had she thrown all away, or had he? If she had remained at Gallhiel, would he have left her there month after month awaiting him? No! The word blazed in her mind. She remembered how he had held her so few hours earlier. That was not false! Was he giving her a choice or bidding her go?

She turned to stare in the direction he indicated. Her heart felt no pull towards England. She looked at him. His eyes were watchful now, but unrevealing. Must she plead? Tears burned her eyes.

"I am your wife." The words came from between numbed lips. "Are you sending me away?"

His mouth twisted bitterly. "I swore once to hold you against your will and all others. But, aye, you are my wife, and I'll have you willing— or not at all."

"I married you willingly." Her voice quivered traitorously.

"Words of a priest."

"No!" Unbelievably she felt angry. "The words were of my heart. Did you vow falsely?"

"Nay, Dara, not falsely." His voice was deep and warm and urgent.

"Then take me with you. Take me to Athdair and love me until I am again with child, then take me home—home to Gallhiel."

Chapter XXVII

Laochlain slipped into the darkened room and moved to stand beside the bed where his wife lay sleeping in exhaustion. The dark smudges beneath her eyes tore at his heart. His gaze traveled over every inch of the still form outlined by a light coverlet. A fire blazed in the hearth so that the room was warm, even for January, but he felt an urge to cover her more heavily. Without the burden of the babe, her body looked ethereal in its slenderness. Garda had assured him the birth was normal, but fear of that other time haunted him.

Nestled beside the wife who had become the very heart of him, his daughter stirred, pulling his gaze to her. A smile tugged at his lips. His daughter. Dara, he knew, had desired a son, thinking to give him that which they had lost. He had given the matter little thought, caring only that Dara should come to no harm through the birth. But he found himself well pleased, now, at the images that raced through his mind of a little girl looking more like her mother with every year that passed.

With great care, he eased the baby from the cocoon of blankets. She was so tiny as to fit almost entirely in the palm of one of his broad hands, but Garda had promised him she was strong and healthy. And she did look healthy with soft skin that glowed and dark, silky curls. As she protested the movement from her warm nest, he cradled her against his chest. His heart-beat, as her mother's had done, soothed her, and she quieted at once.

Laochlain eased to the chair placed by Dara's bed only to look up, startled at the sound of her voice. "Art pleased?"

"Aye," he said softly, and she knew from his expression that it was true. "But you scared me, lass. 'Twas such a long birth."

"Garda said it was not."

"For me it was a lifetime. I wanted no child as much as I wanted you safe."

"And now?" Her eyes twinkled, for he was holding their daughter as if she were all the treasures of the earth.

A rueful smile touched his lips. "And now she is as much a part of me as you. She *is* you." He reached out the hand not cradling the baby and watched as Dara placed her small hand in his. "I love you," he said, joining the two of them together in his mind and in his heart, "and I'll never lose you."

"Never," she agreed softly, knowing she would never regret the choices she had made, for this man was all she would ever need in this world and the next.

WINNER OF THE
GOLDEN HEART AWARD!

Sweet Treason

By Patricia Gaffney

Exquisitely beautiful, fiery Katherine McGregor had no qualms about posing as a doxy — if the charade would strike a blow against the hated English. But her certainty turned to confusion when she was captured and confronted by the infuriating Major James Burke. Now her very life depended on her ability to convince the arrogant English officer that she was a common strumpet, not a Scottish spy. Skillfully, Burke uncovered her secrets, even as he aroused her senses, claiming there was just one way she could prove herself a tart...But how could she give him her yearning body, when she feared he would take her tender heart as well?

_____2721-6 $3.95US/$4.95CAN

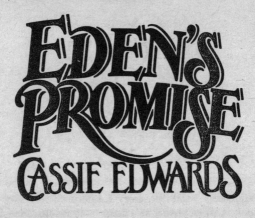

FOREVER GOLD

Catherine Hart's books are "Beautiful! Gorgeous! Magnificent!"

— *Romantic Times*

FOREVER GOLD. From the moment Blake Montgomery held up the westward-bound stagecoach carrying lovely Megan Coulston to her adoring fiance, she hated everything about the virile outlaw. How dare he drag her off to an isolated mountain cabin and hold her for ransom? How dare he kidnap her heart, when all he could offer were forbidden moments of burning, trembling ecstasy?

_____2600-7 $4.50 US/$5.50 CAN